COUNTING
TO ZERO

By the Author

COUNTING
TO ZERO

by

AJ Quinn

2016

COUNTING TO ZERO

ISBN 13: 978-1-62639-783-5

THIS TRADE PAPERBACK ORIGINAL IS PUBLISHED BY
BOLD STROKES BOOKS, INC.
P.O. BOX 249
VALLEY FALLS, NY 12185

FIRST EDITION: DECEMBER 2016

CREDITS
EDITOR: RUTH STERNGLANTZ
PRODUCTION DESIGN: STACIA SEAMAN
COVER DESIGN BY SHERI (GRAPHICARTIST2020@HOTMAIL.COM)

Acknowledgments

Endless thanks to Radclyffe and Bold Strokes Books for providing the platform from which my characters and their stories can spring to life. To Ruth, editor extraordinaire, for always being there to teach, listen, and encourage. To Sandy, Cindy, Connie, Sheri, Lori, Toni, and all the others who work so tirelessly to make everything possible. And especially to you, the readers, who welcome me into your lives through my stories. Thank you for your emails, your words of encouragement, and your ongoing support. It's an honor and a pleasure to spend time with you.

To Korie for showing me the magic of the desert
and so much more

PROLOGUE

Everything in Paxton James's world came crashing down around her without warning.

One minute she'd been standing in a slow-moving queue, music thundering in her ears drowning out the cacophony of voices around her. Doing her best to ignore the heat and humidity while idly waiting to pass through customs at Ngurah Rai International Airport in Bali.

In the next moment, a hand touched her lightly on the elbow. Turning, she saw a uniformed customs officer with a scarred face, nearly black eyes, and an even darker expression. She tugged the earbuds from her ears when he indicated with his head toward the carry-on luggage by her feet. The same suitcase Carrie had asked her to watch just a minute before while she dashed off to find a washroom.

"Is this yours?" he asked in faintly accented English.

Paxton shook her head and smiled apologetically. "Not exactly. It actually belongs to my girlfriend. I'm just watching it for her."

Dark eyes narrowed and assessed her. "Passport please."

Unconcerned, Paxton reached into a pocket and handed over her passport. She watched as the officer looked it over, studied her face against the photo in her passport, then carefully examined the luggage tag on the suitcase. "You are Paxton James."

"Yes."

"Suitcase tag says it belongs to Paxton James."

Even as she automatically shook her head in denial, she stared in surprise at the luggage tag he had just indicated. A tag that clearly had her name on it, printed in Carrie's recognizable writing. Even though the suitcase belonged to Carrie. Uneasiness began growing somewhere in the pit of her stomach, spreading and manifesting as tension between her shoulder blades.

"I'm sure Carrie can clear this up as soon as she gets back." She looked around, trying to spot Carrie so she could explain the mix-up. But for the moment, all she saw was a wall of strangers. "There's clearly been some kind of mistake."

"Yes, but I think it was you who made the mistake," the officer answered. He gripped her arm more tightly and pulled her and the suitcase in question toward a table. There, another officer opened the carry-on bag and began to go through its contents.

It was haphazardly packed in typical Carrie fashion, but she could see a couple of Carrie's familiar T-shirts, a bikini, a pair of shorts, and the lacy red thong she'd used to try and rekindle Paxton's interest, along with three paperbacks. There was also a foil-wrapped package, about four-by-six inches in size, that Paxton had never seen before.

What the hell?

"I don't know what that is. It's not mine."

The officer beside her grunted a command, moving her to the side of the table away from the line of slowly moving people and gesturing for her to spread out her arms. Without another word, he began to pat her carefully, moving down the outside of her arms before working his way over her hips and legs. At the same time, the second customs officer tore a small corner on the foil package, licked a fingertip, and stuck it inside. It was covered in white powder when he withdrew it.

He growled something in Balinese, but Paxton only needed to understand one word.

"Cocaine."

"Oh, Jesus," she whispered, half expletive, half prayer. "That's not possible."

She knew she was no angel. Had never really been. But her domain consisted of cyberspace. Firewalls and program codes. And when things got too close, too intense, she would simply go dark for a few weeks—or a few months. Do things like trek through Nepal or explore Cambodia and Vietnam as she'd most recently done. Whatever it took to restore her equilibrium.

But not drugs.

Never drugs.

And if she needed proof her world had just slipped off its axis, she could see multiple signs scattered throughout the airport, proclaiming: *Death penalty to drug smugglers.*

The crowd around her ceased to exist. The endless announcements of flight arrivals and departures went silent and the din of loud voices evaporated. Struggling to make sense of what was happening she started when she saw five soldiers moving toward her, heard the unmistakable clatter of rifles coming to bear, safeties going off, and knew they were all aimed at her.

Denying the monster in the closet was a child's game and she had never truly been a child. She swallowed, swallowed again as primordial fear crested along with adrenaline and confusion. She held her breath, felt a faint and distant tremor of reaction over the pounding in her chest, and threw her arms in the air. "Hey, no need for this. I'm unarmed."

"Down on the floor. Arms out, legs out."

Paxton immediately dropped to her knees then assumed a spread-eagle position face down on the floor. She remained motionless as someone straddled her, winced as he dragged her arms back and cuffed her wrists. Felt the finality of the action as the cuffs clicked into place.

In disbelief, she struggled to raise her head. Still trying to understand. Still trying to find Carrie so she could explain this was all a mistake.

And then she spotted her.

Beautiful Carrie, whose touch and smile had once lit something inside her, but now succeeded in only making her sad.

Playful Carrie, who had pleaded to stop over in Bali for a couple of days rather than fly back to New York as Paxton had originally planned once they departed Hong Kong.

Deceptive Carrie, who had casually asked Paxton to watch her carry-on luggage while she went in search of a washroom.

For a heartbeat, forever frozen in time, their eyes met and locked.

Carrie mouthed something. It looked like, *I'm sorry. It was you or me.*

For a moment, it seemed as if there was something else she wanted to say. But no. In the space of a heartbeat, she simply backed away, disappearing into the crowd that had gathered to watch.

CHAPTER ONE

W elcome to Bali.
    Before today, Emma Thorpe believed the mere mention of Bali would have evoked thoughts of paradise. Images of temples and beautiful beaches. Endless blue skies, spectacular mountain scenery, and lush rice fields. Warm and friendly people and a culture steeped in tradition.

It was more than a place. It was an aspiration. A state of mind.

Reality, however, proved to be quite different. At least on this particular day.

Walking out of the airport meant stepping into mayhem, and the warmth of the welcome quickly paled as humidity enveloped her and a wall of sound assailed her. People coming and going, taxi drivers shouting prices, horns blaring, vendors trying to outdo each other. And that was before she climbed into the back of the car prearranged to pick them up and began a thirty-minute ride best suited for a carnival.

The driver merged into a steady stream of traffic, where it seemed everyone was determined to drive in a style antithetical to an island known for spiritual retreats. Cars and trucks, motorcycles and scooters all swerved aggressively around street hawkers, changed lanes without signaling, and took traffic lights as merely suggestions, rather than law.

Already trapped in a no-win battle between adrenaline and jet lag, Emma looked at her hands and slowly unlocked her fingers.

"I think it works better if you don't look," Dominic Creed muttered on her left.

Turning toward him, Emma felt a smile tug at her mouth. "You're one to talk," she said dryly. She could feel his tension escalate when their driver barely missed a family of four crammed on a scooter—only to put their car on the same path as an oncoming taxi.

Dom scowled and his jaw muscles flexed as he bit down, no doubt on a sarcastic comment he was about to make.

"At least it's only supposed to be a thirty-minute trip," she reminded him.

"We should be so lucky." He sighed and rubbed his eyes. "It might help if we focus on something else. Anything. Like how you want to handle things when we get to Kerobokan. During the flight over, you said you were still mulling things over, considering all your options. Have you made any decision? Do you know what approach you want to take?"

As distractions went, his questions worked well and Emma was grateful. Not only because Dom reminded her of a decision she needed to quickly make, but because it also gave her a bona fide reason to look away from the road ahead and not consider herself a coward.

Putting her game face on, she accepted and opened the file Dom handed her. She tried to organize her thoughts and caught herself staring once again at the photograph sitting on top of the thin stack of papers. Staring and pondering how they were going to approach a woman who'd existed only in rumors prior to three weeks ago—a seemingly innocuous moment in time when Emma was told she could have her choice of anyone she wanted for the team of cyber specialists she'd been charged with assembling to deal with an ever-increasing threat to national security.

Everyone except one.

Paxton James.

She had to be on the team. That, according to the only person above Emma who truly counted, was a nonnegotiable.

I need you to do this.

Need, not want, Emma had thought, and found it telling.

I'm asking you to do this and I'd consider it a personal favor.

She was nobody's fool. She didn't mind having someone powerful owe her. And this one meant POTUS herself would owe her one, which never hurt.

But it didn't make complying any more palatable.

Emma didn't need to be reminded they were dealing with a viable and imminent cyber threat to national security. She knew they'd been lucky in that there'd been no loss of life—so far. But each of the unrelated computer system failures carried with it potentially devastating results.

Three different airliners briefly lost control of their cockpit avionics systems.

A train derailment averted only at the last minute following a computer glitch.

An oil supertanker dangerously off course, threatening a spill that could have destroyed the fragile ecology of the Gulf Coast of the US and Mexico.

The incidents had all come on the heels of a major breach in the Army Corps of Engineers computer systems, giving someone highly sensitive information about the nation's over eighty thousand dams. And they had left the government grappling to identify an unknown enemy. One Emma and her team believed was preparing to unleash a new kind of warfare.

Cyber warfare.

Without needing to be asked, Dom had immediately started digging into the background of the mystery inside an enigma that Ms. James proved to be. Perhaps not surprisingly, he didn't unearth a lot. "Sorry. It's all I've been able to come up with, but I think you'll find it's enough."

What she'd found was mostly rumor steeped in myth and mystery. It left Emma wondering how much of the woman was actually real. And what her connection to the president might be.

By the time she finished reading Dom's report, she realized she didn't know much more than when she'd started, but for one thing. Whether it was creating breaches or finding solutions for computer security or other cyber-related problems that could never be made public, Paxton James was the best.

It wasn't just consensus. It was unanimous. And that was what she needed. The best.

Having Dom agree so quickly was surprising enough that it made Emma sit up and take notice. In the years they'd worked together, she had learned to trust him, value his opinion. He was the most experienced field agent reporting to her and a key member of her team. Moreover, he seldom rushed to judgment.

Somehow, what he'd managed to uncover had convinced him the president was right. And not because openly disagreeing with President

Catherine Winters would be career suicide. He truly believed Paxton James was the key they would need to succeed.

There was one major challenge he had discovered, however. One Emma would need to overcome rather quickly.

"What do you mean she's in prison?"

Dom's rueful shrug did nothing to downplay what was already looking like a complete cluster-fuck. Emma's head began to pound as he explained the computer genius she'd been told to add to her team was not only in prison, she was in the notorious Kerobokan Prison in Bali. Facing the death penalty for trafficking drugs.

And muddying the waters even further, it turned out she'd been set up. By a dirty NSA agent.

Nicholas Perry.

Emma had never thought much of Nick Perry—and certainly nowhere near as much as he'd always thought of himself. But while she had sometimes quietly wondered how he afforded his lavish lifestyle, she had difficulty accepting one of their own could turn down such a dark path.

According to Dom, the former NSA agent and current federal prisoner had only admitted what he'd done after he'd been swept up in an unrelated DEA sting operation. Realizing he was trapped and knowing they were trying to locate Paxton James, he'd reached out to former NSA colleagues and offered up what he knew in the hope of cutting a deal for himself.

And wasn't that the ultimate irony, Emma thought. Getting Paxton out of prison would be easy when compared with convincing her to join the very organization that had indirectly landed her in jail.

❖

The woman's photograph had been her first surprise when Emma initially opened the folder Dom provided. Even knowing he was watching her, waiting for a reaction with a grin that spelled trouble, she'd still been caught off guard to the point of stammering. She should have been better prepared.

Paxton James—*Dr. Paxton James, PhD*—was a wizard, a term used by hackers to describe those rare few who achieved the highest level of skill.

But that was just it. Knowing she was a wunderkind, a computer genius with multiple degrees from MIT by the age of fifteen, she was so not what Emma had imagined. She had expected—well, hell. She wasn't really sure what she'd expected.

What she got was—well, *damn.*

Even in a photo, Paxton commanded that kind of attention and something stirred faintly in Emma that she'd thought safely dormant. Despite feeling foolish, the same reaction happened each time she glanced at the picture.

She had glanced at the picture far too many times over the last three weeks as they worked to build the case that would free Paxton, and she wondered if Dom had somehow deliberately set her up. Had chosen to insert that one photograph, suspecting it would elicit some kind of response.

That he got one possibly spoke to how long it had been since she'd even been attracted to someone, and Emma called herself every kind of fool.

But it didn't stop her from being drawn, time and time again, to an intriguingly angular face with flawless skin, framed by clouds of silky dark hair. Her eyebrows were dark arcs that stood above laser-blue eyes. And her incredibly sexy mouth was flanked by dimples.

There were subsequent photos in the file completing the overall picture, adding a long and lean frame, most often covered by a leather jacket and blue jeans. But it was her eyes that kept drawing Emma back to the original photo. Shadows played in those eyes. It made them seem mysterious, unreadable, and caused her to lose track of her thoughts.

Of course, Emma reminded herself, the photographs depicted what Paxton James had looked like fourteen months ago. *Before* she was locked away in an Indonesian prison notorious for its brutality, drug abuse, squalid conditions, and severe overcrowding.

Automatically, Emma flexed her right hand, still swollen and bruised. She could still barely make a fist and knew it would be at least a couple of more days before that changed. But while she'd clearly forgotten how hard a human jaw could be, she couldn't deny the satisfaction she'd gotten from seeing the damage she'd done to Nick Perry's face.

"Clearly, he shouldn't have called Paxton James a dyke," Dom said.

"You're really getting too good at reading my mind," Emma said. "I'm not sure I like it."

"That's funny," he replied. "Wasn't it what you wanted when you asked me to be part of this operation? You said I needed to know what you were thinking and be prepared to act on it before you thought of it."

"Damn you for remembering that." Emma laughed for a moment before her smile faded. "The truth is the bastard showed no remorse at putting an innocent woman in prison and actually thought it was funny he'd sent a lesbian to what he said would be like going to dyke heaven. But you know what? That wasn't the worst."

"Emma—"

"No. The worst was when he didn't bend or break her—when Paxton James didn't reach out and beg to be allowed to do whatever it was the bastard wanted her to do—he left her sitting in that jail, waiting to be executed by a firing squad. Damn him."

She fell silent as she stared out the window. It took more effort than it should have, but gradually she could feel her heartbeat settle back down to a slow and steady cadence.

"I guess that's why his team always called him Nick the Prick," Dom said a minute later. "And I hope he enjoys spending the rest of his life in federal lockup. But I need to remind you that you're supposed to be the brains in this operation and I'm supposed to do the heavy lifting. Try to remember that next time. Shelby and Kinsey were all over me when they saw your hand."

Emma released a soft sigh. He was talking about the core of her new team. Women who were exactly what she needed. Independent freethinkers, creative rule breakers. But she also knew how protective both women could be.

The team didn't usually work face-to-face. Although it did happen on occasion—they had an office, after all—much of what they did could be done just as well from far-flung locations. But when the new task force had been put together, the general consensus was that the situation could escalate and change so quickly that working as a unit in close proximity could make a critical difference.

So Emma's task force had come together, new team members mixing with old, and they were in the process of bonding. And though at times they might get overprotective of her, Emma had no doubt everyone would have her back if needed. Especially Shelby and Kinsey.

In her midthirties, Shelby Jarrett, much like Emma, had been recruited by the NSA straight out of college, and Emma had brought her along with her on every promotion. She could think on her feet, had a way with technology that outdistanced most people, and best of all, she could put up with Dom, giving as good as she got.

Kinsey Dane, on the other hand, had recently been recruited out of the CIA and already Emma knew she had a keeper. She'd come highly recommended. More importantly, although younger than most of her colleagues, she had meshed well with the others from the start and had razor-sharp instincts Emma was quickly learning to trust. Not only that, she could put a bug on a telephone line with her eyes closed.

As she thought of the team and the two women in particular, Emma tried to flex her hand again, cringing as their driver went through a red light. "I know, but as I explained to both of them, I can't let you have all the fun."

"You also need to remember James is not exactly an innocent in all of this," Dominic said. "If even part of what we've learned is true, she's used her unbelievable computer skills and built a reputation as a top-of-the-line hacker. Christ, rumor has it she hacked into the CIA just to show a couple of her professors at MIT how she could do it and get back out again without getting caught."

"Maybe so, at least it was CIA rather than us." She looked at Paxton's photo again and thought of shades of gray. "More importantly, she's not a drug smuggler. She's not selling death to schoolchildren. And those computer skills? They're the very reason why we need her."

"You're right." Dom shrugged. "She's also quite stunning, isn't she," he added appreciatively.

"She is that," Emma agreed and found herself wondering what her voice might sound like. Somehow she imagined it as dark and sensual. But no matter. So far, Ms. James had remained stubbornly silent. Apparently had nothing to say. "Just remember you're not her flavor."

"Sadly, true." Dom grinned. "But you are, aren't you?"

"Don't go there," Emma said wearily. "If all goes well over the next couple of days, Paxton James will be leaving Bali with us. We get to right a serious wrong and get her to work closely with us for the foreseeable future. That's all we're here to do."

Frowning, she stared out the window again all too aware her annoyance was directed at herself, not at Dom. It left her feeling beyond foolish, knowing she had been captivated and continued to be haunted by a damned photograph.

Especially when the truth was she didn't do personal relationships. At least, not successfully. More often than not, her career saw to that, and in a way, this obsession was even worse because the photograph that held her attention was of a woman who stood on the opposite end of the spectrum from Emma's own beliefs about right and wrong. And honor.

But it didn't change her reaction. And the inexplicable, foolish attraction didn't fade.

For a moment she wished she was here in Bali to simply stand on one of those magnificent beaches framed by waves that every surfer dreamed of. Standing in the refreshing water while feeling the sun on her skin, as warm and soothing as a lover's touch.

Then she thought of Paxton James again, locked in a prison considered Bali's most notorious while waiting to die, and came to a conclusion.

"I can see you thinking," Dom said. "Why don't you think out loud so I can see where you're going?"

"I'm thinking we're going to play this straight."

Dom narrowed his eyes and stared at her. "What does that mean?"

"It means an innocent woman has spent the last fourteen months of her life in some kind of living hell. We both have a pretty good idea what she's gone through. Someone owes her and I'm not going to make coming to work with us a condition of giving her a get-out-of-jail card."

"And if she refuses—if she won't work with us?"

"Then President Winters will no doubt be less than pleased with me." Emma shrugged. "That's mine to own. But I'll still get her out of here and get her back to the US. It was a dirty federal agent that put her in here, so it's the least we can do. We owe her that much."

She fell silent, lost in thought for the remainder of the drive.

Chapter Two

The prison, once built for three hundred fifty inmates but now housing more than one thousand, was nestled amid the narrow streets of Kerobokan. In a ramshackle area not greatly touched by tourism, it stood like a monolithic temple, with graying walls rimmed by razor-sharp barbed wire.

Emma had already learned that within those walls, a United Nations of prisoners were crushed together in misery. Petty criminals, thieves, and unlucky tourists who'd seen their holiday dreams become a living nightmare after being caught with a few tabs of Ecstasy shared cells with murderers, rapists, and drug traffickers. She shuddered, knowing it didn't bear thinking about it.

Leaving their driver to await their return near the front of the prison, they got in line for an entry procedure that proved laboriously slow. Or maybe it was just fatigue starting to weigh her down. But after a long wait and various security checks, Emma and Dom each received a purple stamp on their wrist that identified them as visitors and would allow them to leave when it came time.

They were then brought to the visitors' area, which turned out to be nothing more than a square of concrete floor with some thin reed mats and a corrugated iron roof that trapped the humidity in the still air. The temperature, as a result, was stifling and the small, crammed space held competing scents of spicy food, stale sweat, and despair.

It was also loud as visitors and inmates mingled, some talking, some crying, some groping in corners, while still others gathered in prayer circles holding hands.

After indicating who they wanted to see, a guard instructed them to wait. It took some time, and a sliver of doubt sliced through Emma's mind, but she remained still. Waiting until a woman who could only be Paxton James showed up, shoulders hunched, hands buried deep in her pockets, and a wary expression on her face as she cast narrowed eyes around the room.

She looked young—much younger than her actual age—and was dressed in faded, baggy cargo shorts and a plain navy blue shirt with the sleeves rolled to her elbows. The long dark hair was gone, replaced by a short asymmetrical cut, damp from sweat and the heat, and haloing her pale, angular face.

There were signs of strain evident in the lines carved around her mouth and in the shadows under startling blue eyes that had seen too much. She was much thinner than she'd been in her photographs, but the muscle tone in her arms and legs suggested she was fit.

Still, she was instantly recognizable. And she still had one hell of a face.

Emma took a step toward her and offered her hand. "Ms. James— Dr. James. Thank you for agreeing to see us. My name is Emma Thorpe. This is my associate, Dominic Creed."

Paxton's shoulders straightened, squared, even as she looked at Emma's hand for a confused instant, as if not quite certain it was real. Her eyes widened and then she offered her own hand to each of them, her grip surprisingly firm. "It's Paxton—or Pax, if you prefer. As you might guess, we're not really big on formalities in here. It becomes too easy to forget."

Emma took her hand, then smiled into her eyes. Good eyes, she thought. Bright, steady, clear. And her voice? It was as smooth as honey. Low and husky, it slid over her skin and left a disconcerting sensation in its wake.

Paxton led them to a corner where a female guard was standing, and spoke in a hushed tone to the woman in Balinese. After a quick, subtle exchange took place, the guard nodded, smoothly pocketed whatever she'd palmed, and walked away.

Her frown deepening, Emma continued to watch, uncertain what she had just witnessed. All she knew for certain was if drugs had just been exchanged, this meeting would quickly come to an end—no matter what Catherine Winters wanted. "You speak Balinese."

"I've been here a while with little else to do." Paxton slanted her a look before wrapping her arms around herself, hands clamped tight on her forearms while her body vibrated with nervous energy.

"Fair enough. What did you give her?"

Something flashed in her eyes, the only change in her expression, but Emma thought Paxton looked a little irritated by both the question and her tone. Good, she thought. Better a bit angry than the faintly glassy-eyed confusion she had initially presented.

Angry or not, Paxton turned and studied her face for a span of several heartbeats. Her expression shifted slightly, became devoid of emotion, and for an instant, Emma believed she had played the scene wrong.

But then Paxton released a soft sigh. "Once you get past the initial shock of finding yourself here, the first thing you learn is that everything works on the barter system." She spoke quietly as they sat on the concrete floor in the corner the guard had vacated. "And you learn very quickly or you don't survive."

Dropping to a reed mat on the floor across from Paxton, Emma watched her closely, searching for any hint of deception. She saw her pulse beat steadily beneath smooth skin at the base of her throat, but nothing else. "Barter system?"

Clearly aware she was being scrutinized, Paxton faced her without flinching and Emma could see an enforced poise reasserting itself. See the strength of will it took on her part to slip that calm back into place. *Interesting.*

"It's really quite simple," Paxton said. "You want something to eat beyond a daily handful of rice, you barter. You want to be separated from a cell mate who gets off on beating the crap out of you, you barter. I'm told the same rules apply for sex, drugs, and alcohol, but I can't say for certain because I've never been interested enough to find out. At least not so far. Time will tell."

She paused, stared at the battered Nikes on her feet, then glanced up again. "Look, one thing I've learned since I've been in here is that when you're in survival mode, you make the best decisions given what you know, and then you move on. I don't know who you are or what you want from me, Ms. Thorpe. All I know is, other than my court-appointed lawyer, you and Mr. Creed are the first people, let alone the first Americans, who've asked for me by name since I was locked up in here. It made me curious enough to agree to meet with you, but until I can figure things out, a corner is the best place to talk without everyone knowing my business."

"All right. And it's Emma."

"Well, Emma, allow me to explain that corners are prime real estate in here, especially for people with spouses or lovers. They are always the first spaces taken. So the guard, Lintang? She just made sure there was a quiet corner available for us to talk."

"Makes sense, I guess," Emma said mildly. "Can I ask what it cost you?"

"Six cigarettes. Ordinarily, it would have been more, but I've been teaching her to use a computer late at night when everyone else is sleeping, so she lets me off easy."

Emma tried not to laugh at the image of one of the world's best hackers teaching a Balinese prison guard who spoke no English how to use a computer. "I'm sorry. Will you be all right without the cigarettes? If we'd known, we could have brought you some."

"That's okay, I don't actually smoke. I keep cigarettes on hand strictly for bartering. Haven't you heard? They're bad for your health." The corner of her mouth lifted slightly as if appreciating the irony of a woman on death row believing smoking would be detrimental to her health.

Gallows humor. But the smile transformed her.

She remained unquestionably beautiful, but the smile made her seem more real. More approachable. Unguarded. And sexy as hell.

Although Emma doubted the good mood would last, at least momentarily the ice was broken. "Be careful," she said, trying not to stare at the faintly smiling mouth. "I might get the idea you have a sense of humor that's still intact."

"Sorry. That's not allowed in here." The grin widened infinitesimally. "They make you leave it at the door when you check in. And since there's no checking out, at least not for me—"

Just as quickly, Paxton's expression changed. Her smile disappeared as if it had been an illusion, her body tensed, and she became quietly pensive.

Emma felt the mood shift as if it was a physical thing. And though Paxton's expressive eyes were still an amazing blue, she realized in that moment they'd become stark and empty once again, devoid of any humor or emotion. Devoid of anything at all as she shut down.

"Now, how about telling me who you are and what you want from me," Paxton said quietly. "Just please don't tell me you're reporters looking for the inside story of sex and drugs on death row. I'd hate to think I wasted six cigarettes for nothing."

❖

"Believe it or not, Dom and I are here to help you."

Paxton blinked slowly as she heard the words echo in her head, and took a brief moment to align them in her mind. They were words she'd spent the last fourteen months waiting to hear. Longing to hear. She'd waited so long she found herself dangerously close to being willing to deal with the devil himself if it meant getting out of this hell.

She tuned out the chaos around her and silently studied the two people sitting on the floor across from her.

Dominic Creed appeared to be exactly what he most likely was. A fortysomething career federal agent with short dark hair and dark eyes, dressed in a dark suit that didn't come off the rack. He probably had a whole closet full of them, she thought wryly, and he had to be sweating in the oppressive humidity of the visitors' quadrant. But he showed no obvious sign of discomfort.

Tall and lean, his face had strong features and his nose had clearly been broken at some point in the past, edging his look toward dangerous even as he kept his expression carefully blank. But there was something in his eyes, in his characteristic stillness, that told her he could be lethal.

The woman was a different story altogether. Emma Thorpe. One thing was immediately clear. It certainly seemed like the devil knew all of Paxton's weaknesses and had chosen his representative well.

Midthirties, slender, slightly taller than average height, with a fair complexion and shoulder-length honey-blond hair. Cool, understated beauty in a dark blue power suit and white silk T-shirt. Add the obvious intelligence visible in her changeable hazel-green eyes and Paxton felt a string being plucked somewhere deep inside her.

Still, lessons learned the hard way were impossible to forget and she, of all people, knew how easily one could be fooled. Paxton held a fleeting image: Carrie walking away, leaving her prone on the floor, handcuffed, with multiple weapons aimed in her direction.

She shut it down.

"Right," she said. "How foolish of me not to see that right away. Of course you're here to help. That's because you're from one of those wonderfully philanthropic organizations like the Innocence Project or Truth in Justice—um...no, that's not right. Wait a minute, I know. NSA. You're with the NSA. How am I doing?"

"That's very good." Emma swallowed visibly. "Actually, we're with the American Cyber-Research Institute—"

"Which is an NSA front," Paxton responded. "A think tank specializing in computer crimes. Same game, different club."

"You're right. Unfortunately, I'm not at liberty to tell you more. At least, not yet," she added softly, clearly trying not to alienate Paxton. "What I can tell you is we're part of a rather special group that answers directly to the president's office—"

"And you could tell me more, but then you'd have to kill me?"

Startled, Emma smiled. "I wouldn't go that far."

Paxton's own wry smile returned as, in that moment, she realized something. Despite the horrific circumstances of the last fourteen months, she had somehow managed to hold on to not only most of her sanity, but apparently her sense of black humor as well. The thought pleased her.

"You should work on that smile, Emma. It's not very reassuring. But worry not. You just have to wait. It seems the government here has a firing squad that will take care of that bit of business. I'm told I'll even be given a choice—whether I want to be blindfolded or not."

Emma opened her mouth but only released a strangled sound. Paxton chose to ignore it as she continued. "I've been giving it some thought, and personally, I think if someone is going to go to the bother of putting a bullet in me, I'd like them to look me in the eye. But I don't know. I guess I won't know for certain until the time comes."

Emma squared her shoulders and drew a deep breath. The movement outlined her breasts against the silk of her shirt. "Believe me, Paxton. We're not going to let that happen. You need to know we've been negotiating for your release with the prison governor since before we got here. Most of the *T*s are crossed and it should only take another day or so before we have you out of here. In the meantime, I'd like to offer you a place in our organization."

Paxton closed her eyes for a second as something inside her stirred. Maybe hope? It had been so long she wasn't certain she recognized the sensation anymore. "And you can't tell me more than that? I'm supposed to take you on faith?"

"For now, yes. I'm sorry."

She nodded, considered. "For argument's sake, let's say I believe you. Why me?"

"That's simple." Emma smiled again. "Because we need you. Because intelligence seems to be the only thing there's never enough of—anywhere in the world, but especially in the intelligence community. And I've got a file that says you're damned smart. That you test off the scales."

"Not smart enough to stay out of here. Didn't even see it coming," Paxton murmured mostly to herself. Her nerves tingled and she could hear a note of caution somewhere in the midst of her swirling thoughts. "Beyond being bloody smart, do you have any idea who I am? What is it you want or expect me to do for you?"

"I believe you'll find we know fully well who you are and that you're exactly what we're looking for," Emma said mildly. "You are a certified genius, but computers are your specialty. You're twenty-seven years old, obtained postgraduate degrees in computer science and engineering from MIT by the time you were fifteen. You're considered one of the two, maybe three best hackers in the world. It's suspected you can get in and out of any system without leaving a trace. Of course, since you've not been caught, it's a difficult thing to prove. Still, on occasion you've been known to tell organizations how to prevent others from doing what you just did. But that too could be part of the myth. So for now, all we have to go on is rumor and innuendo. Have I left anything out?"

The unquenchable flicker of hope that had broken free began to fade. Squaring her jaw, Paxton slipped into her own façade of control. "Only what it is you want from me."

Emma assessed her quietly, then leaned closer and lowered her voice. "You were right. We're a unit of NSA. But we're not like any other unit. We're not discussed in Senate committees, have fewer rules and hoops to jump through, less bureaucratic red tape, more funding. I recognize it's a bit to digest, but what you need to know is that Dominic and I are recruiting a team. The team will be second to none. The best of the best at everything. And according to my boss, quite frankly, all we're missing is someone like you."

"There's no one else like me."

"Exactly why we want you onboard, Paxton. We need your undeniable talent and you want your life back. I see it as a win-win proposition—"

Hope shattered.

"Damn." Paxton closed her eyes and smiled sadly as she listened to yet another federal agent tell her how she would be used. It had all been scripted beforehand, and she should have known what was going to happen. Opening her eyes, she rose to her feet. "I have a feeling I already know the answer to this, but tell me something. Do you know an NSA agent named Nick Perry?"

There was only the slightest hesitation. "Yes."

"Then I assume you will also know that the last time an NSA agent tried to recruit me, I somehow ended up with a suitcase full of cocaine in my possession when I said no. I was tried, convicted, sentenced, and here I sit—waiting to face a firing squad." She shoved her hands into her pockets and straightened, her heart hammering so hard she could feel it down to her running shoes. "But at least there's one piece of good news."

"What's that?"

"Over the last few months, at times things got so bad in here I often wondered if I'd eventually be reduced to agreeing to do Nick Perry's dirty work for him. Anything. Just to be free of this place. It seems I needn't have worried. I've got my answer."

"Your answer?" Emma asked quietly.

"My answer is no, Ms. Thorpe. I'm not for sale. Not to anyone and not at any price. I am not willing to do your dirty work. No more than I was willing to do Nick Perry's. And although you're a hell of a lot more appealing than Perry, I am not willing to be your whore any more than I was willing to be his."

Before either Emma or Dominic could react, she left the visitors' area and disappeared into the dark bowels of the prison, heading back to her cell.

❖

The room was almost completely dark.

But he was fine with that. Not only did he prefer the darkness, he didn't need any additional light to scan the emails he had been receiving all evening. Routine status checks from watchers he paid good money to, assuring him everything was in order. On schedule.

All but one had checked in without fail.

He exhaled and reminded himself these things happened. He had chosen his people carefully, paid them well. To date, things had been going smoothly and there were countless reasons why one watcher could be late reporting in.

So why had he developed an uneasy feeling over the last few days? He couldn't put a finger on anything that would account for it. He just knew to trust his instincts. They'd served him well in the past.

Was it possible things had been going too well?

No. He was simply allowing paranoia to get to him and he couldn't let that happen. Couldn't let it change his course of action. Not when he was so close. Too much planning had gone into ensuring his success. All the initial test runs had gone without a hitch. And he had potential buyers clamoring to outbid each other.

Not that it mattered. This wasn't about money. Yes, by the time it was done, he'd have enough money to retire to his own private island and live like a king. But more importantly, he'd have recognition. And power. He'd have it all and then…

His computer dinged softly. Finally. The email he was waiting for arrived, accompanied by an attachment. A photograph.

The news—that a cyber terrorism group within the NSA was bringing in an expert to try to counter his offensive—wasn't entirely unexpected. *As if anyone could*, he told himself.

Humming quietly, he dismissed the email and turned his attention to the attached photograph. He tried to anticipate who thought they might be up to the challenge but drew a blank.

With only a few deft key strokes, he altered the screen resolution. His system was cutting edge. Ultra-high-definition. He watched the image become larger. Sharper. And felt his pulse kick up a notch as he realized it was a face he had committed to memory years ago. Could it be?

"I'll be damned."

Unbelievable. The woman on the screen was thinner than he remembered and she had cut her hair. But her blue eyes were unmistakable. Shadowed and too serious. Haunting.

He had thought of her often over the years, had done what he could to follow any news he could find about her. Her name was whispered in rumors and people said she could do things that bordered on magic.

Based on what he knew, he had no doubt just how good she was. A long time ago, he'd seen her work firsthand and time would only have enhanced her abilities. But he was equally certain she'd have no idea what she was up against. He knew his own skills had grown. He was better than ever. Likely better than her.

Not arrogance, he told himself. Just facts.

He stared a moment longer at the woman on the screen, then began to laugh. And just like that, the game changed.

CHAPTER THREE

Traffic proved to be heavy by the time Emma and Dom left the dismal environment of the prison behind. Thankfully, they didn't have far to go, and as luck would have it, most traffic was heading in the opposite direction from their hotel.

Resting her head against the back of the seat, Emma rubbed her temples and sighed. She knew she should be feeling elated. They'd made a misstep in their first attempt to convince Paxton James to join them, but at least they'd concluded a successful meeting with the prison governor and had accomplished the most critical part of what they'd set out to do.

By day's end tomorrow, Paxton would be a free woman and they could use that as a show of faith. A stepping stone toward convincing her to join forces with them.

But somehow, instead of satisfaction, all she could feel were knots of tension in her neck and shoulders and the onset of a headache.

Not surprisingly, she could feel a similar tension emanating from Dom. But there would not be an opportunity to debrief about the day or discuss any further plans until they were checked in to their hotel. Away from the possibility of eyes and ears that might see or hear something they shouldn't. After they had a chance to sweep their suite for bugs. And preferably, she thought wryly, after she had a glass of single malt scotch in her hand.

One thing was clear. Paxton James had more secrets than she did, and something deep inside Emma wanted to know what they were, why she kept them.

An hour later, having grabbed a quick shower and changed into jeans and a soft cotton T-shirt, Emma stood on the hotel balcony enjoying a soft breeze while staring out at the beautiful panorama. The evening was hushed, the sun low on the horizon, while the sky, the Indian Ocean, and the shadowed beach were painted with a palette of golds and reds.

She breathed in salty air and listened to the surf and the birds squawking as they skimmed the water searching for fish. Paradise itself could scarcely have been lovelier.

In the suite behind her, she heard Dom speaking softly on the telephone, arranging to have a light dinner brought up to their suite. A minute or two later, he joined her on the balcony, remaining silent while she took a slow sip of her drink. It had definite restorative power, she thought, breathing out when it ran smooth and warm down her throat.

She turned with her eyes fixed on Dom and asked, "How much do you know about Nick Perry? You were there for all of it when he tried to cut a deal. I was only there for the finish. What exactly did he want with Paxton?"

If Dom was surprised by her question, he didn't show it. "Money."

He said it as if that was all there was to tell. And in a way, he was right. Didn't it always come down to money? But instinctively knowing there was more, Emma crossed her arms over her chest and waited.

Dom shrugged. "Perry said he'd been originally approached to facilitate locating a top-notch hacker for the head of one of the drug cartels. Seems they wanted to use technology to launder money—and maybe funnel some away from the competition. Pretty clever, actually."

"Maybe. Who wanted her?"

"Hector Escobar."

"Oh, Jesus." Emma felt ice run through her veins as she pictured Escobar. A ruthless killer in his forties with dark hair, dark eyes, a cruel mouth, and a history of lethally enforced loyalty.

"I hear you. Knowing what we now know about James, it would not have ended well. But it doesn't matter because before it got to that, Perry changed his mind."

"Did he say why?"

"He decided Escobar was on to something. By then he was on to James, and he decided he could have her do the same thing Escobar wanted. Except have her do it for him instead. Use her skills to access bank accounts he would identify for her."

"Whose accounts?"

"He's never said. Likely drug lords, since that was what Escobar wanted to do. Perry had been undercover as part of the NSA/DEA joint task force for quite some time, and would have had a lot of inside knowledge. He said he wanted her to crack the encryption codes guarding the accounts, then transfer the money into a series of offshore accounts he'd set up."

"Okay." Nodding to herself, Emma lifted her head and looked at Dom. "What else?"

"I'm not sure what you mean."

Emma narrowed her eyes fractionally and stared at him, before allowing a bite of censure into her voice. "What else did he tell her he wanted?"

Dom shoved his hands into his pants pockets and leaned back against the railing. "You mean about being his whore?"

Emma hardened her voice to steel. "Tell me what he wanted."

Dom swore. "Look, I really don't know the specifics, but I can guess. So can you. I mean, he's a cold-blooded, arrogant bastard and she's—well, just look at her."

"I get it. She's gorgeous and Perry wanted her. And he likely figured he was entitled, since Perry always believed he should get whatever he wanted," Emma finished for him.

"He had a reputation. Not all of it good, and over the last few years, it got worse. There were a lot of rumors circulating about him when he began working on the task force. Although I'm certain he positioned himself as a better option than Escobar. The devil you know—"

Emma rocked back on her heels and closed her eyes as she recalled the look on Paxton's face, her eyes dark and unguarded for a brief moment. *I am not willing to be your whore any more than I was willing to be his.* "I should have known about this before I approached her. I could have ensured there was no doubt—"

She stopped, suddenly uncertain. No longer sure she was any better than Nick Perry. Had she allowed her inappropriate and misplaced attraction to Paxton to show itself somehow? What in bloody hell had she done?

"Don't go there," Dom said quietly. "Nick Perry not only wanted to force an unwilling woman to steal for him, he wanted her to become his plaything. He didn't give a damn about what she wanted or that she had no interest in him. Or any man. In fact, knowing Perry, it's likely that was part of what drove him. Part of the appeal. He wanted her and when she turned him down cold, he decided to see how far he could bend her before she broke."

Emma picked up her drink intent on finishing it, but set it back down on the table without tasting it. "How did he get to her? She said she didn't see it coming. If she's so damn smart, why didn't she see it coming?"

"He hit her close to home where she'd least expect it. He used her girlfriend to set her up. Carrie Nolan. She's some kind of model—"

"Jesus, Dom, you can't be serious." She let out a sigh of exasperation. "Carrie Nolan may be well into her thirties, but she's still considered one of the top five runway models in the world."

"Maybe so, but a traitorous bitch in my books nonetheless. Perry claims he found out she had a fondness for cocaine. She was just about to sign a multi-million-dollar contract to be the face of some design house or other in Paris, and he threatened to make her habit public knowledge. She stood to lose a great deal. Or she could plant the shit on James and convince her to spend a couple of days in Bali before heading back to New York." Dom shrugged. "We all know what she decided."

Dinner arrived while they continued to talk, and though the rich scent of spices wafting in the evening air was meant to entice, Emma discovered it wasn't enough to work up an appetite. She toyed with her food, restlessly pushing it around on her plate before finally giving up any pretense at eating.

Pushing away from the table, she bid Dom a good night and headed for her room. But before she had even reached the door, the phone rang and she paused while Dom answered it.

It didn't take long after that for her to realize they had a serious problem on their hands.

❖

Paxton stirred. Her heart thudded painfully and during those initial few beats she discovered two things.

Pain slashed through her, searing white and to the point of blinding her, telling her she hadn't dodged enough to completely avoid the razor-sharp knife. The pain kept coming like waves, building layer upon layer and leaving her dizzy in its wake. But it also told her something more important.

She was still alive. And that trumped everything.

"Ms. James? Paxton. Can you hear me?"

She blinked, licked her upper lip, and found herself barely able to open her eyes. Her vision tunneled and all the grays and shadows blurred together. Every inch of her ached as she tried to focus. Her head didn't split as she feared likely, but she had to work to keep it from spinning.

She also had to be hallucinating.

All she'd done was try to intervene when she'd come upon a young inmate being attacked by two older and much larger inmates. Seeing the girl shoved, pushed, punched, and beaten rather badly reminded her of things better left forgotten and she'd simply reacted. Jumping into the fray, she'd taken a couple of shots of her own and had gotten stabbed for her effort.

Now the woman from the NSA, Emma Thorpe, had somehow materialized beside her bed in the prison infirmary. She just couldn't be this unlucky.

Concentrate on your breathing. Hell, just concentrate.

She coughed. A mistake, because the pain in her side became so intense she nearly passed out again, and she closed her eyes as a shiver racked her body. But when she managed to reopen them, Emma Thorpe was still there.

"Why are you here?" At least that's what she tried to say. She had to tense to keep her teeth from chattering as she shivered again and her words came out garbled.

"Welcome back. It's nice to see you've rejoined us. Even better to know your cheerful disposition is still intact."

Paxton's head resumed aching and she tried to raise her hand to her temple, but was only able to lift it partway before she let it fall back onto the bed. "And you've not gotten any better at answering questions since the last time I saw you."

That got a laugh. "Sorry," she said, but she didn't sound very sorry. A moment later, she extended her hand. "Hi. Emma Thorpe. Nice to meet you."

Paxton's brows came together in confusion. "What are you doing?"

"Starting over."

Paxton stared at the hand Emma had thrust toward her an instant longer, and managed to reach up to meet it. "Paxton James. Nice to meet you."

"There," she said. "That wasn't so hard. How are you holding up? Because I have to tell you—you look like hell."

The side of her mouth that wasn't bruised pulled upward in a half grin but her voice was raw with strain. "Oh, yeah? You should see the other guy."

"Actually, I did. Both of them, I might add," Emma said dryly. "They could pass as linebackers for the Panthers. What the hell were you thinking?"

"That two against one was unfair and they were twice the kid's size." Paxton sighed as she looked up and caught a glimpse of Emma's grin. "I'm never living this one down, am I?"

Another laugh. "Probably not."

Paxton remained silent for a long moment. She shifted on the bed to get a better look at her visitor and instantly regretted it. The pain was immediate and searing and she had to fight through it. "Will you please tell me why you're here?"

"That's easy. I've come to get you out of here."

The words set off an echo as they rattled in Paxton's head, stirring hope and disbelief in equal parts. "Today's not my birthday, and your timing's a bit off for an April Fool's joke." She frowned and felt the pounding of her heart in her throat as she met Emma's gaze. Because in spite of an innate distrust in human beings, she so badly wanted to believe. "Are you real?"

Emma nodded. "Very real. I did tell you we'd been negotiating your release. The governor reviewed all of our evidence this afternoon, including a signed confession from a former NSA agent admitting that he set you up. In honor of the long-standing relationship between our countries, the governor has agreed to release you into my care, the paperwork's signed and sealed, and everything is good to go."

"Oh, God—"

"In fact, we'd have taken care of it all tomorrow, but now we've run into a bit of a problem. A slight snag, if you will."

It took her two tries to get the question out. "What kind of problem?"

"The incident this evening needs to be investigated. The governor wants to know where the guards were and why it took so long for them to respond. More importantly, there are questions about how one of the inmates was in possession of a knife—a real knife, not a shiv."

"Um…sorry. I don't understand. What does any of that have to do with me?"

"If you are still here come morning, you'll become a key witness in an internal investigation that could last weeks. Perhaps months."

"Then"—Paxton hesitantly licked her lips—"I'm guessing I shouldn't still be here in the morning."

"My point exactly. So if we're going to get you out of here, it has to be tonight."

She tried to consider what the words meant. The pain in her side was increasing, but she wasn't going to say or do anything that would stop Emma from continuing to tell her what she most needed to hear. Instead, she focused on breathing. Slow and steady.

"Are you still with me, Paxton?"

"Yeah, sorry." Paxton nodded and winced. "I know how badly I want to get out of here. And since you're the only game in town, I guess I'm going to have to believe you."

"How reassuring." Emma's tone was dry. "Dom has a car and driver waiting to get you out of here as quickly and quietly as possible. Now. I recognize you're hurt and in pain, but this can't be helped. Is there anything you need to get from your cell?"

"No. The only thing I would need or want is—"

Emma reached into a pocket and withdrew an American passport.

"—my passport." She stared at Emma for a couple of heartbeats, still not fully accepting or ready to believe this was happening. "Oh, Jesus. This is real?"

"Very real. Can you—are you able to move?"

Paxton closed her eyes, moved her legs tentatively toward the side of the bed, but then stopped as if suddenly uncertain in her ability to make a decision. "If I let you do this…if I let you save my ass, it doesn't mean I'm coming to work for you. You understand that, don't you?"

"It would mean working *with* me, not *for* me." Emma smiled, gave her a patient look, and moved closer to help. "But I don't want you to worry about it right now. Consider this a get-out-of-jail-free card on behalf of the NSA. After having had to deal with the likes of Nick Perry, I'd say we owe you one. And just so you know, he's locked up in a federal prison."

Paxton swallowed. "He's locked up? For real?"

"For real."

"I'm guessing Armani doesn't make prison jumpsuits. And orange really isn't his color." She tried to picture it and released a small laugh. "Damn. I wish…just once, I wish I could see him like that."

"Maybe we can arrange something once we get you stateside. We can talk about it later. For now, can you stand?"

"I'm good, I think." With a concerted effort, Paxton pushed up and made it to her feet. Barely. She was light-headed, every cell in her body hurt, and the stitches in her side pulled with every move she made. One step later, her legs started to fold and she staggered, automatically reaching out for anything to help keep her upright.

She should have fallen to the floor, but before the worst could happen, a pair of strong, solid arms slid around her, holding her. Supporting her.

"I've got you," Emma assured her. "Why don't you lean on me and let me do most of the work? It'll make this easier on you and maybe you won't hurt as bad."

It was strange having someone concerned about her and Paxton felt her throat tighten as she leaned into Emma's strength. "Thanks."

"Not a problem. Do you think you can do this? Make it to the car?"

"Probably…yes. Does it really matter? If it takes crawling over broken glass to get out of here, then that's what I'm prepared to do."

"I don't think that'll be necessary. Just lean on me and we'll make it out okay. But you know, you really should have let them give you a transfusion to replace the blood you lost. The doctor Dom and I met with had some choice words regarding your refusal."

Having experienced the doctor's bedside manner firsthand on

a couple of occasions, Emma's rebuke was almost enough to make Paxton laugh. "No thanks. I've heard too many horror stories about where the blood comes from and how it's collected. As it is, I'll be lucky if the infection from the dirty knife and the stitches in my side don't kill me."

Emma didn't bother trying to conceal her amusement.

"Oh, hell. Let's just do this." As she leaned in to her, Paxton turned her head and saw Emma's face clearly, inches from her own. Real and solid as Paxton smiled weakly. "And in case I pass out or anything and forget to tell you—thank you for saving my life."

Chapter Four

As the driver made his way from the prison in the darkness, Paxton took a deep breath of clean night air, then leaned her head back and closed her eyes.

Her face was an unreadable mask, but in the intermittent lights of passing cars, Emma could see flashes of tension in her jaw as she fought the pain she was clearly feeling. It was concerning. Her color was off, her skin was clammy and her brow damp with sweat even as she shivered. There also appeared to be fresh blood on her side, an indication that one or more of her stitches had probably let go.

As soon as they got her to the hotel, Emma decided, she would make it a priority to have a doctor check Paxton out. At a minimum, a fresh set of stitches and some antibiotics would top the list.

"If you're making a list, I also need some clothes," Paxton said, her voice soft as she opened her eyes. "In the short term, once I get out of the extra-long shower I plan on taking, if I could at least borrow a pair of jeans and a T-shirt from you? Personally, I want to burn everything I have on. Even if I disregard the blood, my stuff all smells of the prison. So anything you don't mind lending me would be appreciated."

"Not to worry. We'll find something for you, even if it's from the hotel boutique. Because I somehow doubt anything I own will fit you."

"What makes you say that?" When Paxton lifted her head, pain, hot and raw, shone in the depths of her eyes. Emma watched her swallow back a moan then hold her breath as she waited for the pain to abate before continuing to speak. "I know I'm a bit taller, but at a guess, I'd say we're roughly about the same size."

"Maybe a year ago we were."

"What does that mean?"

Emma laughed. "Paxton, when was the last time you looked in a mirror?"

"Um...I'm not sure. I think it was shortly after a gang of inmates cut my hair off. I believe it was part of some ritual initiation. A welcome-to-the-cell-block kind of thing."

Emma's smile froze and words battled for dominance in her throat before she swallowed them. "They shaved your head?"

"Shaved? Hell, no, that would have been kinder. It was more like they hacked my hair off. Left a few clumps to go with the bruises they gave me. After a couple of weeks, one of the transplanted Aussies who would come by to visit prisoners befriended me and fixed it somewhat. She's continued to keep it trimmed, and since I truly didn't give a damn, I let her do whatever she wanted. Made it easier to keep clean with what little fresh water we had access to, so having it short wasn't a concern."

"Pax...shit." Emma felt a stillness slow her heart rate as the image hung between them. "I'm sorry. I don't know what to say."

"It's all right, Emma," Paxton said. Her voice was flat with acceptance, but even through the fatigue in her eyes, Emma caught a glint of arrogance. "I know many people believe a woman's vanity is connected to her hair, her appearance. And maybe so, but other than my instincts and my intellect, I've never given much thought to vanity."

Emma choked. "You're kidding, right?"

"Thanks." Paxton's smile appeared momentarily and her dimples winked from both cheeks. "I think I'll take that as a compliment."

"I would think so."

Paxton nodded, the lines of stress and strain bracketing her mouth more visible as she grew pensive once again. "The truth is with everything else I witnessed in that place over time, I know I got off lucky. I learned very quickly how to defend myself. It wasn't as if there was a lot to do anyway, so I exercised. Learned and practiced martial arts with a couple of Thai prisoners. And after a couple of tussles didn't go their way, the bullies left me alone."

Emma remained still a moment longer. She watched Paxton put a hand on her side. Saw her palm dark with blood when she drew it away. "I can already see you're in pain. How badly are you bleeding?"

She waited a moment when Paxton failed to answer. Waited a second or two longer before looking closer and reaching to check her pulse. Her breathing had slowed and was shallow, but she could feel her heart beat in a steady rhythm and she realized Paxton had all but passed out. "Dom—"

"Way ahead of you," he reassured her. "Worry not. I arranged to have a doctor on standby while I was waiting for you to bring her out. He'll meet us at the hotel. It'll just be a couple more minutes."

"I think we need to hurry."

"It's all right, Emma," Paxton said from beside her. "I was just resting my eyes for a minute."

"Nearly passed out from blood loss is more like it," Emma countered. "The good news is we're just about there. Will you be able to make it in on your own? If not we can check if the front desk can lend us a wheelchair. And if all else fails, Dom can always carry you."

She wasn't certain, but in the shadowed car, it looked as if Paxton rolled her eyes. "Thanks. I'll make it on my own steam."

"All right. You probably also need to eat. Should I order anything special for you?"

Paxton shook her head. "I have two simple goals in mind when we get to wherever we're going. A very long, very hot shower. And ten hours of sleep in a real bed. Other than some aspirin, everything else can wait."

"You'll see the doctor first," Emma told her.

"Emma, I don't mean to sound ungrateful because believe me, I'm not. But I'm dealing with limited and rapidly diminishing resources. If the doctor's there before I make it to the shower, all well and good. If not, quite frankly, he can see me in the morning."

❖

As promised, the vacationing American doctor Dom had arranged to check Paxton over was waiting in the lobby when they arrived. Once in the room, he wasted little time.

"How do you feel?" he asked her.

"I'm fine," she answered automatically. She wasn't entirely sure. But she didn't question it. Not until the doctor began to remove her bloodstained shirt so he could check the damage she'd sustained. That was when she heard Emma's gasp and saw her push Dom out of the room ahead of her.

Looking down at herself, she saw a rainbow of bruises and a weeping wound on her side that looked nasty. And yeah, maybe she could stand to put on some weight. But she didn't think any of it warranted the reaction she'd elicited.

The doctor remained mostly silent during the next few minutes while he checked her thoroughly. "How long have you been running a fever?"

"A few days."

"Did the doctors at the prison infirmary give you anything for it?"

A moan escaped Paxton's clenched teeth as she shook her head. Her body was begging to shut down but her mind refused. She inhaled and hissed the breath out through her teeth.

The sound caused the doctor's eyes to narrow, cool and steady, as he focused on hers. "What about for pain?"

"No."

"Nothing?" He sounded skeptical. "Are you on anything at all? Drugs of any kind?"

"No." She scowled and bit out the words. "I don't do drugs."

Something in her response must have made him believe her. Without any further argument, the doctor began the process of cleaning, re-stitching, and bandaging her side, before shooting her full of antibiotics.

Finally, after several silent minutes had passed, he said, "You're in surprisingly good shape, considering what I understand you've been through. But I'm concerned with how malnourished and dehydrated you are. And while I understand it's not what you want to hear, the best place for you tonight is a hospital."

Paxton groaned. She was mentally exhausted and didn't have the energy to get into any kind of discussion. Not with the doctor and not with the two NSA agents in the other room. But neither was she prepared to have anyone making decisions for her. After fourteen months of being told what to do, when to do it, and how, enough was enough. Game on.

"Doctor, I appreciate what you're trying to do for me, but I don't think so. No hospital until I'm out of Bali and preferably safely back on US soil. All I need right now is a very long hot shower followed by some sleep. Then I'm going to catch the first available flight I can get to

New York. If you really want to help, do you think you could find a way to protect this bandage long enough for me to get clean?"

The doctor gave her a long, hard look, but he finally did as she requested. Maybe he could sense that she still felt caged. That the prison was still much too close in proximity, both physically and in her psyche. And that she wasn't about to let anyone take her anywhere except home to the States. At the earliest opportunity.

First things first, which meant going to New York. Nick Perry appeared to have been dealt with. If he really was in federal lockup, there was nothing more for her to do. But there was still Carrie.

After that?

Maybe she'd go to Patagonia.

She didn't want to think about whatever Emma Thorpe wanted her to do. Didn't want to think about the fact she might owe this woman who had given her back her life. Who had taken her out from under the threat of death and had freed her from a hellish, never-ending nightmare.

But damn it. She hated owing anybody anything.

Rock? Hard place? Meet Pax.

Once the doctor left her, going no doubt to confer with Emma and Dom, Paxton struggled to her feet and made her way to the bathroom. Although she had to move gingerly and her body trembled from the effort, she hoped the shower would succeed in washing away the filth and ever-present stench of the prison that had been clinging to her for much too long.

She tossed her bloodied prison clothes into a wastebasket in a corner, then turned the water on as hot as she could stand it, and stood still under the pulsing beat. It stung at first, then soothed as she let it slowly warm away the chill that accompanied her fever.

As the steam began to rise and the tight muscles in her neck and shoulders started to loosen and untie, she reached for the soap and began scrubbing herself, not caring that her side throbbed and she was bruised all over. Fatigue was also a weight bearing down on her, but she couldn't recall the last time she'd been truly clean.

She had missed this simple pleasure. So damn much. Just the feel of the hot water and the scent of the soap slowly replacing the odors of the prison.

As she reached for the shampoo, she closed her eyes, and in that brief instant, she was assailed with shutter-flash images. Familiar images she had to struggle to hold back. The ones that had taken shape and form every single day since her arrest at the airport in Bali.

Damn it all. She was normally so good at compartmentalizing her emotions. She'd been doing it since she was a child. But while her time in prison made up only fourteen months out of the twenty-seven years of her life, right now, it seemed to define her.

She knew she would need to find a way to deal with the images. She would need to work on replacing them with older, happier memories. Or better yet, by making new memories. But she also knew not to expect healing to happen immediately. Or that anything would completely erase the past fourteen months. She just knew she had to start somewhere.

To Paxton's absolute horror, tears stung her eyes. Except she didn't believe in crying. She'd learned that lesson long ago and she wasn't about to start now.

As steam filled the bathroom and enveloped her, she wanted nothing more than to howl in grief and rage, and felt the scream trapped in her throat, begging for release. She fought back. Fought the urge to rail at the unfairness of it all. It would change nothing. But she was physically and emotionally spent, and her knees slowly buckled seconds ahead of a long-overdue and well-deserved meltdown.

❖

After seeing the doctor out, Emma stopped and spoke briefly with Dom. "The doctor seems more concerned with Paxton's emotional state than with her physical condition, although he'd still prefer she went to a hospital. He said she doesn't seem to realize how fragile she is and thinks we should keep a close eye on her. I'm inclined to agree."

"We can do that," Dom said. "But try to remember Paxton didn't survive her time in that prison by being a pushover, and in spite of everything she's been through, she seems to be holding it together."

"Or she's simply showing us what she wants us to see."

Dom nodded. "That's always a possibility. We still don't know enough about her to do more than hypothesize. The good news is I've got Sam and Theo working on trying to piece more of her background together, trying to find out more about who she is, where she's been, and what she's done. Maybe we'll get lucky and find something that will help. In the meantime, let's just concentrate on getting her back to the States and convincing her to work with us."

"And if she won't?"

"My money's on you. But if we can't convince her, we'll have to see if the president can." Dom's mouth curved up a tiny fraction and he let out a low laugh. "Catherine Winters wants James working with us. Stands to reason she must have some influence she can exert. Don't you think?"

Emma shrugged. "Why do you suppose that is?" She hated not knowing and softly sighed. "What possible connection can there be between the president and a former black hat hacker half her age?"

"I can't begin to guess." Dom laughed. "And it's not something we're going to solve tonight, so why don't you try to get some sleep? We've got a lot to do over the next couple of days, not the least of which is a long flight home."

She was still contemplating the possible connection between Paxton and Catherine Winters when she bid Dom good night and went to her room. But she couldn't stop the litany of questions, and as she lay in the darkness listening to the sounds of the surf, Emma's eyes remained wide open. Sighing, she rolled onto her side and attempted to get comfortable. She knew she needed to sleep. Needed to stay sharp, and this wasn't helping.

Twenty minutes later, in a move that defied logic, she abandoned the bed, slipped into a T-shirt, and silently left her room. Taking a deep breath that did nothing to fortify her and calling herself a fool, she knocked gently on Paxton's door.

Faintly concerned but not overly surprised when she received no response, she twisted the knob and went inside. It was immediately obvious the room was empty, and for an instant, Emma thought Paxton had taken off. But as silence settled around her, she realized she could still hear the sound of the shower running.

That wasn't right.

She could also still hear the doctor's warning about the shape Paxton was in—physically and emotionally—and with increasing concern she walked to the bathroom, knocked, then opened the door.

Emma didn't know what she expected. What she found was Paxton sitting on the floor of the shower, hot water spraying over her bowed head as she rocked herself back and forth. Bruised and battered, she appeared lost. Fragile. And the thundering sound of the shower seemed to echo her unvoiced screams.

Without thinking, Emma reached for the plush white robe hanging on a hook by the door, then turned off the water. Slowly Paxton looked up, her eyes swimming with pain, her expression dark and filled with too many shadows for her to sift through.

"What are you doing here?" Her voice was rough with unfiltered emotion.

"I thought I might be of some help," Emma said and offered her hand. As Paxton looked at it, Emma could see her body tense and expected her offer of help to be rejected.

She was right—but only to a point. She watched Paxton rise to her feet on her own with surprising grace, but then she surprised Emma as she accepted her help in wrapping the thick robe around her body. And there was only a slight hesitation before she allowed Emma to lead her out of the bathroom and into the bedroom.

They ended up sitting side by side on the bed. Emma knew she couldn't afford to say or do the wrong thing. If Catherine Winters was right—and there was no cogent reason to doubt her—countless innocent people's lives depended on her gaining Paxton's trust and cooperation. One wrong move could undo all the goodwill gained by negotiating her release from prison.

"You're covered in bruises, Paxton," she said mildly. "Can I get you anything? An ice pack or maybe some aspirin?"

Paxton stared at her wordlessly before she shook her head. "I'm okay. The doctor gave me something that took the edge off."

"All right. Do you want to talk?"

She'd surprised her with the question. Emma watched her expression switch from somber to startled, and in that instant, it seemed as if Paxton was actually seeing her for the first time. "No."

It was more a breath than a word, but Emma heard her. She realized she'd wanted Paxton to trust her, wanted it more than she could explain. But as she watched her struggle with what to say, Emma knew it was wishful thinking that Paxton would be able to take such a large step right now.

She could see an enforced control reasserting itself, along with the strength of will that enabled Paxton to slip a mask of calm back into place. Even then, she could see a desire to believe warring with a doubt fixed by experience. But she could also see the effort was costing her, to the point she wasn't certain Paxton was breathing.

"Okay. I can live with that. Just know I'm here and I will listen to whatever you want to say, whenever you want to say it. For now, could you do me one favor?"

"If I can."

"Just take a breath." She said it gently but firmly. Paxton was still disturbingly pale and she kept a close watch, waiting for her to take a breath. "Good. Now take another one, please."

Paxton again did as she was told, and as they sat in awkward silence for a long moment, the air seemed to crackle with intensity. Emma tried to read what Paxton was feeling, but couldn't. Paxton had somehow smoothed away all emotion from her face until it showed nothing, but Emma watched her knuckles turn white where she gripped the bed.

Uncertain what to do, Emma reached over and laid a hand on Paxton's. She didn't look up, but neither did she flinch or pull away.

"Amazing," Paxton whispered. "You've just done something I didn't think was even possible anymore."

"What's that?"

"You've surprised me."

A moment later, Emma felt a faint tremor under her hand and saw Paxton's eyes fill with tears. She was losing her grip on the tightly held control she'd exhibited since their meeting in the prison. Reacting instinctively, Emma reached and drew her into her shoulder, mindful of the bruises she'd seen on Paxton's torso. Offered a soothing balm for her lacerated soul.

"I can't begin to imagine what you've been through. I can only tell you that in time, it will get better," she said. "Give me a chance. Let me help."

She knew better than to promise things would be good right away. She knew nothing but time would ease the sting of betrayal and fade what Paxton had witnessed and experienced over the past fourteen months.

Emma remained silent and held Paxton until she stopped shivering. Until she lay quiet and still, curled in her arms with her head tucked safely beneath her chin. Until she closed her eyes and drifted away.

In the silence, broken only by the distant sound of the waves breaking against the beach, Emma continued to hold her, watching her sleep. Tomorrow, she told herself. Tomorrow she would let the questions come, let the doubts in, but not right now. Right now she was doing the one thing she'd wanted to do since she'd first laid eyes on Paxton's photograph.

She held her as she slept until just before the first light of day came through the windows. And then she slipped quietly from the room.

CHAPTER FIVE

As the early evening flight banked away from Bali and made its way through a darkening sky toward New York, Paxton stared out the window and tried to let the drone of the engines lull her into sleep. But sleep was impossible because she knew, somewhere behind her, Emma Thorpe and Dominic Creed were waiting for her to decide what she was going to do.

No, that wasn't right. They were waiting for her to decide she was going to help them. Work with them and their team of cyber specialists to resolve some kind of global cyber threat—something they'd yet to talk about or explain.

There was no question she was grateful to both of them. They'd gotten her out of prison. Gotten her out from under the ever-present threat of the firing squad waiting to carry out her death sentence. Gotten her away from the squalor and misery that had been all she'd known for more than a year.

She was aware Emma had held her for most of the previous night, enabling her to have the best night's sleep she'd had since Carrie walked away from her at the airport. Just as she was aware the two NSA agents had arranged for her to travel back to the US on a diplomatic flight out of Jakarta rather than on a commercial airliner, somehow intuiting she desperately needed room to be alone with her thoughts without someone intruding into her space.

Even better, the flight departed in the early evening, which had allowed her to spend most of the day by herself on the beach. Racing across the sand to the sea, she'd dived under the waves. The salt stung all of her cuts, but she didn't care. It was cleansing.

For the first time, she'd realized she was truly free. She heard her heart beat, felt the sun and wind on her skin, felt alive, and gloried in the feeling.

When she tired of swimming, she'd rolled lazily onto her back, floating in the unbelievably clear water while allowing the sun to chase the prison pallor from her face. She felt the normalcy of the people sharing the beach with her. Enjoying their vacations. An interesting sensation, considering she'd never had a normal life. Ever.

When she'd finally returned to the hotel room, she discovered Emma and Dom had bought her some new clothes—the jeans and brightly colored T-shirt she was wearing—that, together with signs of a slight sunburn, enabled her to blend in with all the tourists at the airport, heading home after a vacation in paradise.

Even more remarkably, Emma had let her borrow a laptop. Clearing any emotion other than polite calm from her face, she'd stared at Emma. "Knowing who and what I am and what I can potentially do with this, you're leaving me with your laptop?"

Emma simply nodded. Paxton knew Emma wanted her to trust her—in fact, needed her trust for this venture to be successful. But she clearly understood it wouldn't come easily.

"Paxton, sooner or later, you and I are going to have to start trusting each other. I'm thinking it might as well start now. All I ask is one thing from you."

"What's that?"

"After we land? Please don't run. I'm sure you're well aware reintegration can be difficult and we—my team and I—can help you with that. All I'm asking is that if it gets difficult for you, please don't disappear. We can and will find you. I think you know that. But it will go so much smoother for everyone if we don't have to."

Paxton weighed her words. Part of her wanted to agree, but then she slowly shook her head. "I'm sorry." She let out a long breath. "When I make a promise, I keep my word. Otherwise, what's the point? But I'm not sure of anything right now, so I don't think I can promise that."

"All right." Emma sounded disappointed, but not surprised. "Maybe the best we can hope for is that you'll at least try."

She walked toward her seat, leaving Paxton tilting her head and silently staring after her, momentarily distracted by the gentle sway of Emma's hips as she walked away.

Trust. Such an elusive thing. Hard to give. So easy to lose. She'd already taken too many hits in life to trust easily—if at all.

Her relationship with Carrie came to mind as a perfect example. Before that final trip, the mutual lust that had bound them together had run its course, their initial friendship wasn't strong enough to sustain them, and the relationship had been easing toward an inevitable conclusion. It was something they had both recognized. But she had still trusted Carrie. Right up to the moment when she walked away, leaving Paxton with a suitcase filled with cocaine she couldn't explain and weapons trained on her, daring her to move.

Now Emma and Dom said they wanted her help, and in an act of faith had gotten her out of prison, no strings attached. But that didn't really matter because she knew she owed them. That in itself weighed heavily as a condition of her freedom.

Except she couldn't deal with this. Not any of it. At least not right now. Not until she was able to put some time and distance between her and the prison in Bali. And not until she'd had time to think things through. Time to regroup.

For a few minutes, she listened to the ambient sounds around her—soft conversations, muted laughter. Listened until the captain gave permission to use electronic devices. She then turned on the laptop and immediately connected to the plane's WiFi.

It was time to find out what had been going on in the world while she'd been locked away. There were people she needed to contact, bank accounts she needed to access. And more importantly, a life she needed to reclaim. Everything else could wait.

❖

"Are you planning to talk to her before we get to New York?"

Turning back from the cloud formations that had held her attention, Emma nodded and thought about Dom's question. She'd already been contemplating slipping into the empty seat next to Paxton and having a serious one-on-one conversation. She just hadn't decided on the best approach.

She'd actually wanted to at least start this conversation while they'd still been in the hotel. She'd heard Paxton get up around five, but had chosen to give her space rather than check on her. Just after seven, she got up and found her on the balcony drinking coffee, and for the first time since meeting her, the half smile on her face seemed real.

Below them, waves were breaking with a deceptive, lazy grace. She watched them hold Paxton's attention, captivate her, and in that moment, Emma decided against disturbing whatever peace she'd momentarily found and let the silence settle between them.

After a minute or so, Paxton looked up and pointed to the table where a tray held coffee, orange juice, and a basket filled with sweet rolls. "I hope you don't mind. I really needed coffee. It's quite good and since I didn't know what you might want, I opted for continental."

"Continental's perfect for me, although Dom may want something more substantial."

"Actually, he's already gone down to the restaurant. He muttered something about needing more sustenance than this. Said he needed something more manly."

Emma had laughed and helped herself to the coffee. Let the caffeine flow through her system. When no other comments were forthcoming, she turned and saw Paxton's eyes briefly close as she turned her face to the sun and visibly relaxed. And just like that, any serious conversation was put off until later.

Later appeared to have arrived.

With a terse nod, Emma slipped past Dom into the aisle and slowly moved to where Paxton was seated. She appeared comfortable, her face intent while her fingers flew across the laptop keyboard. Emma knew the moment Paxton sensed her approach. Her shoulders stiffened and her hands stopped in midmotion as she turned to look at her.

"Am I interrupting? I was hoping we might talk."

Paxton's gaze narrowed a bit at the careful but casual way she said it. Her smile showed effort, but she also looked curious as she shifted in her seat and pushed the laptop back. "It's all right. I've probably done as much as I can deal with from here. Will you want some coffee or something stronger for this talk?"

Emma's eyes moved in the direction of the glass Paxton had by the laptop. Watched her reach for it and drink some.

"It's just water," Paxton said mildly. "You'd be amazed how good it tastes—kind of like freedom. But get yourself something stronger if that's what works for you. I was told one of the advantages of being on a diplomatic flight is there's a lovely selection of wines on board." She hit the call button.

"Actually, tea would be nice. Even better if you've got chai," Emma said to the attendant who silently appeared beside her, then used the time until he returned to settle her mind. She needed this to go right and that meant she needed to establish that elusive, subtle line of trust between them.

They'd not had the best of starts, and there was still the ghost of Nick Perry to contend with. But she needed to move forward, needed to convince Paxton that working with her team was in everyone's best interest. And she feared she only had the remainder of their flight to plead her case and make it happen.

She felt the intensity of Paxton's eyes watching her and eased into the conversation, keeping her tone even. "We told you we want you to work with us. I thought perhaps we could talk a bit more about that, and maybe clarify a few things."

"All right. Why don't you level the playing field for me? Tell me what I need to know." She spoke casually and took another drink of water, but Emma could see her body had gone to alert. "Even if I didn't know you're with the American Cyber-Research Institute, the fact that you want to involve me already tells me it's a cyber issue. And serious enough that you went to great lengths to find me and get me out of a bad situation."

Emma frowned. "You were set up. That should have been reason enough to get you out. But I admit the problem is serious. I'd go so far as to say the cyber attacks we're facing present a very real threat to our national and economic security, and the magnitude of the threats is growing every day."

"Considering my background, I'm not about to disagree with you," Paxton said dryly. "At least in general terms. But clearly there was something specific that sent you looking for me. Why don't you start by giving me the fifty-thousand-foot view? We can worry about the details later."

The details would only be important if Paxton agreed to help. Clearly the time had come to convince her.

"All right. The number of cyber attacks into secure government systems has been skyrocketing. Initially, we were dealing with

Distributed Denial of Service attacks, except they lasted far longer than expected, caused loss of revenues, and eroded trust."

"In other words, the DDS attacks did exactly what they are supposed to do."

"Yes. I suppose so. But then the attacks began to change, resulting in the theft of intellectual property that could pose a threat to national security. There've been a number of high-profile system breaches, including the State Department, the DOJ, Homeland Security, and the Office of Personnel Management."

"What was accessed at the OPM?"

"Security clearance applications. Highly detailed information on everything from where an applicant has lived and worked, to personal references, family members, friends and associates, drug history, and intimate health information. Virtually every government employee and contractor who holds the top echelon of US security clearances has been impacted."

Paxton was silent for a long moment, her face pale and set. "Interesting. That kind of information could be used for anything, including blackmailing government workers, so it could net a hacker a tidy profit."

Emma nodded. "But it gets worse, because the attacks are crossing the line from data mining and disruption to potential destruction. For example, the USACE computer systems have been hacked, giving someone highly sensitive information about the nation's dams. The data taken includes their location and condition, and the potential for fatalities if the dams were to be breached."

"If that kind of information falls into the wrong hands, the flooding and the disruption to the electric grid could result in loss of life and damage to the economy beyond what occurred after 9/11," Paxton said.

"That's the fear," Emma agreed. "And it doesn't stop there. We've gotten reports from two—no, three—different airlines where the pilots have temporarily lost control of their onboard computer systems and had them remotely taken over by someone, either on the plane or somewhere on the ground. We're not sure. But something similar happened with an oil supertanker in the Gulf of Mexico. In each case, the loss of control was temporary and was returned in time to avoid a disaster and any loss of life. It's almost as if—"

"Someone was testing their ability to take control," Paxton finished for her.

"That would be the consensus opinion. And if they can do it at will, it renders meaningless all the security protocols that were put in place post 9/11. Terrorists won't need to train pilots, hijack planes, or deal with air marshals because the threat doesn't have to be onboard the aircraft. It can be accomplished remotely through computer systems."

Paxton gave her a penetrating look. "I assume you're aware the technology in the Dreamliner and the A350 was actually designed to allow for remote control intervention in the event an emergency were to happen in the air?"

"Yes. Except this isn't intervening in an emergency situation, is it?"

"No. This is any given day of any given week when countless commercial aircraft suddenly become vulnerable to having their onboard computers hacked and remotely taken over. All too doable, I'm afraid, and the potential loss of life would be horrific."

Emma hesitated. "Could you—?"

"Yes." Paxton's expression didn't alter. "But it's one thing to test and stretch technological boundaries, breaching security systems. Another is being responsible for countless lives being lost. So the real question you should be asking is *would* I, and the answer to that is no."

"I'm sorry. I knew that, but I had to ask."

Paxton's lips curled in an approximation of a smile. "It's all right, Emma. I understand. Now tell me what else you know."

"It would be easier to tell you what we don't know," Emma responded. "We don't know how many different groups we're dealing with. We don't know whether we're dealing with terrorist groups from hostile nation states trying to destabilize Western interests, or high school kids working out of their parents' garage. Just as we don't know whether the endgame is a series of senseless, devastating accidents and catastrophic loss of life or whether it's an attack followed by an attempt at blackmail, using the compromised systems as hostages, as bargaining chips. Force governments to free political prisoners. Or for money. We simply don't know. All we know is that we keep getting hacked and they've gotten into secure systems they should never have been able to access."

"Except every system is vulnerable and every cyber attack is a reflection of some vulnerability in the system," Paxton said matter-of-factly. "Welcome to the Wild West, cyber style, where at the end of the day, there are only two kinds of computer systems. Those that are known to have already been hacked and those that have been hacked, but people don't know yet."

"Not exactly what anyone wants to hear."

Paxton shrugged.

"I admit we've long known it's only a matter of when, not whether, we'll have a catastrophic attack, and the fear is growing that attackers will shut down our financial system or our electric grid. There's been an increase in chatter. Suspicions point to the Chinese and the Russians. We continue to work closely with the Germans, the French, and the British. But no one's been able to turn up any tangible leads."

When Paxton remained silent, Emma leaned her head back. She chewed her lip then glanced at her. "We are living in a time when the public turns to computers to handle everything, from finances to storing personal information. And while most consumers believe they are adequately protected by firewalls and antivirus software, the reality is quite the opposite. The same holds true for governments. We are significantly exposed to a cyber attack, the consequences of which could exceed our darkest imaginings. That's why my boss decided to put a special ops group together, answering directly to her."

"Under the guise of the American Cyber-Research Institute."

"Yes. She asked me to head it up. To recruit the best of the best. To identify, locate, and deal with terrorist cyber threats. And then she reminded me of an old adage. Something about it taking a thief to catch a thief."

"So you went looking for a hacker in the hopes of catching a hacker?" Paxton sighed.

"Yes, something like that. Except my boss doesn't want just any hacker. She actually suggested you."

"Your boss? Are you saying your boss sent you in my direction?"

"Yes."

"So who do you answer to? And how the hell does she know me?"

Emma stared at her in surprise. "I thought I mentioned it to you. I answer directly to the president. Catherine Winters. It works for me. I like having a short reporting chain."

Paxton suddenly looked pale and her voice was reduced to a whisper. "You're saying Cat's the one who wants me working on this thing with you?"

"If you mean the President of the United States, then yes." With questions circling in her head, Emma almost missed the brief change in Paxton's expression before she regained control. "Paxton? I'm sorry—did you just call the president *Cat*?"

Paxton nodded and ran a hand through her hair in an oddly vulnerable gesture.

"Oh, hell."

CHAPTER SIX

All too aware that Emma was closely watching her, Paxton tried to sort through a jumble of thoughts while trying not to become overwhelmed. Except it was easier said than done. Especially since her emotions had been in a state of constant flux from the moment Emma and Dom first appeared at the prison.

She needed to remain focused. Stay in the moment. But damn, it was hard, because Catherine Winters was the only person with whom she had an outstanding IOU. She owed her. Would do anything for her. Without question.

Cat had been there and come through for her at a time when she had so badly needed help. At a time when there'd been no one else to turn to. Was this her way of calling in that long ago marker? If so, it left her with little choice but to work with Emma and her team.

Actually, it left her with no choice at all.

"Paxton?" Emma's voice broke through her thoughts. "What is it? Can I do anything to help?"

She found herself oddly pleased by Emma's words. Still, she shook her head. She could feel nerves shimmering because in that moment, her world had just shifted off its axis and there was nothing anyone could do. Because just when she'd least expected it, the past had raised its ugly head. *Her* past. And just like that, her life had managed to become even more complicated.

Emma reached out, touched her arm. "Will you at least answer one question for me? Do you or do you not personally know Catherine Winters?"

"Yes."

"Do you want to tell me how?"

"Not particularly."

Emma brought her head closer. "Paxton, I assure you whatever you tell me stays here. Between us. Please. Believe me when I say I don't want to use it. But I do need to understand. I work best when I've got all the facts. When I'm not about to get blindsided. And I've been trying to understand this ever since President Winters made recruiting you an imperative."

Paxton didn't bother to hide her skepticism.

"You don't believe me?"

"Oh, I believe you," she said. She could have dropped it there. Should have dropped it there. But some impulse made her push. "I believe you want to know what connection could possibly exist between the president and a hacker because you can't picture it. Because it can't possibly be real. Because the president is a powerful woman who is above reproach while I'm—"

"I'm sorry."

"Don't worry about it." Paxton sighed, briefly closed her eyes, and felt as if she was walking an emotional tightrope. *She doesn't have a right to know*, she thought, but then the words just spilled as she found herself reciting details, unleashing the past slowly.

"If you must know, it happened about fifteen years ago. The police brought a twelve-year-old girl into the emergency department of a Boston area hospital. She was in pretty bad shape, having been beaten to within an inch of her life by her stepfather."

"You? Oh, Jesus, Paxton. I'm so sorry. But why?"

"Because I refused to continue using my computer skills to steal for him."

Emma's eyes widened and Paxton could see she was trying to control her reaction to what she had just heard.

"It's all right, Emma. This story actually had a happy-ever-after ending. Because as luck would have it, the doctor who operated on me became my friend, for no reason other than he liked to talk with me. He'd come to visit after his shift ended and we'd play chess. He said I challenged him."

Emma gave a soft laugh. "I don't doubt that."

"And he had a wife, who happened to be a damned good lawyer, and she not only became my friend as well, she offered to help. So what could have been one of the worst times of my young life turned into one of the best."

"Do you know what emancipation means?"
"If we're talking about emancipation of a minor, it's a legal process that gives a teenager who is sixteen or older legal independence from his or her parents or guardians. Except I'm nowhere near sixteen."
"If you're smart enough to have broken in to all those computer systems, you should be smart enough to trust your lawyer."
"You're my lawyer?"
"Right the first time. I knew you were bright."

The silence stretched until Emma asked, "Are you all right?"
"Sorry, just momentarily replaying the past."
"The lawyer who helped you. That was Catherine Winters?"
"Cat, yes." Paxton's voice softened as she met Emma's eyes and wondered what it was about this woman that had her admitting things she wouldn't normally share with any living soul. "She was really something to see in action. She took my case pro bono and got me my freedom. More than that, she believed in me, had me tested, and got me into MIT on a full scholarship. She opened the door to a world of limitless possibilities and showed me I could do anything, be anything. And along the way, she even showed me how to look after myself and how to cook enough that I wouldn't starve to death."
"I'm impressed. I guess it also explains why we've been unable to find any intel on you before MIT."
"That's because there is no intel before then. I was a ghost until Cat and Paul saved my life. I didn't exist." For an instant, Paxton felt a flash of the helpless impotence she'd lived with for so long. The sense of being invisible.
She closed her eyes as her chest tightened. She worked to unclench hands that had formed into fists. Slowly took a deep breath. In. Then out. In. Then out. And then she opened her eyes. "Like I said, Cat was something to see. But it was more than that. She saw something in me, accepted me for who and what I was, then helped me become more."

"You don't have to sell me. I don't just work for her, I voted for her," Emma said and offered a small smile. "What about your mother?"

"Frank threw her out when I was nearly nine. Told her he would kill her if she tried to come back and get me away from him. We'd seen what he could do and we both believed him." She saw the shift in Emma's expression, caught the horror, and wiped her own face clear of any emotion. "It's in the past. It was a long time ago."

"Not so long. It left you alone with your stepfather for about three years, if I'm doing the math correctly. And you were only a child."

She stared at Emma, fighting through her discomfort as an involuntary shiver crept up her spine. She didn't talk about her childhood. Period. Visiting old pain was useless, especially when nothing would change. "It was a long time ago," she repeated. "And trust me. I wasn't a child even when I was a child."

Emma looked as if she wanted to press and Paxton tried to quickly armor herself. To shut the door. But then Emma surprised her by changing course. "Did you ever find her? After Catherine Winters got you free of your stepfather, did you ever find your mother?"

Paxton nodded. "We managed to reconnect briefly."

"Good for you. And your biological father?"

"There was no one to find. He died before I was born. He was in the military, on shore leave having a drink with some mates when someone blew up the bar he was in. Simply a case of wrong place at the wrong time."

"I'm sorry." Emma felt a fierce anger begin to simmer just under the surface for all that had happened to Paxton.

"It is what it is. I've had a long time to come to terms with it."

The words were said with calmness, but for just an instant, Emma saw the truth in her face—the still raw edge to Paxton's emotions. She could feel it and knew she was walking on fragile ice.

Some things are best left buried. The words echoed in her mind, an apt warning, even as she veered away from talk of family and moved the conversation forward cautiously. "The fact that the president helped you fifteen years ago doesn't show up anywhere. Is that your handiwork?"

"Yes."

"Why? Why hide it?"

"I did it for Cat. Think it through, Emma. If you were Cat Winters, would you want your name that closely associated with a known computer hacker? It doesn't matter that her heart was in the right place and she brought a world of possibility into the life of one mixed-up kid."

"It was a long time ago," Emma said.

A half-mocking smile touched Paxton's lips. "Not so long. Politics has a long memory and Cat was already being groomed for something big. The best I could do for her was stay away. Well, that and to donate to her campaign for the senate, and again for the presidency. Admitting we knew each other could only hurt her. People would find a way to use it against her. Especially at a time when, as you said, the greatest threat to national security is cyber warfare. I owed her too much to allow that to happen. So maybe I took some liberties and buried some history."

"Okay, maybe. But I still don't understand. Why did you continue hacking after President Winters got you into MIT? I saw some of your records. You tested off the scales and I understand from your professors there were corporations lining up to hire you."

"Why? Because I'm good at it. Everyone has certain talents. Mine just happens to be hacking."

"No." Emma stopped her. "That's not good enough. What's the real reason?"

Paxton shrugged as if recognizing the moment for what it was. "Probably because I was a kid. Too smart for my own good, but just a kid. And sometimes my need to see if I could figure something out—or prove that I could—simply got the better of me. I wanted to find the secrets to operating systems, computer security systems, cell phones. Anything that stirred my curiosity, my desire to learn about technology, and my need for intellectual challenge. And I didn't want to be constrained."

"You make it sound like it was a game."

Paxton smiled.

Emma reminded herself not to stare.

"In a way it was," Paxton said. "I've always loved games that challenge me. Like one time I saw the CEO of some company talking on CNN. He said his security system was foolproof. Said no one could get in."

"So you decided to see if he was right?"

"Something like that. I even went the white hat route afterward and told them where the security flaws were. But I seem to have the devil's own luck and even before I was done being a student, along with the corporations that wanted to hire me, certain people appeared in the periphery of my life. People like my stepfather and Nick Perry who figured out what I was capable of doing. How much it might be worth."

"They wanted to use you."

"They wanted me to make them rich. And they made sure I understood no wasn't an acceptable answer." Memories darkened Paxton's eyes and made her smile disappear, her mouth becoming a grim line.

"Damn it, you were a kid."

"Actually, I was a survivor."

"I don't understand. Why didn't you reach out and ask for help? Call—"

"There was only Cat and she had already done enough. Risked enough. And there were other reasons."

"Like what?"

Paxton paused in thought. "For one, my stepfather's attack was as close to dying as I wanted to get. And truthfully, I was already hooked on the shadow life. The other life, the one that was supposed to be real, just didn't seem real anymore. The highs and lows and the sheer adrenaline of what I was doing had become all-consuming."

"How did you survive? Find any balance?"

"I made a deal with myself. On any job I was pulled into against my will, I insisted on thirty percent. Ten percent for me, sent my mother ten percent, and donated ten percent to organizations I felt would do some good with it. Places that support runaway street kids or wildlife or refugees."

"Are you saying you compensated by turning into some kind of Robin Hood?"

"Not hardly." Paxton offered a tired laugh. "And I don't want you to think I'm making excuses, because I'm not. I'm just talking about choices. When it comes down to it, most people's lives hang on just a few choices. I know what I did, just as I know the responsibility I bear for my choices."

"But they weren't all your choices alone."

"Maybe not. I made some, had others made for me. Some right and some maybe not so much. But the truth is, though I may have had a rough start, I've made a very good living for myself along the way. I live well. And over time I figured out how to untangle myself from certain connections and chose to become more gray, and then more white than black. That was a conscious choice. Just like not working for Nick Perry was a choice. I just didn't anticipate how determined he was to use me or the possible consequences of my refusal. And it certainly didn't occur to me that Carrie would set me up to save herself. Go figure."

"Will you go see your mother now that you're back?"

Paxton shifted infinitesimally. "No. She died about a year after I found her. My stepfather—he finally found her and killed her."

Jesus Christ. "God, I'm so sorry. What about him? Your stepfather. Does he still pose a danger to you? Is he still any kind of threat?"

"No."

"How can you be certain?"

"Because he's dead. He chose a coward's way out and used his service revolver on himself before they could arrest him for killing my mother."

Emma frowned. "Service revolver?"

"He was a cop. She met him in a park she'd taken me to when I was maybe six months old. She was young and lost and he seemed kind and she thought he was a good choice. A safe choice. She thought he would protect the two of us. Make us into a family."

Paxton's voice seemed to echo the emptiness she was clearly feeling. She'd been running on adrenaline, Emma realized as she listened to her voice. And it was fast running out. The thrill of being released from prison would only carry her so far, and then she would crash. Physically and emotionally.

Emma hated having to push. Having to ask the question. But she needed some kind of indication that Paxton would work with her before they landed in New York. She needed something she could present when she met with Catherine Winters. "Thank you for trusting me with this. And I'm truly sorry, but I really need to ask. What happens now?"

It was clear the question shut something down inside Paxton, who sighed and looked away, but not before Emma saw a shadow

COUNTING TO ZERO

move across her eyes. "I'm sorry too, Emma, but the best I can say is I honestly don't know what happens next. Over the years, I've discovered I'm not particularly fond of agencies like the FBI or CIA and I'm not exactly happy at the prospect of working for some government agency, let alone the one that employed Nick Perry."

Emma considered that and half smiled. "Well, I can assure you that you won't be working for either the CIA or FBI. We may use their assets as resources, but that's as far as it goes."

"Thank God for small mercies," Paxton observed dryly. "In any case, I know I owe Cat. Just as I know I owe you and Dom for getting me out of that hell in Bali."

"I told you that was a get-out-of-jail-free card."

"Call it what you will. But everything's happened too quickly and I haven't had time to process anything. And that's what I need. Some time alone. Time to think. I don't deal well when I'm surrounded by too many people. That's why I go to places like Cambodia and Vietnam. Or hike the Inca Trail to Machu Picchu."

Emma waited when Paxton paused, all too aware she'd just been given a clue that would hopefully help in the days and weeks to come.

"I appreciate that time is of the essence. But I've not had any time alone for a very long time. And I need it before I can make any decisions. The best I can do is promise you I'll be in touch. One way or the other. And now, I'm done talking about this. Thanks for lending me the laptop."

The conversation was over and silence returned.

Acknowledging it, grateful Paxton had given her as much as she had, Emma rolled her shoulders and stretched her legs as she slowly returned to her seat. She handed Dom the laptop. "I want Shelby to go over this computer and tell me where Paxton's been. I want to know every site she visited, every connection she made. And I want Paxton followed from the moment we land."

"It went that good?"

A muscle worked in her jaw before Emma shrugged. "It's still undecided. But as much as I told her we'd find her if she tries to disappear, I'm not certain how realistic that is."

"I thought you were trying to establish trust with her?"

"I was—I am. But she's not just bloody brilliant, she's street smart. I don't doubt she's got connections we don't even know about.

And she likely has the financial resources to stay in the wind for a very long time. We can't afford to lose her. So I'm going all in on this one."

Dom accepted the explanation and didn't push for more. "Understood. I'm on it, boss."

CHAPTER SEVEN

P axton knew she was being followed before she left JFK.
Unperturbed, she fought against an impulse to wink at her initial tail as she grabbed a to-go coffee and a toasted bagel and took a cab to her first destination. After that, she walked.

She knew walking was simply making it easier for whoever was following her, but she had always loved walking, and she used the time to become reacquainted with the sounds and scents and energy of the city. She heard snatches of conversations, felt the sun on her face, and enjoyed simply being able to go anywhere she wanted to go without being stopped by guards and walls and bars on windows.

She used the time to think and come to some decisions she hoped she could live with.

It took longer than she'd originally planned. But as the day waned, she'd managed to deal with most of the mundane necessities of a return to her life—a current driver's license, credit cards, money transfers, several cell phones, and a pair of fully loaded laptops she had custom built with help from an old acquaintance.

By then, she was in tune with the rhythm of the interchangeable pair of NSA agents who were taking turns following her. One male. One female. They were pretty good, she'd give them that much. But Paxton knew the streets and the people who lived between the cracks, having been there often enough herself.

She also knew how to disappear, if that was what she wanted to do. But disappearing wasn't on today's agenda.

The male agent had short dark hair, the body of a runner, and sunglasses covering his eyes. Earlier, she'd managed to snap his photograph with her phone and run him through a facial recognition program when she stopped at an internet café. It gave her everything she needed.

On the other end of her search, she found NSA agent Theo Landry, thirty-five years of age. After a stint in the military, he'd done time with the counterterrorism unit before moving to NSA's cyber operations, and reportedly possessed an incredible ability to absorb and sift through intelligence. Current boss: Emma Thorpe.

No surprise.

Having identified Landry made it easier to track the woman working with him. Paxton simply tapped into Emma Thorpe's team files and quickly found Samantha Carson. An ex-CIA threat analyst whose focus was finding patterns and connections.

Attractive, athletic, with shoulder-length dark hair and a faintly exotic look to her sharp cheekbones and dark eyes. Her hair was pulled back in a ponytail, which made her appear too young to be of consequence, but the intelligence in her eyes was unmistakable.

An interesting woman. And the longer Paxton thought about it, one who just might work perfectly into her plans for the evening.

She waited for the next changeover before kicking into action. Increasing her pace, she moved along the crowded sidewalk filled with New Yorkers hustling in every direction, all studiously avoiding eye contact with each other. And when the time was right, she ducked into a Vietnamese restaurant, maneuvered past harried staff as she ran through the steam- and scent-filled kitchen, and came out in a shadowed alley.

Only a skinny tabby, perched on the edge of a dumpster, stood watch as she made her way in the gloomy light toward the street. Once she reached the end of the alleyway, a quick glance showed her two tails, standing on either side of the busy street, looking decidedly unhappy while clearly communicating with each other.

After a short discussion, the woman slipped inside and checked the restaurant Paxton had disappeared into. A few minutes later, she returned to the sidewalk, shaking her head and shrugging her shoulders as she and her counterpart discussed what to do next. Paxton slipped in behind her.

"Agent Carson, be a good girl and tell Agent Landry to report back to Emma Thorpe at the office," she whispered in her ear. "Tell him there's no need to worry. We're simply changing the rules of engagement. You are going to continue watching me for the rest of the day, only we're going to do it much more openly."

She felt the agent stiffen against her and watched as she turned around and met her gaze. She held still, kept herself relaxed and open to the woman's scrutiny, and waited without saying a word. She saw reality settle in and knew the moment Samantha Carson agreed before she heard her tell her partner she would be spending the rest of the day with Paxton.

Theo Landry wasn't a happy man and clearly wanted to argue. But by then it was obvious Samantha Carson had made her own decision. Turning her back on her protesting partner and decreasing the volume on her PRR, she gave an effervescent grin.

"If we're spending the day together, call me Sam and I'll call you Pax. Can you tell me where we're going?"

Paxton liked her already.

She knew she had piqued Sam's curiosity and saw something in her eyes as she tried to process what had just happened. Leaving her to her thoughts for a moment, Paxton hailed a cab, indicated Sam should get in beside her, and gave the driver the address for her loft.

Traffic moved slowly, but the sun was still bright, the sky clear, and the ride gave her time to think and plan. She appreciated that Sam remained quiet, her eyes watchful, taking it all in when they finally stopped in a neighborhood of cobblestoned streets and historic warehouse buildings that once housed poets and artists and writers.

Cat and Paul Winters had helped her when she'd decided to buy a place to live on the East Coast, and the Manhattan loft had turned out to be the first and only place Paxton had looked at. Her bolt-hole.

For the first time in her life, she'd fallen in love with a place—both the city and the loft. Manhattan made it possible for her to remain alone while surrounded by people. The full-floor loft gave her a sense of space that was enhanced by the large windows, barrel-vaulted ceilings, exposed brick walls, and four exposures.

And while the loft was still relatively lacking in furniture, to her it was perfect.

"Wow," Sam murmured as Paxton led her inside. "This is gorgeous. And maybe I'm wrong, but for a place you've not been in for more than a year and a half, your home has a definite lived-in look. Do you have a house guest, Pax?"

Paxton shook her head. "Not one that's here by invitation. A squatter's more like it and not for much longer. I just need to make a couple of quick calls, and then we'll talk. All right?"

The calls included making arrangements for the locks on the front door to be changed and making some alterations to the security system. There was also a call to a young hacker Paxton knew well. Very well. She'd contacted him by email while on her way back to New York, so her call came as no surprise.

"I need some help, Tommy. I need clothes for a friend for this evening. We'll be going to Jimmy K's so I need you to make it something sleek and sexy." She glanced at Sam before continuing. "Size six. And she'll need shoes."

"Size eight," Sam said without being asked, her expression curious.

"Size eight. I've also got some stuff left behind at my place by a former friend that needs to find a new home. It's going to be a bit impractical for the kids down at the center or the women's shelter, so tell me what you think you can get for all of it, keep ten percent, and give the rest of the money to Sister Kate. She'll know what to do with it."

Once she got off the phone, Paxton walked through the loft with Sam trailing her. There were signs of Carrie everywhere, from clothes carelessly tossed on the unmade bed to the scent of her perfume in the still air.

The scent stirred memories. Not all of them good.

It shouldn't have surprised her that Carrie had set her up, let her take the fall, and then continued to live in Paxton's New York home. But it did. It also hurt, but after tonight, she wouldn't give Carrie another thought.

"She left a lot of clothes behind," Sam said as she peered into one of the closets in the master bedroom.

Paxton scowled. "It appears that's not all she left."

There, surrounded by jewelry, perfumes, and an assortment of creams and lotions, was a small fortune in cocaine, sitting in a Waterford crystal goblet Paxton didn't recognize. Picking up the glass and holding it in one hand, Paxton stared at it long and hard.

The loft receded until she was aware only of the sudden pounding of her heart and the sound of her own breathing.

"Pax? Are you all right?"

Even as she heard her name called, for an instant she was back at the airport in Bali, sprawled on the floor with her wrists cuffed and multiple weapons aimed at her head. Watching Carrie walk away.

"Pax? You've gone kind of pale and—oh, damn, is that what I think it is?"

Paxton licked her lips and slowly nodded. Without saying a word, she walked to the bathroom and emptied the powder in the goblet into the toilet, then flushed it out of sight. When she finally looked up, she saw Sam leaning against the door frame watching her.

"Okay. Change the locks—check. Dispose of cocaine—check. What's next on the agenda for this evening?" Sam grinned. "Did I hear you say Jimmy K's?"

❖

"Did I hear you say Jimmy K's?"

Emma's stomach tightened as she pressed the phone to her ear and tried to separate what Dom was saying from the background noise, both at his location and hers. She hoped she'd misheard.

"Paxton James walked in a few minutes ago. She looked so hot Landry almost swallowed his tongue. And a funny thing. She had a woman on her arm who looked a lot like Sam Carson, only she was wearing some hot little number. Actually, they're both dressed for a night on the town. And Jimmy K's? What's not to like?"

Emma blew out a sharp breath and rubbed the fatigue in her neck. "It wouldn't be the first place I'd choose." *Actually, it wouldn't make the top ten.*

It might have been a long time since she'd been out with a woman, but she still preferred quieter, more romantic venues—soft jazz and candlelight. But just because it wasn't for her didn't detract from the club's popularity.

"Let's remember Paxton just spent the past fourteen months in prison, and if a night on the town helps speed her decision to work with us then let's cut her some slack. As long as Sam's inside with her and you and Theo have the outside covered, I don't see a problem."

Dom cleared his throat. "The problem is James has been taking care of business all day and she's been a busy girl. So far, she's been to the DMV, several banks, electronics stores, and several places where I can't begin to guess what they do."

"And—?"

"And I believe the next order of business just might be her ex."

Emma closed her eyes and tried to keep a sudden headache at bay. "You think Paxton is looking to settle the score?"

"Could very well be. I'm told Jimmy K's is Carrie Nolan's favorite place to see and be seen and she usually makes an entrance around midnight if she's in New York, which she happens to be."

"All right. Tell me what you've got."

"I've got Landry outside with me and Shelby and Kinsey on the inside, plus Sam. But after your talk on the flight, you're the only one with any sense of connection to James so far, so I'm thinking you might want to make an appearance before things get too out of hand. The last thing we need is for Paxton to get arrested again."

"Shit." Emma glanced at her watch. According to Dom's timetable, she didn't have a lot of time to change into something appropriate and get to Jimmy K's.

If Paxton was looking for payback, Emma could hardly blame her. But she had no interest in having to bail her out of jail or having Paxton's picture all over the morning papers. That would potentially alert people who were best kept in the dark about her whereabouts, making it something they could ill afford to have happen.

By the time Emma arrived at Jimmy K's, she had used up every one of the twenty minutes Dom had given her, plus an extra ten. And even that was a miracle, she thought wryly, given it was after midnight on a Friday night in New York.

She hesitated briefly as she slipped inside the club. Paused long enough to absorb the scents and sounds, the heat and vibrations. Long enough for her eyes to adjust to the lighting as she scanned the faces around her. Long enough to gather her wits, knowing it was likely she would need them.

Laughter and music mixed. Alcohol flowed like honey. Cash was king. Moving through the crowded club, she spotted Kinsey near the bar and followed her line of sight until she found her target—and paused, slowly running her eyes over her. Because this woman looked nothing like the one she'd met in Bali.

She was dressed in a tuxedo. Silk jacket. Pants. Skinny black tie.

Black boots. Nothing else. Gone were the wariness and vulnerability. In their place, this version of Paxton James looked edgy and dangerous as she stared down at her famous ex.

There was no denying there was a powerful sensuality to her, one Emma had first sensed in her photographs and one she found so much more appealing than any of the overproduced quartet of blond models standing opposite Paxton and Sam.

But there was also a coiled tension in her body that was impossible to miss. Considering this, Emma knew she would have to move slowly and carefully.

According to Dom, Carrie Nolan and her entourage had arrived just a few minutes ahead of her, and what had already gone down was anyone's guess. But as Emma watched the standoff, it was clearly long enough to have already inflicted some damage.

Interestingly, Paxton's face was quite expressive when she didn't deliberately shut down. At the moment, she was pale, making her smoke-shadowed eyes seem so dark they looked more black than blue, and myriad emotions flickered across her face.

An instant later, all thought of moving slowly and carefully vanished as she watched Carrie Nolan stretch out her hand and stroke Paxton's cheek as she said something that elicited a look of pain on Paxton's face.

When she saw Paxton reach up, her eyes were no longer flat and expressionless, but instead they appeared to have ignited into cold fury. But whether she meant to simply remove Carrie's hand from her face or escalate, Emma could only guess. Thankfully, she got there before anything could happen. She grasped Carrie's wrist and forcefully drew her hand away, then replaced it with her own on Paxton's cheek.

"Hey, darlin'. Sorry I'm late."

❖

The voice close to her ear was familiar, but Paxton blinked twice when she realized it was Emma Thorpe standing there. Only this Emma Thorpe didn't look anything like the woman in well-worn jeans and a silk T-shirt she'd left behind at JFK. Nor did she look like the one she'd first met in the prison, the one in the dark blue suit who was all business.

No, this one was dressed with seduction in mind and she looked… *damn.*

Paxton shook her head and tried to clear the vision. But the vision that was Emma Thorpe remained where she stood. An instant later, Emma leaned in and pressed her lips against her in a kiss that threatened to grow hot much too quickly.

For one interminable second, Paxton was sure neither of them took a breath. She could feel Emma's heat pouring into her. Could feel it igniting her own heat and, for a heartbeat, she wished they were somewhere private, not in the middle of a jammed club with Carrie watching them from mere feet away, a frown marring her beautiful face.

She was breathless by the time the kiss ended and braced herself. But Emma didn't immediately pull away. Instead, she looked intently into her eyes, as if to confirm what she suspected, then whispered, "I'm right here. She's done enough harm already. Don't give her a chance to hurt you more."

She kissed her softly one more time before she drew back. But she remained at her side, her arm wrapped around Paxton's waist as she turned and sent a coolly disdainful look in Carrie's direction.

"Hi, I'm Emma. Thanks for keeping Pax company until I could get here." She extended her hand, but seemed neither surprised nor perturbed when Carrie ignored it.

Carrie stared at Emma, clearly angry and confused, her eyes narrowed as she tried to understand the tableau in front of her. "Isn't Pax a little young for you?" The chill and derision in her voice could have formed icicles.

Emma went deadly still. "I don't know. Since I believe you're my age, why don't you tell me?"

Full of rage and fury, Carrie turned to face Paxton. "I wouldn't think she's your style. Is she the reason? Is she why you won't give me a chance to make amends?"

"Jesus, Car. It may be hard for you to believe, but you actually don't know me well enough to know my style." Paxton felt Emma's arm tighten around her. Strangely comforted, she looked at Carrie and started to laugh. "Only you would think you could set me up to take a fall, walk away and leave me to go to prison, and then think another woman's the reason I won't give you a second chance."

"We were good together."

Anger burned through the numbness. Aware Carrie's voice was getting louder and was starting to draw attention, Paxton shook her head and kept her voice cool and controlled. "Lie to yourself if you want to, but don't lie to me. We stopped being good together long before that last trip. And we both knew it. But no matter how bad things had gotten, I never would have used you to save my own ass."

When she started to turn away, Carrie reached out and grabbed her arm, driving her long red nails into Paxton's skin, something akin to desperation coloring her voice. "Damn it, Paxton, don't do this to us. Don't be angry. Let me make it up to you. Can't you see I had no choice? Nick left me with no choice. I'm sorry, but if I didn't do what he said, he would have destroyed me, my career, everything I'd worked so hard to build. Everything."

Paxton stared at the hand holding her arm. Her expression must have shown more of her thoughts than usual, because Carrie quickly released her. "There is no us, Carrie. Not anymore. And you don't need help destroying yourself and your career. Your fondness for coke will do that for you. Jesus, if you want to question the truth of what I'm saying try taking a hard look at yourself in a mirror."

Carrie's reaction was both instant and predictable. "Fuck you."

Paxton saw the slap coming. She could have stopped it, but she didn't bother trying. Her face stung ridiculously as Carrie's hand made contact. The people around them gasped and a buzz went through the crowd. But she figured it was the last thing she owed Carrie. "We're done."

"What the hell does that mean?"

"Just that. We're done. And just so we're clear, I've changed the locks and security system at the loft and the concierge has been told not to let you in, so don't bother trying to sweet-talk him."

Carrie blinked. "Wait a minute. I still have stuff at your place. Just let me pick it up and I'll be on my way."

"That won't be necessary. It's all gone. And the proceeds from whatever was at the loft that wasn't mine went to Sister Kate."

"What? Look—fine. Fuck it. I don't care about the clothes or jewelry. I guess I owe you and if you want to give whatever you got for my things to Sister Kate, that's your choice. But I have—" Carrie's breath caught as desperation edged her words.

Paxton sighed tiredly. "It's gone, Carrie. All of it. I flushed it. So there's really nothing left for you to come back and get. No need for me to see you again." Turning back to Emma and Sam, she made contact with Emma's watchful eyes and nodded in the direction of the nearest exit. "Do you mind if we get out of here?"

"I don't mind at all. It's a beautiful place filled with beautiful people, but not exactly my kind of venue."

"You don't like beautiful people?"

"Only when they're real." Emma paused, reached closer, and gently touched her lips to Paxton's cheek, where Carrie had made contact. "But if we're going anywhere else, you might want to put some ice on that first. She got you pretty good."

Paxton nodded. She searched for something to say and failed. Because as near as she could tell, no one in her life had ever kissed her where it hurt.

CHAPTER EIGHT

Perhaps not surprisingly, the passenger compartment of the cab was filled with a restless silence as it slipped through the busy streets.

Beyond giving the driver an address, Paxton simply slid into the backseat, leaned her head back, and closed her eyes. She appeared lost in thought—or maybe just lost—and she paid no attention to the group of NSA agents who had followed her to the sidewalk outside Jimmy K's.

She never acknowledged when they separated into two groups. Never acknowledged when only Emma got in the cab beside her. It was as if the confrontation with Carrie had burned away the last vestige of her energy and she had no more left to give.

While they cut across the city, Emma watched the colors of the city fall across Paxton's face at different angles. Each passing light rippled and flowed, creating new shadows and highlights that made her face appear both beautiful and mysterious. Unearthly. Stunning.

She knew Paxton wasn't asleep and wondered what she was thinking. Whatever it was, it was clear her thoughts weren't peaceful. A frown perpetually creased her forehead and her hands were clenched into fists.

When at last the cab came to a stop at their destination, Paxton roused herself long enough to pay the fare, before leading the way inside.

As she crossed the threshold, Emma stopped. Her breath caught in her throat and all she could do was stare. The open-concept loft was enormous and did not have much in the way of furniture. But it had art. Everywhere. Murals covered every dividing wall, while finished and unfinished canvases in bold primary colors leaned haphazardly against each other and against walls.

None of it would ever be mistaken for a soothing touch of art over a mantel. Instead, chaotic colors creating frantic depictions of life jumped out at her—layered with emotions and edged with a touch of madness.

"This is incredible." It was powerful and moving and it was very personal. And she didn't need Paxton to confirm she'd been the one holding the paintbrushes that created this kaleidoscope of color.

Emma tried to take it all in, tried to make sense of what she was seeing. Slowly, she turned in a circle and tried to find a pattern. But there were too many scenes, too many colors.

"I'm surprised Carrie didn't have it all whitewashed while she was using the loft," Paxton murmured. "She always hated this—all of it."

"That would have been criminal." Emma paused with her hand stretched out, touching the outline of a woman's face on the wall closest to her. Saw the same outline reoccurring in several other places. "But I suppose for a woman whose entire livelihood is tied to her face, she couldn't have been happy you left hers unfinished."

Paxton smiled. "Carrie was even less happy when she discovered it wasn't her."

With a frown, Emma studied the outline closer. But it was just that. An outline with no features surrounded by blond hair and a shadowed body, reappearing in different forms in various murals. Running to catch a train. Reflected in a shop window. Disappearing into a crowd on a busy midtown street. "If it's not Carrie, who—"

"I don't know." Her smile dimmed and the stoic façade returned. "She just keeps appearing. Sometimes I don't even notice she's there until I sit back in the morning and look at what I've done during the night. Painting…it's just the way I relax. I love the colors. The textures. How it feels when an idea takes form and becomes reality."

Emma looked at her more closely. "Do you ever sleep?"

"Not a lot." Paxton shrugged. "As a kid, nighttime was always a magical time when my…when no one was around and I could do anything I wanted. I could get on my computer and just be myself and connect with others. With people who used a language I understood."

"Hackers?"

"Mostly, but not always. After I left MIT, when I moved to New York, nighttime also became a time for running. Through Central Park or along city streets. Or for getting on my bike and redlining it and getting lost in the rush. Or for simply painting on walls with no one to tell me I couldn't."

"It sounds potentially dangerous—and lonely." Emma could have bitten her tongue as the words slipped out.

But Paxton didn't seem to mind. She nodded, as if aware she was revealing too much, but seemingly willing to try something different. Something new. Something that looked a lot like trust. "Maybe that's where she comes from," she said, indicating the not fully formed woman that kept showing up in the midst of the chaos on her walls.

"She's not going to be able to protect you or keep the loneliness at bay until you give her shape and form. Until you make her real and let her fully in. You know that, don't you?"

Paxton raised a brow, appearing to weigh the situation. "You mean like letting you in, along with the cadre of agents you had with you at the club? Let me see—I'm pretty certain I counted Kinsey Dane, Shelby Jarrett, Theo Landry, and Dom. And of course Sam, who arrived with me. Did I miss anyone?"

"No." Emma laughed. "That's really very good."

"Isn't that the reason you want me?"

Yes, but only part. Emma held herself very still as heat seeped from Paxton's body to hers. Knowing she was being baited, she worded her response carefully. "Because you're very good? The best? Of course. There's no denying it. But then you still haven't agreed to work with us, have you?"

Paxton shook her head and managed a rueful smile. "Not yet, no. I had things I needed to take care of today before I could give consideration to your request."

"You mean things like a driver's license? Credit cards? Some new technology? And of course, dealing with Carrie?"

Paxton stared at her for a moment, blinked, then tilted her head and laughed with a fierce kind of pleasure. "Touché. Damn. I think I could like you, Emma Thorpe. How about you give me what's left of tonight to think things through and we'll talk in the morning?"

"All right." She was being dismissed, Emma realized, a habit of

Paxton's she would have to deal with at some point. But it was also as good as she was likely to get, and she worked to ignore the stab of disappointment. "Will you paint tonight?"

"Oh, God, yes." The expression on Paxton's face was a curious mix. Part longing, part desperation, possibly indicating how close she was to the ragged edge of self-control. "It's been much too long. I want to start so badly my hands are shaking."

"Then I'll leave you to it. But don't forget to put some ice on that cheek and please try to get some sleep."

❖

In the wake of Emma's departure, Paxton felt strangely restless. Emotions surged through her, too jumbled and powerful to identify individual feelings. But the aftermath left her shaking.

She wandered through the loft as whispers eddied from the depths of her memories, and she recognized the signs. Under normal circumstances, she kept those memories at bay, tucked away safely in the past where they belonged. Where they couldn't touch her anymore.

But these weren't ordinary circumstances. She'd been running on adrenaline all day and now she was starting to crash.

Sleep would not be the worst idea, she thought wryly, especially when she considered how crazy her life had been over the last few days. But that was before she walked into the master bedroom. As she stared unhappily at the rumpled sheets on the unmade bed, she knew there was no way she would be sleeping there. Not just yet.

She rubbed her forehead and fought against the temptation to walk out of the room. But reality dictated she'd have to deal with this sooner or later. Without giving it further thought, she stripped the bedding that still held Carrie's scent, only to discover there were no clean linens in the closet.

Trying hard not to feel a resurgence of anger toward Carrie— trying hard not to think of Carrie at all—she tossed the load of sheets into the washer and turned her thoughts to Emma instead. She'd been surprised by Emma's reaction to her paintings.

She painted for no one but herself. It held back the demons. Sometimes. Or maybe it simply released them so her mind cleared and she could go back to working on code and searching for system vulnerabilities.

But where Carrie had seen only chaos and color and had complained about the smell the oil paints left hanging in the air, it seemed Emma had looked and seen much more.

The thought somewhat disturbed her. Pulled at her. Mostly, it left her feeling unsettled. Because when all was said and done, she knew how much the paintings revealed of her disparate nature if someone chose to look closely. Because everywhere one looked they would find traces.

Traces of the computer wunderkind with the precise, compartmentalized brain. Traces of the hacker who approached life fast and loose. Even traces of the woman whose constant reminders of childhood were a series of fine, spidery scars—so faint, most people didn't notice them.

She stared at the walls as the silence of the loft surrounded her and filled her with bruising memories. Thoughts of sleep vanished and she quickly changed into sweatpants and a loose cotton shirt that had seen better days. And then, with her emotions still in flux and nothing to distract her from her dark thoughts, she turned the lights off, tuned in a jazz station, pulled out her paints, and approached a large canvas waiting to be filled.

Almost immediately the restlessness began to dissipate as she picked up a brush, dipped it in green, and began to paint. She used shape and color to paint emotions, but how the image would turn out was still an unknown. She simply let herself go and got lost in what was inside her. Used painting to ease the scars in her soul.

Time passed. How much, she wasn't sure, just that there had been several aborted attempts to sleep. But by the time she stopped painting and took note of where she was, the light coming in through the windows was a thin, misty gray from the clouds that hid the rising sun.

Surprised to realize the night had passed without much notice, Paxton stretched her back and shoulders as she tried to ease the ache. But as she looked at what she'd produced, she felt what she always did after a night of painting. Calmer. More focused.

Painting was like a hit of pure oxygen. It cleared her senses and deepened her ability to concentrate. Left her ready to make some decisions, or possibly to acknowledge they'd already been made.

Putting down the brush, she wiped her hands on her paint-splattered shirt and began the meticulous process of cleaning up before heading for a much needed shower.

She felt better by the time she was clean, then put on her favorite jeans and shrugged into a blue Henley. Her reflection in the mirror showed a tired face and red-rimmed eyes from too little sleep. But she thought she also saw a shade of determination, and after months of feeling nothing more than a basic need to survive, she'd take what she could get. One step at a time.

She paused at the window, spent some time just watching the light touch the nearby buildings and rooftops. *Nice.* She'd missed this. Enjoying the dawning of a new day. The view. The ability to come and go as she pleased.

Before leaving the loft, she looked up the address she would need. A minute later, she slipped her earbuds in, grabbed a well-worn leather jacket, tucked a cell phone into her pocket, and hitched a messenger bag with one of her new laptops on her shoulder before heading out.

❖

It was barely past noon. But already Emma's eyes were burning after a morning spent reading endless pages of reports on intercepted transmissions. Added to the mix was an unhappy conversation with her boss, and she could feel frustration riding her back and settling somewhere between her shoulders as she headed to the renovated four-story brownstone that served as their station.

The building they'd chosen was narrow and old. It was nestled in a tree-lined street in a mixed-use neighborhood where apartments shared space with small businesses—shops, restaurants, medical offices, cybercafés—and as such, the American Cyber-Research Institute attracted little to no attention.

True to her word, Catherine Winters had come through, ensuring there were no budgetary restrictions, allowing Emma to equip a team that was second to none with state-of-the-art technology and software. Satellite capability. Links to Homeland Security, the NSA, and the

CIA as well as DGSE and other European counterparts. And access to intelligence from thousands of surveillance posts.

It was a work in progress, but by the time they finished, their technological capacity would be incredible. In other words, it was everything she could hope for. With one exception.

She stared at her watch and cursed softly. She had been convinced she would hear from Paxton this morning. Positive that when she'd left her last night, Paxton had all but decided to come on board to work with them. To play a pivotal role in defending the country from cyber terrorists. To help identify these potential threats and stop whoever was behind them before they could launch attacks that could paralyze the nation.

If there was anything Emma hated more than being wrong, she didn't know what it was.

In keeping with her nature, she took stock of everything that had happened, forced herself to review all the details, and wondered how she could have done things differently. But for the moment, she had no answers. Only questions.

As she walked into the building, she became immediately aware of a difference—an excitement—in the air. She could see several team members huddled, focused on the large flat screens and other electronic displays that sat on tables drawn together in the open-plan main floor, and the intensity was tangible. "Anything new going on?"

A couple of heads popped up. "Hey, boss. You've got to check this out," Kinsey said with a grin.

Emma approached the table while trying to read Kinsey's expression. Not easy, because truth be told, she looked like a cat with a mouthful of cream. Turning toward the screen Kinsey indicated, she saw a satellite image appear, then split and divide several times as Kinsey closed into street level. "Tell me what I'm looking at."

"Paxton came by early this morning and worked some magic on our systems. I've gotta tell you, she's bloody brilliant. She managed to get us access to a few pieces of hardware in the sky I didn't even know existed. I swear we can now look into someone's kitchen window if we want to. And then she did something that's got our signals hopping on and off networks and bouncing all over the galaxy, so fast no one's ever going to figure out who or where we are."

Ah, hell. Whose satellites? Emma's eyes narrowed, but before she could probe, the realization hit her. "Paxton was here? Damn it, why the hell didn't anyone call and let me know?"

"Easy, Emma," Shelby murmured. "We knew you were waiting for a call from the boss. And Paxton told us not to disturb you."

"It wasn't Paxton's decision to make." She heard the sharpness in her voice and struggled to tone it down. "How long—how long ago did she leave?"

"Actually, she's still here." Shelby nodded toward the room Emma had been using as an office and looked infuriatingly amused. "I know she used your desk and worked on her laptop for a while, but the last time I checked, she was sleeping on the couch."

Emma closed her eyes and breathed a sigh of relief. Had Paxton said anything? She wanted to ask, but then decided it wasn't important. What was important was that Paxton had come. Had helped the team. And had stayed.

Uneasy that they were linked to what were clearly military satellites of undetermined origin, she remained long enough to understand Paxton's actions were helping, not hindering, the work at hand. She then quietly entered her office and shut the door behind her.

She spent a few minutes quietly observing Paxton, earbuds in, asleep on the couch. She watched the rise and fall of her chest. Felt the warmth of her body. Inhaled the soft scent of sandalwood and vanilla. For an instant, Emma's gaze rested on her shadowed eyes and on her cheek, faintly bruised from her encounter with Carrie. She frowned, but then let it go. *At least she's here. Be grateful for that.*

Resisting the urge to wake Paxton, she took a seat at her desk. A moment later, a chill shot up her spine as she realized her computer had been accessed. Shit. Not only had it been accessed, it was quietly humming as it processed some kind of instructions.

Damn it. What had Paxton done?

CHAPTER NINE

Paxton stirred and slowly stretched, blinking as she attempted to orient herself. It took her a moment to shake off the remnants of bad dreams. Her stitches itched and she scratched her side while trying to make sense of her surroundings. More specifically, why Emma Thorpe was sitting a few feet away staring at a computer, her expression darkened like a storm cloud occluding the sun.

Probably because you bypassed all her security protocols, accessed her computer, and programmed it to conduct a search for you.

Sometimes the pragmatist in her head could be quite annoying. But this time, it also happened to be right.

Maybe it hadn't been the smartest way to start things off. But she trusted her own instincts and it had seemed the most expedient course of action at the time. Just like now seemed to be the best time to start making amends. Tugging the earbuds out and easing up onto her elbows, she cleared her throat. "Sorry, I didn't mean to fall asleep."

Emma looked up, pale brows still furrowed. "No, I expect not. But tell me, Paxton. Just what did you mean to do?"

Bewildered by the level of heat in Emma's voice, she breathed a ragged sigh and got to her feet. "Damn. You're angry with me."

"That comes as a surprise?" Emma snapped. "I was so damned pleased when I came in and found out you were here. That you'd started helping the team. And then I walk in here and find you've not only breached my security system and accessed my computer, you're running an unidentified program on it. What am I supposed to think?"

"My mistake." Paxton searched for the right words, only to realize she didn't have any. "I might remind you that you knew who and what I was when you came to me and asked for help. The problem is you don't know if you can trust me. And we can't work together if you don't trust me."

Emma closed her eyes and sighed. "I know that."

Paxton realized the thought bothered her more than it should and she took a moment to study Emma's face, but could find no alternatives. "No problem. Let me grab my jacket and laptop and I'll get out of here. But just so we're clear, I've no intention of letting you or anyone else send me back to that godforsaken prison, so don't even try."

For an instant, Emma looked confused. "Why in hell would anyone send you back to prison?"

"You got me out so I could work with you. If we can't find a way to work together—"

"I didn't say we couldn't work together." An expression that was both weary and faintly amused crossed Emma's face. "I was simply agreeing that it can't happen without trust. I want to trust you. More than that, I know I need to trust you. Just like you need to trust me. But if you think I'd send you back to that hellhole in Bali, then clearly we have trust issues on both sides."

Paxton stood still. "Well, damn. You might have a point."

"Are you saying you agree with me on something?"

"Actually, yes." She blew out a short breath, trying to relieve some of the tension in her neck. "Look, I'm the first to admit that as a rule I don't trust anyone. But while I'm trying like hell to trust you, part of the problem is that you confuse the hell out of me."

The unexpected comment forced Emma to pause. "I confuse you?" she repeated. "How do I confuse you?"

"You keep sending mixed signals."

"I send mixed signals?"

"Yeah. You do. Like right now, you look like you can't decide between getting me out of your office and grabbing and kissing me until neither of us can breathe." Paxton smiled. "Oh, well, another time, Agent Thorpe."

❖

Well, hell.

Emma stared as Paxton shrugged into her jacket and hooked her computer bag to her shoulder, leaving her earbuds dangling around her neck. Watched as she reached the office door and started to open it. Knew that a second or two longer was all it would take before she slipped away.

She didn't want to examine why Paxton had gotten so deep under her skin in such a short time. All that mattered right now was she had. And that she wanted her with an intensity she hadn't felt in a very long time. Her heart pounded in her throat and she fought against the instinct to run. Away from Paxton? To Paxton? She wasn't sure.

Without further hesitation, Emma moved forward, pushing the office door closed before Paxton could completely open it, while grabbing Paxton's hand. She pulled her deeper into the office, removed the soft-sided leather bag from her shoulder and set it on the desk. She then helped her ease out of her jacket before tossing it onto the couch, aware of the faint trembling in her hands.

Paxton remained silent, her expression filled with caution and a glimpse of emotion that stirred Emma even as she caught her around the waist and pulled her hard against her chest. Her mouth was a breath away. And then she kissed her.

"Just so that there are no mixed messages, I've wanted to do that since the moment I first saw your picture," she whispered. And then she kissed her again, longingly and with total surrender. Effectively melting away any resistance from Paxton.

She was smiling when she finally drew back. She paused for a moment and pushed Paxton's hair off her brow then watched the dark strands sift through her fingers. "We need to figure out how to communicate and learn to trust and work together. As for the other—"

"I'd say we have no problems as far as the other's concerned," Paxton murmured and laughed. She drew her arms around Emma's shoulders and held her tight an instant longer.

Emma swallowed, her voice suddenly deserting her. She was saved when her computer made an innocuous sound, indicating whatever program Paxton had initiated had run its course. "Will you tell me about the program you were running?"

"Of course." Paxton sounded surprised. "I didn't plan on being asleep when you got here. If I hadn't been, perhaps things wouldn't have gone off the rails so quickly."

"I'd say you fell asleep because you were exhausted." She ran a gentle fingertip on the shadows still evident under Paxton's eyes. "And you look like you could still use some more sleep. Did you get any sleep at all last night, or did you spend the whole night painting?"

Paxton shrugged. "Mostly painting."

"Why?"

"Because every time I closed my eyes I could still hear the rats that would come out at night in the prison and I kept having premonitions about ending up back there."

"Oh, Jesus. Paxton, no. That's not ever going to happen, you have to trust me on that." Emma couldn't see Paxton's expression, but her body had become taut and her shoulders were a rigid line. Reaching over, she touched one shoulder, knew Paxton registered the contact and felt the heat coming from her body. Beneath the soft Henley, she could feel the muscles between her neck and shoulder. They were hard, tense, and she began to rub gently.

After a minute or so, she glanced at her watch, then allowed her gaze to flick around the office before momentarily lighting on the computer. "There's a deli up the street. Why don't I send someone out for sandwiches and coffee? After we've all had a bit of a break, maybe you can update everyone on what you were running on the computer. And what new hardware you've linked us to."

Paxton nodded and grinned weakly. "You mean satellites like Meridian? Skynet? Cosmos?"

Shit. Emma felt the blood drain from her face. Explaining they were piggybacking on British and American military satellites she could handle. All in a day's work. But Russian satellites—especially highly secretive Russian military satellites—was another matter. At best, she could kiss her career good-bye. At worst…she didn't want to think about it.

She reminded herself that just a few minutes ago, she had said they would learn how to trust each other and work together, but damn it, Paxton was making it all but impossible. She needed to remember President Winters wanted Paxton working on this with her. Surely if anyone knew what Paxton was capable of, it was Catherine Winters. Lost in thought, for a moment she forgot how to breathe.

"Emma?"

Emma turned her head and saw Paxton staring at her.

"Do me a favor and breathe, Emma. Take a deep breath and let it out slow. Focus on me." She waited until Emma followed her directions then repeated herself. "That's good. Now take another one and sit down before you fall down. I'll ask someone to see about getting some food and coffee, maybe get you one of those chais you're so fond of, and then I'll be right back."

Feeling foolish, Emma nodded and did as she was told.

"And keep reminding yourself that your boss knew what she was doing when she told you she wanted me on your team. Okay?"

❖

With the team gathered around a table for the impromptu meal, Paxton sat and watched closely while Emma ate. She was pleased that by the time Emma dusted off the crumbs on her plate and reached for her second cup of coffee, most of the color had returned to her face.

But she was all too aware her every move was being monitored while the people around her maintained ongoing discussions. Biding her time, she nibbled on carrots and drank too much coffee until all pretenses at conversation disappeared.

It's showtime.

She looked at Emma. "Where would you like to start?"

Emma's expression gave no indication of what she was thinking. "How about the program you were running on my computer when I arrived earlier?"

Emma's suggestion caused an immediate stir in the room. The team was clearly aware of Paxton's background, and although she had earlier demonstrated both her willingness and ability to help, there was still a high level of suspicion she would need to cut through.

Paxton sent a nod to Emma, acknowledging she knew she'd just been tossed in the deep end. Clearly it was time to see if she would sink or swim. "All right. Let me first say I don't believe an aggressor nation is behind the latest cyber threats."

She wasn't surprised when people at the table started to protest. She waited until Emma signaled for them to be silent and listen, and then continued unperturbed. "That's not to say a less than friendly nation won't quickly become involved if whoever is behind this starts meeting with large-scale success. That's the greatest risk. But for now—"

"Wait a minute. You think an individual is responsible for taking remote control of commercial jets?"

Paxton looked at Dom and shrugged. "An individual. Or possibly a small group working together for a common goal."

"Like Anonymous?"

"Yes. Basically a group of like-minded individuals coming together for a cause they believe in. Catching them is the challenge. Encryption tools may not be perfect, but they're good enough to end any investigation trail almost all the time."

Theo pushed away from the table in obvious frustration, getting to his feet and staring at her with thinly disguised challenge in his eyes. "So you're saying we're screwed before we start and we got you out of jail for nothing?"

Emma stiffened, but before she could say anything, Paxton responded sharply. "I need to say two things. If after I've finished, you're still unhappy, perhaps you and I can continue this discussion off-line. Will that work for you?"

Forcing herself to ignore Emma, she stared at Theo and waited until he gave a reluctant nod. "First, no one's screwed. Forensics can still be done on Tor. Encryption and secure deletion tools are not perfect. And don't disregard the power of human intelligence. Online communication was perhaps Osama bin Laden's biggest strength. He had couriers traveling to cybercafés using email on USB flash drives. But in the end, he was still caught."

"What's that got to do with what's happening here?"

"Everything. People get caught in the exact same ways that attackers use to exploit their victims. By finding their points of weakness and vulnerability."

"Maybe so—"

"As for getting me out of jail, I'll remind you I was there because I was set up by a dirty NSA agent who wanted to use me for what I can do. In a way, not that different from what I'm doing to help you and your team. And that's because I'm damn good at what I do. It's as simple and as complex as that."

She delivered the statement without a visible smile. But she was aware it generated one on Emma's face. Theo continued to stare at her for a long moment, then nodded and sat back down. "So what do you think we should be focusing on?"

One crisis averted. "Talent. Earlier, I put together a list of people I believe have the talent to carry out these attacks and started running them through your system. You're looking for cyber signatures. Where they've been. What they've been doing. Who they've been talking to. Since I've been out of the country for a while, my own system isn't where I'd like it to be—for the moment, anyway. Your system made it possible for me to search faster. It also made it easier for me to access a number of systems including CIA, Justice, Treasury, as well as the Brits. MI6 and Interpol."

She noted the less-than-happy expression on Emma's face, but there was nothing she could do. It was about to get worse. "But having the talent to do this is only part of the equation. The cleverest and most dangerous cyber attackers are those who are able to not only compromise a system, but also to evade detection. Sound familiar? It should, because that is also precisely the objective of a government surveillance solution. So they know what you know."

After a brief silence, it was Kinsey who spoke up. "We're not looking for kids working out of their basement or garage, are we?"

Paxton shrugged. "At fourteen, I hacked into the CIA just to prove to an MIT professor that I could do it. Whoever is doing this? Take my word for it. It's not going to be kids. Which means their motivation will be quite different. As will their understanding of potential consequences."

For the next hour, Paxton fielded questions and gained a better sense of Emma Thorpe's team. They were engaged, confident. Had mental agility and were smart enough to recognize the game had just changed, and that she was the game changer.

But as the afternoon waned, Paxton suddenly felt the walls closing in and knew she had to get out of there, at least for a while. She pushed back from the table and grabbed her jacket.

"Where are you going?"

Looking up she heard the concern in Emma's voice as she approached. "I believe I once told you I don't deal well when I'm surrounded by too many people for too long. I think I just need to get some fresh air. Maybe go for a run. I'm not sure. We'll talk later."

Aware she was leaving her laptop behind, but no longer caring,

Paxton grabbed her phone and slipped out the door. Just before it closed, she heard Emma instructing someone to follow her, but she didn't slow down until she hit the street. Only then did she turn and see Sam approaching.

"Have you been assigned to be my tail again today? When is your boss going to learn to trust me?"

"It's not that she doesn't trust you. She just wants to make sure you're okay. As for me being assigned to you, I don't think Emma was too comfortable sending Theo." Sam grinned. "Personally, I think I got the better end of the deal. I heard you say something about a run. Will you disappear on me if I dash in and get my gym bag?"

Paxton shook her head and smiled. "I'll be here. We'll go to my place so we can both change, and then you can show me what a trained NSA agent can do. Loser buys the mojitos."

Sam flexed her muscles and laughed. "You're on."

❖

Setting the latest report on the desk, he sat and stared at it for a moment. He forced himself to reread the words, slower this time, but the facts didn't change. As rage bubbled up, he slammed his fist on the desk.

The fucking bitch. This was all her fault.

Fighting for some semblance of control, he took a deep breath, then another. Reaching into a drawer, he pulled out a half-filled bottle of scotch, poured four fingers into a glass, and downed it. Almost immediately, he felt the warmth ignite and spread through his body. A moment later, he felt calmer.

Before her arrival on the scene, everything had been going his way. He'd been able to hack into government-controlled servers with relative ease, staying one step ahead. But the new system of firewalls and hacker traps she'd created for the NSA cyber-terrorism group she was working with were as good as it got.

Undeterred, he reached for the keyboard, entered a new string of commands, and waited. Minutes passed, and in spite of the cool temperatures he maintained for his computers, sweat began to bead on his forehead. He waited a few minutes longer. And still nothing happened. Staring at his frozen screen, his worst fears were confirmed.

She was successfully blocking him.

Cursing once again, he leaned back and considered his options. He'd come too far to let her interference ruin his plans. And as much as he might have enjoyed the process of proving his superiority, he could not afford to let himself become distracted. However...

He knew the people she was working with. An elite team. Especially Emma Thorpe. A woman with a reputation for being relentless. Perhaps it was time to do something about her.

Chapter Ten

W as I right or was I right?"

Emma glanced up from scanning message traffic within the American intelligence services to find Dom leaning against her door, looking as if he had no plans to leave anytime soon. "I probably wouldn't keep you around so much if it wasn't that you're right most of the time," she said dryly. "What were you right about this time?"

Dom laughed as he entered the office before indicating with a nod of his head toward the other room. Following his line of sight, Emma could see Paxton, huddled over a computer with Kinsey, Shelby, and Sam.

She was in jeans worn nearly threadbare in some interesting places that hugged her in a way Emma couldn't help but admire and a black T-shirt with a colorful dream catcher motif on the front. She'd kicked off her shoes, revealing brightly colored socks with dancing skeletons on them, and appeared to be completely absorbed in something on the computer screen. There was the faintest line of concentration between her brows, and her lips were slightly parted. She looked—

"I was right about the kid," Dom said, bringing Emma's attention back to him. She knew he couldn't have missed the way she'd been staring at Paxton and appreciated that he made no comment as he continued. "It's only been a couple of weeks but she seems to have figured out how to navigate in the spook community just fine. And while I admit I don't always understand her, everything I hear hints at an ability to walk on water. How do you think she's doing?"

Emma made a face. "Shelby says she puts two and two together about as fast as a computer tells the difference between one and zero."

"High praise coming from Shelby."

Emma nodded. "Even Theo's starting to sing her praises. Says she can spot things in a sea of data, make incredible leaps of judgment, and come up with possibilities no one else has even imagined."

"Is he right?"

"She's really that good," she agreed.

"And what does our boss think?"

That was a different story, Emma thought, as she chewed on her bottom lip. "She wants me in Washington this weekend and oh, yes. By the way. Bring Paxton along. Seems she wants to reconnect over a nice and cozy family dinner in the residence at the White House."

"Shit. Won't that be fun?" Dom watched her warily. "Have you told Paxton yet?"

"No."

"Coward." He laughed. "Of course it's not exactly a conversation I'd want to be having with her, so it's not like I can blame you. But aside from talking about a happy reunion with the president, I do think you might want to keep an eye on her."

Emma's gaze sharpened on him. "Why? Has someone said something? Has she?"

"Not exactly."

She saw a muscle flex along Dom's jaw. "Then what is it?"

"Shelby might have mentioned that Paxton never looks rested and that the shadows under her eyes are becoming a concern."

"Oh?"

"I have to admit I hadn't noticed. Men—we don't exactly see things like that when we look at a woman who happens to look like Paxton. But when I took a closer look, I realized Shelby was right. It got me thinking and it seems to me that all Paxton's done is exchange one prison for another. Since she got here, all she does is work or go running. And you said her habit is to paint most nights. So when exactly does the kid sleep?"

Ah. The question weighed heavily. "I don't know. I've tried talking to her about it, and about the nightmares I know she's still having. She tells me I'm hardly one to talk, that I'm in here as much as she is, and it doesn't seem to matter that at least I go home at night and sleep. She says she knows what she's doing."

"Maybe she does at that. I don't know." Dom shrugged. "I do know she's different. And it's not a stretch to think with a mind that doesn't work the same as everyone else's, she'll have different needs. But the human body still has certain basic needs and, from what I can see, she's gone from a nonexistent childhood to MIT where she was miles smarter and years younger than everyone else. A handful of degrees later, she moved into a world of hackers. And now she's surrounded by spooks and terrorists, shrouded in darkness and secrets."

Emma frowned. "Where are you going with this? If you have a point, I wish you'd make it."

"I guess I don't really have one. Look, I like the kid. I also know we need her and I don't want her to crash and burn before we start making inroads on the people we're hunting. So I'm just suggesting it's something you might want to think about. Maybe take her out while you're in Washington and get her to relax. Actually, it might do you both some good."

"Dom—"

"Well, why not? I knew from the beginning that you'd go for her."

"What? You're psychic now?"

"No. I just know you. It was the look in her eyes. You like the wounded ones because you, my friend, have a classic rescuer's complex. And Paxton is not only gorgeous, she badly needs rescuing."

"Damn."

When Emma said nothing else, Dom cocked his head and studied her, then wisely changed the subject. "Does she still have us piggybacking on the Russians?"

"What do you think?" Emma sighed. "The Russians, the Israelis, the French, and the Chinese. At least those are the ones I know about. She keeps changing things up but I have no doubt there are others lurking in the ether. Her basic philosophy is that it's easier to ask for forgiveness than permission."

"In this business, that philosophy's as good as any, I suppose. Are you at all worried?"

"No—okay, maybe just a little bit. But I figure as long as Paxton's confident, I won't worry too much, and based on this"—she indicated the papers on her desk—"I'd say we need all the help we can get."

Dom glanced at all the papers. "Anything new I should be aware of?"

"Not really. Just more of the same. Potentially the most serious was a breach at the White House. We got lucky. It turned out it was an unclassified email system." And maybe that was just as well, as it gave the team time to work on tracking Paxton's list of potential suspects.

In that regard, the team had been putting in endless hours. But it was akin to looking for the proverbial needle in a haystack. Since the public disclosure of intelligence agency surveillance and information collection techniques, suspected terrorist groups had become increasingly difficult to track.

They had begun switching from US internet providers to foreign providers, such as those in Russia, and had moved to increasingly sophisticated methods of encrypted communications, using new software and applications that intelligence agencies were having difficulty penetrating. In the meantime, breaches perpetrated by unknown entities continued unabated.

If there was an early win, it really was in how Paxton had integrated into the team. In a room full of the brightest cyber geeks and intelligence analysts, she was a god and they hung on to her every word. Watched how she worked. Learned from her and gained confidence in their own abilities to think things through.

Theo had seemingly overcome most of his initial reticence and had been creating opportunities to talk to and learn from Paxton. Kinsey's reports were sharper and more insightful. And Sam, who Emma had long suspected could be the brightest of her group of agents, worked closest with Paxton and demonstrated tremendous gains, proving herself to be a quick learner while becoming increasingly effective at making leaps of logic and pursuing ideas.

An even more unexpected by-product of Paxton's integration with the team was the improvement in the fitness level of her normally deskbound agents, as several of them now accompanied Pax when she went running. They used the time to pepper her with questions, suggest scenarios, and try to anticipate what she might do next. An interesting exercise.

Emma had no doubt there were times Paxton would have preferred to run alone. For now, that meant on some occasions she simply slipped her earbuds in and ignored whoever was tagging along.

But most of the time, her earbuds dangled around her neck and she remained open to the endless questions and probes. And she hadn't objected to anyone's presence, Emma thought with amusement, as she and Dom each grabbed their running gear and prepared to join the day's running group.

❖

"No."

"Paxton, please. Just listen to me—"

"Damn it, Emma. No. Absolutely not. Now let it go." Paxton's anger was quick and sharp, disbelief and a refusal to accept what Emma proposed echoing in her voice.

She caught a glimpse of hurt surprise register on Emma's face before she quickly shut it down. But it had been there, no doubt brought about by Paxton's unwillingness to listen. In response, emotions surged through her, and their aftermath left her shaking.

She wanted to apologize. Not only for her sharp reaction, but because she didn't like to think she had hurt Emma or caused her pain. Emma had gotten her out of prison, had offered comfort and kindness, even friendship, with no guarantee Paxton would be able to help her. If nothing else, she owed her.

She started to say something, but stopped herself from saying words she wasn't certain how to phrase. Fearing nothing good would come from it. Knowing she was tired physically and mentally and, inevitably, control slipped by the wayside when she was confronted under circumstances like this.

Acting on part instinct, part impulse, she stood up from the table and walked away, trying not to say another word. Knowing anything she said right now would come out wrong or, at the very least, much too harsh. Grabbing her jacket, she headed out the door, jaw clenched and eyes challenging anyone to try and stop her.

No one made a move.

She had her earbuds in by the time she hit the street, a wall of sound drowning out the world. She chose a direction at random and simply started walking. Resolute. Head down. Rage-driven, aching music slamming in her ears.

She didn't know how long she remained in a fog. Too long, probably, but she didn't really care, not stopping until the aroma of freshly roasting coffee spilling from a nearby shop broke through the cold and angry haze she'd been in. Looking around, she saw people standing in the afternoon sun, lined up to place their orders. Heard soft conversation and laughter, and found the sounds strangely soothing.

With her frayed nerves and edginess abated, she joined the queue at the street-side café. Ordered a large coffee as she got to the front of the line, then abruptly changed her mind and ordered a chai latte—the kind Emma always seemed to be drinking. Taking a cautious sip as she paid, she found the beverage hot and delicious.

An image flashed of Emma's mouth, pressed hungrily against her own. Taking. Giving. Tasting not unlike the mix of spicy and sweet— like the honey, cinnamon, and cloves in the chai.

Potent. Part memory, part fantasy.

Who knew?

Releasing a soft laugh, she heard an all too familiar voice inside her head telling her to stay where she was. Reacting without question, she found a quiet outside table away from the never-ending line. The sun felt good on her face. The faint breeze carried the scent of fall and she was startled to realize the trees were beginning to change color.

She couldn't recall the last time she'd taken a moment to note the change of seasons and as she took another sip of her drink, she laughed at herself again and began to feel more human. In a calmer frame of mind, she replayed her conversation with Emma.

Admit it, she told herself. It was bound to happen sooner or later and, in a way, she was surprised it had taken this long. After all, she was technically working for Cat. Knowing that, Cat would want to reconnect. She had given Paxton time to step up to the plate. And now she was through with waiting, was insisting on meeting face-to-face, and had asked Emma to facilitate it.

So all Paxton'd truly managed to do was avoid the inevitable.

More to the point, she knew Cat wasn't trying to be hurtful. For some reason—for whatever reason—she still cared. She and Paul had cared from the very beginning. Had seen something in her worth salvaging. And yet they'd never tried to fix her. They'd simply tried to help her live and left her to make her own choices.

Just like Emma was doing now.

Yes, Emma needed her help, her skills. But like Cat, Paxton could see that she cared and wanted to help her live again. Wanted to help her move on.

From Nick Perry.

From Carrie.

From being locked up in prison, sentenced to die.

These were the facts. They were neither right nor wrong. They simply were.

❖

Emma paused to catch her breath, having struggled to keep up with the pace Paxton had set from the moment she'd left the station. The only time she'd slowed down was when she'd stopped in front of a pair of homeless teenagers, chatted with them, and reached under her jacket into her jeans, pulling out some bills. Emma used the moment to admire how the jeans hugged Paxton's hips, while the boots she wore accented her long legs.

The stop brought recognition of a different sort for Emma. She'd been spending too much time deskbound, and she vowed to get into better shape. *Possibly go for runs with Paxton more often, and not lose your breath so quickly.*

Now, as she watched Paxton sit, lean back, and turn her face toward the sun, her breath caught in her chest all over again, this time for an entirely different reason.

Damn. She was beautiful.

Letting her eyes linger, she was glad to see the brisk walk and fresh air had put color on Paxton's too pale face, highlighting her classic bone structure, while the play of light and shadow on the planes and angles of her face made her even more striking.

But she couldn't miss the new set of dark circles under Paxton's eyes, making them appear more shadowed than usual. Already haunting, they now verged on haunted.

Emma swore softly. She was usually a keen observer. When had she let her vision of Paxton become so clouded that she missed all the signs?

In those initial moments as she stood watching her, she saw Paxton's face was somber. Almost moody. Her mouth unsmiling. But then some thought must have occurred, because her expression suddenly changed and a ghost of a smile touched her lips.

The change gave Emma the courage she needed to step forward.

As she approached the table, Paxton gave no outward sign that she knew Emma was there. Her eyes stayed closed, her face remained turned toward the sun, and there was no notable shift in her position. But somehow Emma believed Paxton knew she was no longer alone.

"Is this a private moment or can anyone sit down and join you," she asked softly.

Paxton's eyes opened slowly, and though shadows still lingered in their depths, the expression she favored Emma with at least seemed welcoming. "Did I just conjure you?"

The totally unexpected comment pulled a genuine laugh from Emma. "Considering how angry you were with me only a short time ago, I guess it depends on why you would want me to appear."

"That was then. This is now. And in case you're interested, you'll learn I'm not one to hold on to anger for long."

"I'm interested—and it's good to know," Emma said. "Are you okay?"

"No," she said. "No, I'm not okay, but I think I'm getting there."

Emma nodded, uncertain how to respond. "I'm going to get myself a drink. Can I get you another coffee?"

"Another drink would be nice, only it's not coffee. It's a chai latte."

"Um, sure. Okay. Can I ask when you started drinking chai?"

Paxton laughed. "This was actually my first."

Feeling as if the conversation they were having was taking her farther down the rabbit hole, Emma paused. "I guess that means you liked it."

"I liked it fine. It reminded me of the taste of your mouth." Her eyes fixed on Emma's mouth, and clearly aware she had just stunned her, Paxton slowly grinned. "Go get our drinks, Emma. We can talk about it later. Perhaps on the flight to Washington."

CHAPTER ELEVEN

As it turned out, Paxton never managed to have that or any other conversation with Emma during the flight to Washington. LaGuardia proved too crowded; the flight was full and much too short. It didn't help that the closer they got to Washington, the more unnerved she became.

In the end, she closed her eyes and slipped in her earbuds, listening to music while Emma leafed through a magazine and rested her hand on Paxton's arm, helping to ground her.

"I'm sorry," she muttered, finding her legs shaky as they landed at Dulles. "You'd think I've never flown before."

Emma's arm steadied her. "It's okay. Just take it easy. We don't have to be at the White House until seven, so we have plenty of time to check in to our hotel and relax for a bit."

"Good to know, but I still owe you a conversation." Whatever else she might have said, the opportunity was lost when someone called out Emma's name. Turning her head toward the unfamiliar voice, Paxton saw two men approaching them—both fit, dark haired, dark eyed, and wearing nearly identical dark suits. It almost made her laugh.

Considering they were in Washington, it was easy to determine what they were. Phylum: *federal agent*. But subphylum proved a little more difficult, seeing as there were so many choices. But the ease with which the one man greeted Emma made Paxton think they had to be NSA.

Indicating with a nod of her head, she mouthed that she was going to get something to drink. She stepped back and left Emma to pursue a conversation with her colleague, while the second man followed Paxton with his eyes. She didn't recognize him. Couldn't place him. But his continuous stare left her feeling uncomfortable.

She bought a bottle of water, savored it as the cool liquid slipped down her suddenly parched throat, and stalled for a few minutes looking at the headlines gracing the front pages of various newspapers. Problems in the Middle East, terrorists, climate change, political scandals. Some things never changed. When she could find no more reason to delay, she returned to Emma's side, aware she continued to be scrutinized.

"You know, I thought I recognized you," the man who'd been watching her said as she drew near. "You're Paxton James. I'm right, aren't I? You're the notorious hacker that had our Nick Perry all hot and bothered before he got taken down. Are you working with Agent Thorpe now?"

Paxton froze. For an instant, she was catapulted back to the airport in Bali and a kaleidoscope of images flashed in her mind. She felt her blood turn to ice and a wave of nausea rolled through her, followed quickly by anger.

Caught between conflicting instincts of fight and flight, she heard the voice inside her head scream for her to run. To disappear.

What was worse was she had no one to blame but herself. She'd allowed herself to become too comfortable working with Emma and her crew. Had gotten lax when it came to protecting herself. Who she was and what she was hadn't changed, and in her line of work, it had never paid to be recognizable. Especially not by any kind of law enforcement.

And this man? He was NSA.

Moving ever so slowly, she took a first step back and started to turn. An instant later, she found herself stopped. Caught by the pressure of Emma's hand as she reached out and now held her firmly in place. She experienced a brief flare of panic and she tried but failed to pull away only to have Emma tighten her grip on her arm.

"It'll be all right, Pax," Emma murmured, clearly aware of Paxton's discomfort, before turning back to the agent she'd been talking to. "Roger, it was good to see you. We have to go. Give my best to Linda."

Still maintaining a hold on her hand, Emma began to draw Paxton away, leaving her with no choice but to follow. Paxton was aware the two agents were still watching them, but Emma didn't seem to notice or care. Emma didn't pause until they were outside and she had Paxton tucked by her side in the back of a cab.

❖

Paxton continued to hold Emma's hand, but hadn't spoken a word since they'd left Dulles behind. Emma watched her as wordless moments passed, the quiet worrying her. That and the combination of fear and anger she had seen in Paxton's eyes when Jeff Strong, the agent with Roger Frederick, had recognized her.

She needed to say something. Anything to reach out to her. "Paxton? Are you all right? Can I do anything?"

The grip of Paxton's hand on hers tightened for a moment before she finally relinquished her hold. "Just tell me you'll stay by my side this evening with Cat and Paul."

Emma stared at her, surprised by both the urgency in her tone and the request. "Of course. Even if the president hadn't insisted that I be there, I had every intention of going with you. But can you answer a question for me—why does the prospect of seeing them scare you so much?"

Paxton turned her head toward the window, but Emma knew she wasn't seeing slices of Washington life passing by. Ten seconds turned into twenty, then thirty before she sighed and closed her eyes. "Did I ever mention that Cat and Paul Winters wanted to take me home with them when I was released from the hospital? That they wanted to try to adopt me?"

Emma watched her warily. As her mind began to race, she considered dozens of thoughts at once, trying to anticipate where the conversation might be going and weighing the possible implications if she was wrong. "No. But help me understand, what would have been so wrong with that?"

Opening her eyes, Paxton looked at Emma, allowing her to see just how much the past still haunted her. "Don't you get it? They wanted to make me a part of their lives. Even though Cat was already considered a highly sought-after player on the political landscape. Even though they knew what I was. Where I'd come from. What I'd been doing."

"What am I missing, Pax?"

"They had to know I'd never fit in their world. Never meet their expectations. And yet they still wanted to love me. *Me*. How wild is that?"

"Not wild at all," Emma said mildly. "I can see how life as you knew it would do a number on your head, but you don't strike me as a coward. What stopped you from even trying?"

Paxton swallowed. "A man came to see me. He said I would cause irreparable damage to Cat—to her career. He said she was destined for greatness. That she already had a groundswell of support, but people would always question her if I went to live with her. If I let her adopt me."

A flicker of anger flared. "What man?"

"Gerald Hughes."

Emma blinked. "Senator Hughes of Massachusetts?"

Paxton nodded. "That's him. Cat had worked for him at one time as an ADA and I figured he had to know what he was talking about. The last thing I wanted to do was hurt Cat and Paul after everything they'd done for me. So I told them going to live with them wasn't something I wanted."

"You lied to them."

"Yes."

Emma had no answer for the pain she heard echoing in Paxton's voice. The best she could manage was to reach out and hold her hand once again. A lifeline for her to cling to in the midst of her internal chaos.

In her own way, Paxton made it easier. She remained silent for the remainder of the cab ride. Stood expressionless, off to one side, while Emma checked them in. Then followed her to the elevator and up to their adjoining rooms without saying a word.

"I need a shower," she mumbled when Emma opened the door between their rooms. Without waiting for a response, she slipped into the room, took off her jacket, tossed it on the bed, and headed into the bathroom.

Emma waited until she heard the water running before going about her own business. She hung up what she would be wearing for dinner, returned a few phone calls and emails, took a quick shower, then dressed and sat down to wait for Paxton to reappear.

When she did, Emma stilled. Blinked. Her breath caught in her chest and she was torn by conflicting reactions. She was heartened to see that the dark, brooding look had lightened. She was stunned by an instant and nearly overwhelming desire to lock the hotel room door and take Paxton where she stood.

"Thank you—I think."

Emma heard Paxton. Watched her looking at her questioningly then saw her clearly resisting the urge to grin. It was only then she realized she had whispered what she'd been thinking. She'd expressed her desire out loud. The desire to take Paxton there and then.

Closing her eyes, she let out a groan. This was so not like her. She was orderly. Logical. Briefly she wondered what had happened to her vaunted self-control and tried not to fall deeper into Paxton's sensual aura.

But when she opened her eyes a minute later, the vision was still standing there. Wearing slim black pants that emphasized long, lean legs and a cropped black sweater that slid away from her collarbone, inching down to reveal a pale shoulder. A dark angel who had her head spinning and tempted her as no other woman had done in a long time—or possibly ever.

Why now, when a potentially devastating cyber time bomb was occupying most of her thoughts as it slowly counted down to zero? And why this woman, who stood on the opposite end of the spectrum from everything she had always believed in?

But oh my God, she's beautiful.

She was heading for trouble and she knew it. Paxton made her want to indulge in spontaneity. Unpredictability. Outrageous daring. And right now, more than anything, she wanted to thread her fingers through Paxton's dark hair. Wanted to blaze a trail with her lips along her collarbone and see if it was as soft and silky as it appeared to be. Wanted to take her time to explore her mouth and see if it would taste as sweet as she remembered. Wanted to—

Shutting her thoughts down, Emma inhaled unsteadily and licked her lips. "If we're going to get out of here and be on time for dinner, we need to leave now."

As she met Paxton's gaze, something passed between them.

But then just as quickly, it slipped away.

They moved farther apart and without another word, she followed Paxton out of the room.

❖

It promised to be a beautiful evening. The temperature was mild, the sky was clear, and the scent of fall was in the air, crisp and fresh, without the redolent perfumes of summer.

Under normal circumstances, Paxton would have enjoyed herself, walking with an intriguing woman on the way to dinner with friends. Except there was nothing ordinary about this evening. Not the woman beside her or the friends they'd be having dinner with shortly. Nor could she shake off the odd sense of disquiet she'd had since leaving the hotel.

Perhaps it was connected to the nerves surging through her. Nerves that had everything to do with facing Cat and Paul Winters again after so long. Nerves tied to an unspoken fear that she would see disappointment in their eyes when they looked at her.

Then there were the nerves that revved every time Emma Thorpe drew near. And though Paxton didn't normally mix business with pleasure, the dynamic NSA agent was proving harder and harder to resist and had her wondering why she wasn't simply confronting the powerful chemistry that existed between them.

Lost in thought, she heard a shout but she never saw the car that came directly toward them. Not until it was too late. Paxton had barely enough time to push Emma out of harm's way, leaving her off balance as she was struck and flipped onto the hood of a dark sedan before being tossed back to the street.

As she hit the ground rolling, she twisted as much as she could. Just enough to see the car accelerate before it disappeared around a corner in a screech of tires. But it was long enough. Managing to catch most of the plate number, she stared blankly in the direction the car had gone, then rested her head on the side of the road with a groan and closed her eyes.

Awareness returned, bringing with it a pounding in her skull, a searing pain in her side, a throbbing in her knee. She became aware of people all around her. Crowding her. Wanting to help. Making it difficult to breathe.

"Jesus, that guy could have killed them."

"Somebody call for an ambulance."

"I've called the police."

Oh, shit. That couldn't happen, she thought wildly. A white-hot stab of pain flared from her leg and she arched her back to fight it. As it waned, she struggled to sit up, only to feel the pressure of a hand on her shoulder, caressing her even as she was being guided back down. "Pax, please don't move."

Carefully turning her head, she tried to focus on the blurred images until she could more clearly see Emma. On her knees next to her, leaning over her. Paxton could see she was worried, could see it in her face, hear it in her voice. But first—"Emma? Are you all right? Are you hurt in any way?"

Emma shook her head. "I'm fine. You pushed me out of the way in time. You're the one that's hurt—"

"I'm all right. Just bruised, I promise," she murmured. "So no hospital, no ambulance, okay?"

"Paxton, please. Lie still. We don't know how bad you've been hurt. That car hit you pretty hard and you need to be checked out by a doctor. You could have internal bleeding. Or a concussion."

"I don't. Honestly. I've endured enough damage over the years to know." When Emma continued to resist, Paxton reached up and drew her closer. "Emma, please listen to me. Someone just tried to kill one of us, and whether it was you or me, it doesn't really matter right now. What's important is no hospital. No police report. No investigation. No questions. I—neither of us can afford it."

For an instant, Emma stared at her and Paxton could see challenge in her eyes. But then understanding slowly appeared and she nodded. "You're right. Damn it, of course you're right. But I don't have to like it."

No. She didn't have to like it, but a moment later she conceded.

Paxton didn't like it much either. She hurt like hell. But nothing was critical and all of it could wait. What mattered now was the police would be arriving soon and they didn't have much time. They both needed to get out of there.

She inhaled sharply and held her breath as Emma and a man in jeans and a Redskins jersey helped her to her feet. She stood swaying momentarily, waiting to see how her body would react. And then she nodded. "I'm good to go," she said and murmured thanks to the people who had stopped to offer help.

Holding her side and limping, she leaned heavily against Emma as they began making their way back to their hotel room. Once inside, she swallowed some aspirin and stretched out on the bed, gratefully accepted a towel Emma filled with ice, and felt infinitely better.

❖

Paxton was not going to be happy, Emma acknowledged about an hour later as she opened the door and allowed the doctor and his entourage to enter her hotel room. But sometimes life left you with little choice. And in this case, the doctor just happened to be married to the president. The commander in chief. Her boss.

The dark-suited team of secret service agents streamed out of the room, and Catherine Winters followed her husband in and closed the door. As she turned toward Emma, her face was drawn and pale. "How is she?"

Emma flushed and straightened her shoulders. "Paxton's asleep at the moment. From what I could see, she's got a fair amount of abdominal bruising, but she's confident nothing's broken. Her left leg is badly scraped and her knee is swollen. She's got a good-sized knot on the back of her head, which bled some at the scene. And she's mentioned some discomfort in her shoulder, but doesn't believe it's dislocated. Ma'am."

She was slightly breathless by the time she finished reciting the facts and felt a fleeting instant of satisfaction when she saw a look of chagrin cross the president's face. Then she remembered who she was talking to and softly cursed herself. "Ma'am, I'm—"

"No. It's all right. Forgive me, Emma. Sometimes I forget myself and I sounded harsher than I intended. But when you called to say you wouldn't make it for dinner and explained what happened, I…well, knowing Paxton, somehow I imagined the worst."

Emma nodded. "Knowing Paxton, I can understand how that might happen, ma'am."

Her response earned her a genuine smile. "Paul, be a darling and check on our patient," Catherine said, "while I talk to Agent Thorpe and remind her it's still safe for her to call me Catherine when no one's around. Even when I'm being a tyrant."

Paul grinned, picked up his medical bag, and quietly entered the adjoining room where Paxton lay sleeping. As soon as the door closed behind him, Catherine's smile disappeared and she became all business once again. "I'm sorry, but we don't have a lot of time and I need to know. Who was the target? You or Paxton? I have to assume it was you since no one should know Pax is in DC."

"Actually," Emma said, "that's not entirely true. We ran into Roger Frederick and Jeff Strong when we arrived at Dulles. Strong somehow recognized Paxton. He alluded to what happened with Nick Perry and asked if she was now working with me."

"Bloody hell." Catherine began to pace. "I should have never asked you to bring her here. But it's been so long and I just—"

"You just really wanted to see her. And it should have been safe," Emma said. "As things stand, we still don't know for certain which one of us was the target. The truth is if Paxton hadn't reacted as quickly as she did, I would have taken the brunt of the impact. She quite likely saved my life. But it does raise the question of whether some of our work to date has made someone nervous—nervous enough to risk taking one or both of us out in broad daylight."

"And you've no idea who's behind this?"

"Paxton identified a number of potential targets when we first started. The team's been tracking them, tracking their digital fingerprints. Checking electronic and cell records. Looking for any contact with people already on our radar for potential terrorism-related activities, both domestic and abroad. When I check in, I'll see if there's been any unusual activity."

Catherine nodded. "All right. First things first. Do we need to take Paxton off this detail? Should we release her from the team?"

Emma blinked. "No. And I believe if you ask Paxton, she'll give you the same answer, only she'll use much stronger language."

"I could always order her off the team."

"You could do that, ma'am," Emma replied softly. "That's entirely your decision. But you should know that Paxton would undoubtedly continue what she's been doing, only without your support and without the team to watch her back."

The president's mouth tightened, her eyes narrowed, and Emma found herself the subject of rather close scrutiny. "You seem to have gotten to know Pax quite well in such a short time."

"Yes, I have. Believe it or not, once you get past all her walls, she's pretty open. As for the team without Paxton? You'd likely have a revolt on your hands. She's unbelievably brilliant, as I'm sure you know, or you wouldn't have insisted she be a part of this. And she not only makes everyone better at what they do, the team is convinced we'll find and stop whoever is behind these threats as long as we have Paxton. Because she's that good."

Her response elicited a deep laugh. "I'll let you in on a secret. There were times that child's brain and her ability to quickly look at something beyond most humans and have it make sense left me speechless. I remember watching her play chess with Paul, who happens to be very, very good. She thrashed him—every single time."

"I'm sure she was gracious about it."

"Quite the opposite." Catherine laughed again before a prolonged silence settled between them. "Tell me, does she still believe it's easier to ask for forgiveness than permission?"

Emma smiled. "God, yes."

Catherine Winters sighed, her face revealing a mixture of amusement and regret. "All right. I have to tell you I don't like this, but we'll do it your way. Keep doing what you're doing. Only make sure you have a few more eyes watching *both* your backs."

"All right."

"Be careful, Emma. These people we're up against are dangerous and I don't want any more telephone calls like today. Call if you need more backup."

"Yes, ma'am."

"Good. Now that business is taken care of, let's go see how Paul is doing with Paxton. God knows, she could always wrap him around her little finger."

CHAPTER TWELVE

There was a noticeable chill in the air when they returned to New York. The sky was a dull gray, the clouds fat and filled with rain.

Hardly surprising. The flight from Washington had been rocked by severe turbulence on several occasions as it tracked a storm front moving swiftly over most of the eastern seaboard. And that was before the white-knuckle inducing descent into La Guardia.

Paxton pressed her lips together. Her still throbbing head had made the entire flight less than comfortable. On the other hand, it had precluded conversation, for which she was grateful.

She needed time. Time to process everything that had happened in Washington. Time to examine and understand her own reactions. Time to deal with the memories that had been unleashed and were now shadowing her. But the flight was not the right time. Not while she was surrounded by people. That never worked, no matter how hard she tried.

She thought of slipping in her earbuds and getting lost in music, but instead, she pulled out her laptop and began to work. This was what she really needed. She could still hear sounds—the drone of the jet's engines, muted conversations—but she did her best to ignore them. Within the first few seconds, she could feel her tension begin to drain away. And then the world around her receded as her fingers moved over the keyboard and the idea in her mind began to take shape and form.

She didn't stop until the pilot announcing their descent into New York intruded on her concentration. She blinked several times to clear the screenshot that had become embedded in her mind and began shutting down her computer by rote.

The post-cyber-haze headache seemed unusually bad and the pain in her leg told her she'd been sitting in one position for too long. As she rubbed her thigh, her hand encountered the bulk of the bandage on her leg beneath her jeans and her mind flashed to yesterday's accident. She remembered the dark sedan hurtling toward them, striking her just as she pushed Emma out of harm's way. Remembered the burn in her leg and the flash of pain as her head struck the pavement.

Her head swam and she had to work to slow her breathing. But then her senses picked up the subtle scent Emma wore and she breathed more easily.

"Welcome back." A soft voice. Feminine. Emma.

Paxton looked up. "Thanks. Sorry, I didn't mean to leave you like that," she began. She wasn't used to explaining herself. Wasn't certain she knew how. "I just really needed to—"

Emma silenced her with a touch on her arm. "It's all right, Paxton. You needed to shut out the world and managed to do some work at the same time. Quite amazing to watch, although I must confess, as good as I am I've no idea what you were doing."

"Creating a reverse worm." She had no sooner spoken the words when she felt Emma stiffen beside her. Damn. Trust was such a tricky thing. "Emma? I can't change who or what I am or what I do any more than a tiger can change its stripes. So if we're going to work together, you're going to have to accept that our relationship dynamic will be different from what you're used to and you're going to have to trust me. Otherwise, this simply isn't going to work."

She felt more than heard Emma's sigh, saw her nod. "You're right, of course. And I do—trust you, that is," Emma said, while around them people began moving, reaching for carry-on luggage from overhead bins and shuffling along the aisle as they prepared to leave the aircraft. "At least, I want to. So please be patient with me. But after so many years of doing what I do, my reactions are like a conditioned reflex. I really can't control them."

"You mean like Pavlov's dogs?" One corner of Paxton's mouth lifted. "What happens if I ring a bell?"

Emma smiled back. "I guess you'll have to try it sometime if you want to find out. In the meantime, I suggest we get out of here and try to find a cab."

❖

The rain shrouded the city as the cab slowly made its way through endless traffic. Paxton stared out the window, ostensibly watching the raindrops trickle down the glass. But Emma knew she wasn't seeing the rain or anything else, for that matter. Not even her own ghostly reflection.

What was she thinking? Emma knew she'd hurt Paxton when she'd allowed a glimmer of doubt to appear upon learning she was creating a worm. And though there'd been a moment of levity afterward, it had been far too brief and had vanished as if it had never existed.

Now she was left facing a wall of silence and she had no idea how to breach it. But there was still an enemy that needed to be dealt with— along with other more personal reasons—and she had to do something fast. "It doesn't come naturally to me," she said softly.

"What doesn't?"

"Trusting people. It usually takes me a really long time before I can trust someone. That's why most of the people on my team are people I've worked with before. Or people who've come recommended by people I trust. I know what they're capable of and that if things go south, they'll have my back."

Paxton finally turned to face her. "And I'm—?"

Emma couldn't look away from Paxton's face. So close, so beautiful, so perfect. Again she felt the tug of attraction. "I honestly don't know. A complication? You confuse me. You're not like anyone I've known and most of the time I don't know what to make of you. But one thing I do know. I'd like the chance to find out."

Before Paxton had a chance to respond, the cab pulled up in front of her building, leaving Emma to wonder what she was going to say. Or if she was going to say anything at all.

The rain picked up as Paxton stepped out of the cab, pelting her face as she stood waiting while the driver got her suitcase from the trunk. She looked lost, swallowed up by the mist and rain and darkness.

Emma continued to watch her and rolled down the window. Needing to say something but uncertain what to say. "Don't stay up all night painting, all right?"

"I won't." Her words were soft. Less than a whisper as she stood still, the rain soaking her clothes, leaving her hair clinging to the side of her face. For a moment, she looked as if there was more she wanted to say as she chewed on her lower lip. But then the moment passed.

Emma knew it and blew out a long breath. "You'd better get inside. You're getting soaked. I'll wait here and watch for a moment to make sure you get inside safely and in one piece."

She saw Paxton nod, then watched as she made her way to the front door. Just as Emma was about to tell the driver to go ahead, she saw Paxton hesitate, then turn around. Pushing her rain-soaked hair from her eyes, stray tendrils clinging stubbornly, she began the painfully slow process of coming back to the cab.

"Did you forget something?"

"You." Paxton extended her hand toward her. "Please—come inside with me, Emma. Come inside and stay with me tonight."

Emma's brows furrowed in confusion and consternation. "Pax?"

"Nothing will happen between us tonight. I promise. I just want you to let me hold you while you sleep. Do you think we could do that?"

"Yes." Emma smiled. "I think we can do that. In fact, I think I'd like it."

Emma waited while the driver got her suitcase from the trunk, watched Paxton take care of the fare and overtip the driver, and then followed her out of the rain and into the building.

The jolt she got from Paxton's art was no different this time than it had been the first time. It was all so very powerful. Potent. Amazing. Paxton was unquestionably a computer genius but the talented artist she kept hidden away from public view was clearly screaming to be released.

Scanning the walls and the latest canvases, she saw the faceless woman was still there. She had more shape and form, more texture, but she remained an unknown, her face without context. "You keep getting better," she said, aware Paxton was watching her. Taking in her reactions. "But you're going to have to give her a face soon."

"I will," Paxton said wryly. "Just as soon as she lets me know who she is and what she looks like."

She shivered and Emma suddenly realized she was soaking wet. "Jesus, Pax, you're freezing. Go grab a hot shower then put on some dry clothes. I'll rummage in your kitchen and see if I can find something to heat up."

"Good luck with that. If all else fails, there are takeout menus in the top drawer to the right of the fridge."

Emma heard Paxton's laugh fade as she wandered away in the direction of the master bedroom, but luck proved to be on her side when she found some butternut squash soup. She found a pot and had the soup simmering on the stove by the time Paxton returned and stood behind her, peering over her shoulder, watching her stir the soup with a wooden spoon. With her hair still damp from her shower, she was dressed in jeans and a gray T-shirt, and she smelled faintly of her trademark sandalwood and vanilla.

"Something smells good," she murmured near Emma's ear.

Emma swore, dropped the spoon, and spun around. Her mouth immediately sought and found Paxton's while her hands cradled her face. Desire spiraled through her as their lips came together. Tentative at first, but heating quickly, her control slipped a little bit more as she gave herself up to the exquisite pleasure of Paxton's mouth and tongue.

With her breath shuddering, her eyes drifting closed, she deepened the kiss, feeling both her own urgency and the eagerness and heat of Paxton's response. Encouraged, she circled her arms around Paxton's waist and lifted her T-shirt. Her fingers felt hot against the coolness of Paxton's back and she released a moan of pure desire as every inch of her shimmered with sensations she hadn't felt in a long time.

But before she could do more than touch, Emma felt Paxton pull back. "Pax? What is it?"

"Emma—I'm sorry. I can't do this."

"What's wrong?"

"Nothing. Everything." She met her gaze and swallowed. "It's just that I promised nothing would happen tonight and I have every intention of keeping my word."

Suddenly feeling self-conscious, Emma closed her eyes. "I don't understand."

"A short while ago you reminded me that building trust takes time. So how am I supposed to prove you can trust me if at the first opportunity I break my word?"

Emma angled a look at Paxton, meeting her gaze and wondering if she'd find the answers she was looking for there. "And if I tell you it's all right? That this—that it's what I want?"

"Damn." Paxton's smile eased into a laugh, a rich, warm sound that took Emma's breath away. "You wouldn't be making this any easier. But you wouldn't change my mind."

Emma tried to return the smile but failed. "Believe me. It's not my intention to make things easy. But I do need to make sure you understand. You do know I'm not being opportunistic, don't you? I'm not good at flings. And you're not just a distraction for me. There's something about you. About us when we're together. You sense it too. You do, don't you?"

She hadn't meant to reveal so much, but the words were out. Leaving her exposed. To herself and to Paxton.

Paxton leaned in and kissed her forehead. "I do."

It was then Emma heard it. The undercurrent of strong emotion and a soul-deep yearning. Along with regret. Knowing they wouldn't be going any farther down this path tonight, she nodded and sighed. "My turn to make a promise. I don't do it often, but this I promise. I won't ask for more than you can give."

"Emma—"

Emma touched her fingertips to Paxton's lips, effectively stopping her from saying anything. "It's going to be all right, Pax. But right now, you're no doubt hurting and we're both tired. I think we should have some of this soup I heated and then go to bed. Something tells me tomorrow will be a very long day."

❖

In the damp gray light of the early morning, Paxton held a coffee with both hands, absorbing its warmth and savoring the scent as it wafted toward her. It was hot and strong. Exactly how she liked it. Needed it.

Now, as she inhaled the aroma again as she brought the cup to her lips, she could only hope the coffee would prove to be exactly what she needed—something to help her begin to relax. Because so far, nothing else had helped. Not the time spent wandering through misty, still-wet streets that had her injured knee complaining fiercely. And not the music pounding in her ears.

Dawn had come early and it seemed everything about her had been supercharged since she'd awoken with Emma in her arms. Even now, she wasn't sure how that had happened. She certainly hadn't expected to fall asleep as she had. She also hadn't expected to find comfort in Emma's embrace. Or discover Emma fit so well against her, head on her shoulder, their hands intertwined.

She had stayed there awhile, absorbing the incredible comfort of having Emma wrapped around her. Funny, that. She'd never wanted to just sleep or hold Carrie. In fact, she was usually out the door before Carrie awoke. But this was something completely different.

She closed her eyes, basking in the full range of emotional and physical sensations rushing over her again. With Emma pressed against her side, all she'd wanted to do was inch closer. Awaken Emma. Touch her. Taste her. Get lost in her.

Lust was something she could ordinarily control, ignoring it if necessary. She should have been able to push Emma into a corner of her brain and keep her there while she worked. Instead, she kept filling it, and what she was feeling for Emma was something else entirely.

She couldn't remember ever feeling this much. Wanting this much. It frightened her. Enough that she'd run. She was too empty inside, too damaged for a woman like Emma. And she knew if she dropped her guard more than she already had, she'd lose the fight.

Now she was tired and cold, and every bruise the sedan in Washington had left behind was aching. But if the frustrated desire hadn't dissipated and she was still struggling to quell a throbbing need, at least for the moment she was back in control. And that was what she desperately needed to be. Especially now.

She could feel time pressing in on her. The pieces on the chessboard were set, but the players had not yet been identified. And she sensed the next move would be coming soon. They needed to be ready, and for that she needed to keep a clear head. It wasn't about protecting her heart. It was about protecting her life and the lives of others.

At least for now that's what she told herself.

After picking up another coffee for herself and a chai for Emma along with some sweet rolls, Paxton slowly headed back to the loft. She found Emma already up, fresh from a shower and staring out a window at the expansive city vista. She visibly stiffened as Paxton approached, but remained silent as she turned toward her.

"I've brought you a chai," Paxton said. "Or you can have my coffee if you prefer."

Emma's serious eyes narrowed. "And deprive you of what is clearly a much-needed boost of energy?" She sounded cool and in perfect control, as usual. She shook her head. "That would be cruel. Almost as cruel as going to sleep beside you and waking up all alone. You ran."

It wasn't the truth in her comment that stopped Paxton from responding. It was the hand Emma placed over hers. It was the unexpected touch of her fingers and the resulting flare of heat in her blood that had her holding herself perfectly still. "I did. I'm sorry."

Surprisingly, Emma didn't appear ready to debate the issue or push her further, which was just as well. Their mutual attraction had been acknowledged by both. And Paxton's reaction—choosing to run—was now out in the open. How they would deal with it was yet to be determined.

"I'm going to have a shower," she mumbled.

Emma nodded. "All right. I'll wait and we can go to the office together." She paused until their gazes met. "We'll talk later. And Paxton? Make no mistake, we will talk."

Paxton forced herself to take a deep breath and reach for control. But she was still shivering as she climbed into the shower, where she stood for a long time. She let the hot water beat down on her and waited for it to thaw the bone-deep cold that shook her.

She could have stood there all day, but she knew Emma would wait her out. Wait all day if necessary. And if she was being honest with herself, Emma was right. They needed to talk. Later would come soon enough. For now, there was work to be done.

With a resolute sigh, she stepped out of the shower and got ready to face the day.

❖

He winced, as the sun momentarily blinded him, and quickly drew the blinds closed. The room returned to its normal state of darkness, the only illumination coming from the computer screen. But it did nothing to alleviate the throbbing in his head.

He detested failure.

It made no difference that the failure wasn't directly his. He had selected the actor, set the play in motion. That made it his to own. Worse, the failed attack would now have them alert to possible threats, making any subsequent moves on his part a greater challenge.

The longer he thought about it, the more he realized it was time to change tactics. Time to get back to his original plan. He'd allowed himself to become too distracted by an old adversary's unanticipated appearance. And even his potential buyers were becoming restless.

He needed to show them he was still in control. That nothing would distract him from his endgame. And he knew just what to do.

And then?

They said revenge was best served cold. But after all this time, perhaps a little heat would be better.

CHAPTER THIRTEEN

It was late afternoon when Emma walked into the war room. "Is the coffee fresh?"

When no one responded, she shrugged and picked up the pot. At this point, she didn't care. What she needed was something to wash down a couple of aspirin—and a fresh jolt of caffeine wouldn't hurt.

She swallowed the tablets then looked around, sensing something was happening as she picked up a palpable buzz in the room. Felt the tension in the air. She could see Shelby and Kinsey, heads close together, working at a console, while Sam and Theo looked on and appeared to be offering suggestions.

Her curiosity piqued, she wandered closer. "What have you got?"

"We're not really sure," Kinsey said. "One of our listening posts picked up a weird transmission. A live burst. They didn't have time to trace it before it went out of range. Which means it could have bounced off any number of satellites up there. Nor could they make any sense out of it, but it aroused enough suspicion that they sent it over to us."

"It's some kind of code," Shelby added. "I can tell you it's encrypted, but it's nothing any of us have seen before. We've been going through endless data looking for something similar to the encryption and run encryption programs, but so far, nothing. We can't find the key embedded in the code."

Eyes narrowed, Emma stared at the screen. But before she could respond, Paxton entered the room. An enticing view in worn jeans, a black T-shirt, and high tops, she carried the scent of fresh air and leather, and was holding a tray filled with drinks.

She seemed to have managed to bring back everyone's favorite, and Emma smiled when she saw Theo jump up and offer to help as she distributed drinks. That bridge seemed to have been mended. And thankfully, Paxton had brought a chai, which enabled her to quickly dispose of the bitter coffee she'd been holding.

Paxton looked different somehow, Emma thought, but couldn't quite pigeonhole the reason. She was still looking at Emma with a serious gaze that bordered on brooding—the one she'd been wearing since that morning when she'd returned from her run. And she had created some distance again, managing to re-erect the wall she tried to keep up between herself and the rest of the world.

But there was something else. Something Emma couldn't yet identify.

Once everyone had been taken care of, Paxton stood for a moment, sipping her own coffee and looking over Kinsey's shoulder. Her eyes narrowed with interest as she focused on the data stream and she moved a step closer, studying it silently. Intently.

Ten seconds became thirty. Became a minute, then two. "Would you mind if I gave it a shot?"

"Oh, God, please," Kinsey said and couldn't get out of her seat fast enough. "No matter what we've run, we haven't found anything close to the language of the text. Maybe you'll have better luck."

Slipping into the chair Kinsey vacated for her, Paxton began tapping the keys, and then sat back and stared into the screen. Stepping back, Emma watched her.

She heard her laugh at something Shelby said.

Watched the slight tilt of her head as Kinsey and Sam offered commentary that said she was avidly interested in what they had to say.

Saw a change slowly come over her as she stared at the computer screen.

When she tapped the keys one more time, her face turned the color of parchment. Her cheeks became ice pale, her eyes much too dark.

Paxton seldom swore, but she was swearing now, soft and low. Emma could feel the tension in her and hear what sounded almost like disbelief in her voice.

"What is it?" Emma moved closer, glanced at her, and frowned. Paxton's pupils had become pinpoints of shock, her face white and strained. Worse, she looked remote, as if she wasn't really there. Emma touched her gently, a hand to her shoulder, and found it rigid. "Paxton? Please say something."

For a moment, Paxton couldn't respond. But then she sighed and briefly let her head fall back, her eyes closed. "The reason you couldn't find anything similar is because the code is using a mix of extinct languages." Her voice was as empty as her eyes. "The first part of this is using Hittite."

"What the hell is that?" Shelby asked.

"It's an ancient Indo-European language, common to Anatolia—"

"Where's that?"

"Asia Minor."

Shelby stared at her. "What the—"

"It corresponds to what today is the Asian part of Turkey," Paxton said. "It was used from roughly the fifteenth to the twelfth century BC. It's been a long time since I've seen it used, but I'm fairly certain I'm right."

"All right," Emma intervened. "What comes next?"

"The next part…" Paxton stared at the screen again as she worried her bottom lip. "The next part is Hunnic."

"Do I want to know?" Emma murmured.

"That depends, I suppose. Yes, it's another dead language. Hunnic was the language of the Huns. It hasn't been used since, oh, I don't know, somewhere around the fourth century AD." Paxton's voice faded as she tapped a few more keys and mumbled softly to herself.

Emma felt her concern increase. "Pax?"

"This last piece"—Paxton pointed to a section of the screen—"is using Lepontic. That's another Indo-European language, most closely associated with Celtic. Like the others, it's extinct and dates back to around six hundred BC. If I'm putting it all together correctly, the gist of the message says something about…twelve days…or maybe the twelfth day. Damn it, I'm not sure."

"You're doing fine. Now, what else?" Emma encouraged, speaking lightly. "What else does it say?"

"It says something about the sun going down…coming from the east…striking the heart." She stopped, still facing the computer, and bit down hard on her lip. "I'm sorry. It's been a while. I guess I'm out of practice."

The longer Paxton stared at the computer, the more worried Emma became. Wary, Emma placed her hands on Paxton's shoulders and turned her around, forcing her to look away from the computer screen. "Pax, we all know you're a genius. I can't begin to tell you how grateful we all are that you are and that you're on our side. And I'm counting on you to help interpret what that message might mean. But if you could answer one question first?"

"If I can."

"How the hell do you know what these dead languages are, let alone how to read them? What aren't you telling us? Because today is the twelfth and the sun is going down in less than three hours. That doesn't give us a lot of time when we don't know what's coming from the east or where the heart is. And I have to tell you, it's starting to scare me."

Paxton didn't respond for a moment. But when she finally looked up, Emma saw a note of hesitancy in her eyes, along with a shadow of vulnerability. "Maybe it should scare you. Because the code? It's a ghost, connected to my past."

❖

Paxton heard herself say it. Felt the shock of it, of hearing her own voice saying the words. She stared once again at the text on the screen until her vision blurred as she let the memories slide through her mind, remembering a simpler time. But it didn't change anything. And she didn't know how to make it right.

Except for the initial shock, she felt nothing. She tried to make herself feel something else. She thought she should be angry or resentful, but it was as if a switch had been thrown and now she was empty. Numb.

"Pax? What's going on? What are you talking about?"

"It was a lifetime ago, when I was still a student at MIT. I was approached by a couple of other students who'd gotten into trouble. They were older than me, of course. But then everyone was. Still, in some ways, they were like me, or at least they thought they wanted to be." Her voice trailed off.

"They wanted to be hackers?"

"They were amateurs, but yes." After a long pause, she shrugged.

"They'd heard how I'd hacked the CIA and simply wanted to see if they could replicate what I'd done. They were suspected of trying to get into a secure government system, but the investigation was inconclusive. And since they hadn't actually succeeded, they were placed on probation. That was when one of the TAs suggested it might help if they were paired with someone like me. Someone the school believed had turned away from the dark web."

"Except that you hadn't."

"No." Because she could feel her hand begin to tremble, Paxton reached for her drink again and drained it. "So I started working with them. We were all loners, night owls, so there was no issue with staying up all night or working through weekends."

She closed her eyes and fell silent for a moment as the past pulled her, drew her back to a different time in her life. "It started one night. We were working late in a computer lab and somehow came up with the idea of embedding dead languages in our code. It was a totally geek thing to do but so much cooler than using Klingon or Elvish." She looked up and gave a weak smile. "Please try to remember, I was fourteen at the time. And more than a little bored by keeping to the straight and narrow."

She felt Emma staring at her, as she put the tale together and began to understand. "Paxton, are you saying—does this mean you know who is behind this?"

"I think it's a good possibility." Paxton nodded. "If I'm right, his name is Darren Luther."

"That's just one name," Shelby pressed. "You said there were two of them."

"The other was Ben Davis," Paxton said softly. She shrugged and each of her shoulders felt as if they were holding a thousand pounds. "He was killed in a car accident just before he was set to graduate."

"I'm sorry," Emma murmured, even as behind her, they both could see Kinsey and Sam going through the original list of potential suspects Paxton had provided. Looking for Darren Luther. "He's not on your original list, is he?"

"No, he's not. Like I said, it was a lifetime ago, and it never occurred to me that Luther would ever become capable of doing what we're dealing with. Granted, he thought he was brilliant, but at the time, it was mostly ego, with little substance. For the longest time, he got by riding on Ben's coattails…or mine. It wasn't that he wasn't smart. He just wasn't disciplined. He never wanted to work at it or accept he didn't know everything. Or learn anything from me. So I was never truly able to work with him like I could with Ben."

With nothing left to say, Paxton got up and left the room. The truth was she couldn't leave the room fast enough. Even once she got outside, she still couldn't breathe and she needed air.

Darren Luther. Who would have thought he'd become the kind of man she detested, the kind of man who brought only misery to the world.

Her head throbbing, Paxton closed her eyes and slowed things down, trying not to breathe too quickly or too deeply. In a well-established pattern, she got her thoughts to settle. And allowed the questions to come.

So, what does this mean? Where do we go from here?

❖

Emma found her sitting on the front steps of the building. Staring at the nearly empty street and the rapidly approaching dusk, her gaze determinedly forward. Still tense. Arms wrapped around herself as if looking for some comfort.

"Pax? How are you doing?"

Slowly Paxton looked at her over her shoulder, her eyes dark and unguarded for a moment, stark with pain. "I'm not sure. The only positive I can see right now is that you know who you're looking for. No thanks to me."

There was only one way to deal with this. Stepping in front of Paxton, Emma met her gaze. "You're wrong. If you hadn't recognized the languages Luther was using and remembered embedding dead languages into code, we'd be no closer to identifying him. We'd still be chasing our tails. And another thing?"

Paxton considered her for a long moment. "What's that?"

"You're not responsible for Darren Luther." Emma deliberately kept her voice as soft and as gentle as she could. "Not for what he's doing and not for what he's become. He didn't want to learn from you, remember? You were just a kid. He's done this all on his own."

A minute passed before Paxton nodded. Her expression shifted, and Emma was pleased with how she was pulling herself together. Stepping forward, she drew Paxton close and simply held her. Held her for what seemed like a long time, but wasn't really.

"What do we do now?" Paxton asked, her breath warm against Emma's skin.

Emma smiled. "Now we get back to work. We keep doing what we've been doing and leave no rock unturned. Except instead of looking for the proverbial needle in a haystack, we look for Darren Luther. And we stop him before he carries out his implied threats and does real damage."

Just as Paxton pulled out of Emma's arms, Sam came bounding out of the building. She skidded to a halt, an embarrassed half smile on her face as she noted their closeness. "God, I'm sorry, but—"

"It's all right, Sam. What is it?" Emma caught a glimpse of something in Sam's eyes. A glimpse was enough and she quickly struggled to her feet, but kept one hand tucked into Paxton's.

"It's after dusk." Sam swallowed. "On the twelfth."

"What's happened?"

"We just got word. A flight out of Logan." Sam rattled off the details. "The pilot's reporting they've lost computer control. The flight's continuing on its path with no deviation, but someone else is flying that plane."

Emma felt Paxton squeeze her fingers as she processed the information while they hurried inside. "Where? What's the flight's destination?"

"Washington," Sam said miserably.

"The heart," Paxton murmured. "The heart of the nation."

"Jesus. Paxton?" Emma turned to look at her. "Can you—is there anything you can do? Anything at all?"

"I don't know, Emma." Paxton headed for the computer console, nodded gratefully when Kinsey quickly gave up her seat, and pulled her laptop closer, hooking it to the server. "But I think so. I've been playing with an idea…"

Over the next few minutes, Emma watched as Paxton's eyes tracked back and forth, transferring files from her laptop while taking in the data that was flowing so quickly across the main screen it had become a blur.

How could she be reading that fast, let alone reacting to the information? But her fingers were racing on the keyboard as fast as the data was coming in.

Slowly the room fell silent. All business stopped and the energy shifted, everyone's attention captured by what Paxton was doing. Watching the computer as if it was whispering to her, sharing secrets no one else could hear. Knowing there were lives hanging in the balance.

Emma took a closer look. Studied Paxton carefully. She seemed completely oblivious of her surroundings. Unaffected by the pressure she was under to save lives. She didn't seem stressed or worried. Just intent. Focused. And there was a level of clarity in her eyes Emma wasn't certain she'd seen before.

It took an extra moment before Emma realized what she was seeing. Long enough that she laughed softly at herself. Paxton was trying to counterhack and break in to Darren Luther's server. She was attempting to go through the back door Luther had created and was using to control the plane.

She'd known Paxton was off-the-charts intelligent. And this was what she was seeing. Her intellect in action. The wunderkind kid with all those degrees from MIT. The wizard. Damn, she was a sight to behold. Pale and steady. Never taking her eyes off the computer screen.

The only question was how long Paxton could sustain what she was doing.

❖

Paxton knew she needed time to think. But time was the one luxury they no longer had. Everything was about the moment. Everything was about *now*.

A shudder briefly danced along her spine and she took a deep breath, pulling herself together with an effort of sheer willpower. She knew she would have to maintain an iron-willed focus if she was going to wrest control of Flight 192 back from Luther. That was the only thing that counted, how success would be measured on this day. With that thought in mind, she consciously slipped into the zone. The space where training and instinct merged and became one.

Let the games begin.

Time ceased to matter. Everything else stopped as well. Paxton blocked out all distractions and focused on the task at hand. It was like playing a game of chess, she thought, her hands flying across the keys as she worked to stay several moves ahead of Luther while utilizing the team around her.

Somewhere during the intervening years, Darren Luther had learned a thing or two. His transmission was deeply encrypted, he had his signal bouncing around a dozen server locations around the globe, and he had created a sequence of steps that needed to be completed in order before the primer was entered to unlock the encryption. If not, the firewall was alerted and it locked out any intrusion.

But it was nothing Paxton hadn't seen before. And as she prepared to open the firewall, she also prepared to install a reverse worm.

"Shit," Theo murmured. "You are an evil genius."

"Genius? Absolutely." Paxton stifled a laugh while keeping her eyes on the screen. "Evil? Only when necessary."

Her next round of moves included establishing voice communication with the cockpit on Flight 192.

The voice of the pilot in the left seat of the aircraft echoed throughout the war room. She sounded remarkably calm considering the circumstances she found herself in. She also sounded coldly furious.

"This is Captain Stephanie Granger. Who the hell are you and what are you doing to my aircraft?"

"Who I am is your guardian angel. What I'm doing is trying to return control of your aircraft to you. But I can't do this alone. I will need your help."

"You want my help?" Disbelief echoed clearly in her voice. "You do realize that if you don't give this flight back to me in a matter of minutes, you will be responsible for the deaths of two hundred sixty-four innocent people. Or does that not matter to you?"

Paxton took no offense, remaining calm and focused on her battle plan. "Of course it matters, Captain Granger. I'm your guardian angel, remember?"

As her hands continued tapping on the keyboard, she noted they had a very fine tremor. Adrenaline, she realized. But that was all right. Adrenaline helped keep the brakes on time.

She signaled for Kinsey to help transfer additional files, then began gently calming and teasing the pilot, acknowledging the gravity of the situation and explaining what was happening. Over the course of those few minutes, a tentative bond formed. Out of need. Out of hope.

Through it all, Paxton continued talking to the captain, her voice low and soothing.

When everything that needed to be said had been said, she gave last-minute instructions. "Like I said, I'm going to need your help, but I'll only be able to give you one warning. When I tell you, I'll need you to immediately resume manual control. And whatever you do, Captain, keep it on manual. Do not go back on autopilot, no matter what else is happening. That means manual until you're wheels down. You do remember how to do that, don't you?"

"I think I can manage." The pilot's tone was decidedly amused, and she sounded cool and levelheaded. Not only a good thing, but it would be critical that she stay that way.

"Good to know."

Instinctively she felt good about the pilot. The quiet confidence in her voice gave Paxton faith she would come through and would do what was necessary when it became necessary. So for the next few minutes, there was nothing but silence.

Her eyes burned as Paxton intensified her focus, studying the code on the screen for so long the numbers and symbols became like water. Fluid, as they began to swim. But she was ready for them. And when the moment was right, she slid them into place, unleashed her version of the hounds of hell, and spoke one word. "Now."

❖

"Welcome back," Emma whispered amid the laughter, the cheering, the hugs and the kisses while the team celebrated all around her.

Paxton blinked and the world snapped back into regular time. "We did it."

She grinned. It was the grin of a competitor. Exhausted. Drained. Triumphant. And it was the sexiest thing Emma had ever seen.

"You certainly did. Flight 192 inbound from Logan landed safely and is now on the ground at Dulles. And you were amazing."

God, but she wanted to hold her. Kiss her. But before Emma could say or do anything, Paxton took matters into her own hands. Wrapping her arms around Emma's waist, she drew her into a fierce embrace and dropped her mouth onto Emma's in a gentle, searching kiss. It was a tender meeting of lips and mouths with only a hint of the passion that lay beneath the surface. Yet Emma felt a searing heat burn her lips and an undeniable warmth spread throughout her body.

When Paxton drew back from the too-short embrace, Emma simply stared at her, too bemused to say a word.

"I know you have a million things to do," Paxton whispered. "You need to debrief the team. Talk to your boss and the folks in Washington, and do a lot of other things associated with your job and what happened tonight."

"Mm-hm." Emma didn't want to think about any of that. All she wanted was to reach for Paxton's lips once again, savor the taste of her lips, and drift in the warmth of her embrace.

"Emma?"

"Mm?"

"I'll wait until you finish what you need to do, but then I want you to come home with me."

Emma stared at her, unsure. Afraid to trust her voice. "Paxton—"

"Don't," Paxton whispered. "Don't think too much. Don't overanalyze. Just feel and come home with me tonight. I want you, Emma. So damn much."

She looked into Paxton's eyes and saw heat. So strong and direct, she could feel it between her legs, on her breasts, everywhere. And she believed Paxton wanted her, not only because she said so, but because she was clearly feeling that same raging maelstrom of need that threatened to burn her up.

For a long moment, the most she could do was nod. "All right. Let me wrap things up. I shouldn't be too long."

"You will be. Don't kid yourself." Paxton laughed, her voice low and approving. "But I'll wait."

An instant later, Paxton was swept up by Shelby and thoroughly kissed before being passed to Kinsey in a celebration that would wait no more. And overhead, the voice of Captain Stephanie Granger, somewhere safely on the ground at Dulles, could be heard. "Tell my guardian angel to name the place and time. The crew of Flight 192 and I would like to buy her a drink."

CHAPTER FOURTEEN

Night had fallen, still and beautiful, by the time Paxton and Emma left the station and returned to the loft. The rain had stopped, the sky had cleared, and the moon had a clarity undimmed by clouds or city lights.

The moonlight streaming through the windows in the loft was bright enough to illuminate the way, and Paxton succumbed to the temptation to leave the lights off. The darkness had weight and texture and she reveled in the magic of the night, awash in the sensuality of it and the feel of Emma's arm, warmly wrapped around her waist.

Walking into the bedroom, she paused long enough to light some candles, then turned back to where Emma was standing near the foot of the bed. As she looked at her, the realization of just how much she wanted her nearly overwhelmed her, and Paxton's steps faltered.

"You're madness in my blood," she murmured. She tried to keep her hand steady as she picked up Emma's hand and tasted the center of her palm. Emma shivered and the tremors transferred, sending shivers racing up Paxton's spine. "I want you. So very much. But I need to know. I need to be sure that this is what you want."

Her voice was not much more than a whisper in the night air, while she searched Emma's gaze. But it was clearly enough as Emma reached for her, tugged a strand of her bangs, and pulled her nearer. "I thought you'd never ask," she said before leaning in and offering her mouth.

Paxton inhaled sharply, lost in hazel-green eyes. And then there was no longer any time for words. As darkness and heat surrounded them, she closed her eyes and turned off her mind, her questions, her doubts. All that mattered was the moment. And Emma. The rest would take care of itself.

Emma's lips were full and soft and resilient. Her mouth tasted hot. Sweet. An intoxicating blend of heat and desire. And what started slowly as a gentle lover's kiss quickly evolved and became so much more.

Paxton used her lips and tongue to tease Emma's mouth, her teeth to nip her lips, her hands to draw her closer as she drove her fingers through her hair. The simple act of kissing became an erotic mating of mouths and tongues, and the fires stirring and burning deep within her left Paxton wet and needy. Aching. Wanting and craving more.

More demanding, Paxton pressed her mouth against Emma's in a deep, endless kiss as she began to unbutton her shirt. Then, with very little effort, she pushed the soft silk top off Emma's shoulders, down her arms, and onto the floor. A lace bra quickly followed.

Lazily, she trailed one of her fingers across silky skin, starting at her parted lips, down her jaw and neck, to the pebbled tip of her breast. And then she followed the trail she'd blazed with her mouth while her hands slid inside Emma's jeans. Long fingers could be a distinct advantage at times and she used every bit of that advantage, teasing them both in the process.

Pausing momentarily, a low groan reverberated in Paxton's chest as her hands trembled and she fumbled to remove her own jeans. Emma pushed Paxton's hands aside and in no time had Paxton's belt undone, zipper down, and was sliding her jeans past her narrow hips and off, sending a dark red thong to the floor along with her jeans. Paxton's T-shirt quickly followed.

Emma continued to surprise and delight as she pushed her jeans off before dropping onto the bed and drawing her legs apart. She smiled an intimate, welcoming kind of smile, and opened herself farther to Paxton's hungry gaze. Paxton watched a shiver dance across Emma's pale skin, and unable to stop, she moved closer and touched her, sliding her hands across Emma's thighs before her fingers parted soft, hot folds, stroking the wet heat she found there.

Emma released a small, need-filled cry and Paxton required no further encouragement, swallowing hard as a wave of desire crested over her. Her world shrank. She didn't think about what she was doing, she only acted, filled with a primal need and a deep hunger only Emma could satisfy.

She dropped to her knees, leaned forward, and traced a slow, meandering path of licks and kisses before gently putting her mouth on Emma, exhaling softly. Feeling an instant response, she began using her tongue in a circular motion with intermittent pressure that prolonged the pleasure. Swirling, circling, and tasting. Feasting. Devouring her as she slid two fingers inside, unerringly finding the hypersensitive nerves in her inner walls.

Paxton felt electricity shoot through her nerves while emotion and desire melded in her and coursed through her veins. With each greedy swipe of her tongue, she edged the tension higher until Emma was helplessly writhing.

"Please, Pax. Don't stop." Emma grabbed a handful of dark hair and held her in place as tension fisted tight. Her breathing hitched as she leaned her head forward to watch, and her gasps of pleasure galvanized Paxton.

Knowing Emma was watching added depth and complexity to an already overwhelming moment. Driven by desire, Paxton launched a relentless assault, delivering slow, deliberate thrusts while intensifying the pressure from her mouth.

Emma arched her back as both hands threaded through Paxton's hair and held her. An instant later, with Paxton buried inside her, she released a hoarse cry from deep in her throat, begging without words as she was catapulted into a breathless screaming orgasm.

Blessed oblivion followed as they both collapsed in a tangle of arms and legs.

❖

Emma awoke, unbelievably aroused, her hands fisted tight in the sheets as she tried to catch her breath, while tight shudders rippled through her.

She knew without question they were Paxton's hands and mouth that were on her. She had become intimately familiar with them during the last few hours. Now she recognized their texture, their rhythm.

Paxton's hands and those wickedly clever fingers were touching her. Emma felt her nipples rise beneath Paxton's hands, her nerve endings coming to life along with a pulse of heated anticipation in those places that hadn't yet been touched.

A low murmur of approval filled her throat as she was once again seduced by Paxton's lips, her teeth, and her tongue. On her mouth, at her throat, on her breast. Blood rushed to every spot her tongue caressed. Then Emma felt her move slowly lower, her tongue seeking. Her mouth devouring her. Sending her to a staggering climax.

Emma remained silent for a long stretch as the spasms running through her body gradually ceased. Beside her, Paxton let out a long, satisfied sigh and grinned as she lazily nuzzled her ear. "Sorry. It wasn't my intention to wake you. Not really."

Emma bit her and laughed out loud as she looked around the room. The moon no longer illuminated the space and the candles had long since burned out, although the air still held a faint hint of their scent. "Is it morning?"

"Soon. I just couldn't help myself. You just looked so...so appetizing." A slight grin played at the edges of her lips once again and she didn't sound the least bit sorry.

"You're really something." Emma heard the sound of the coffeemaker click on in the kitchen that suddenly seemed miles away. But she didn't move. She didn't want to lose the incredible comfort of having Paxton wrapped around her. "I could get used to this so easily— and to how you say good morning."

"My pleasure." Her words held a resonance of feeling.

Shifting slightly, she felt Paxton's slow breathing and the warmth of her skin, and realized she'd never been so comfortable with someone else. So rare, she thought, and wanted to keep it close.

"What is it?" Paxton asked.

Emma realized she'd been silent too long. Thought she heard the faint, unexpected trace of nerves in Paxton's voice. "It's nothing," she said and smiled. "I guess I was wondering if this is what I can expect from being with a much younger woman."

"I'm not that much younger—"

"Ten years."

"Well, I don't know about what it's been like for you. You know, with other women. And to be honest, I don't really want to know." Paxton frowned and shifted onto her back. "This is just what you can expect from being with me. Do you—are you regretting this?"

She'd unintentionally hurt her, Emma realized and cursed softly to herself as she watched a calm mask slip back into place as Paxton simply buried her emotions. She'd have to proceed more carefully.

In a moment of clarity, she sensed Paxton was afraid. Probably as scared of what she was feeling as Emma herself was. After thirty-seven years of living, she'd never expected to be struck by lightning, and if Paxton thought Emma was about to let her pull away now, she was in for a surprise. All other considerations aside, Emma had never had a woman touch her soul like Paxton had. She wasn't about to let her slip away.

She instinctively reached and slid her arm across Paxton's bare stomach. Both felt and heard her breath catch as she held her. "You're one of a kind, Pax. I no longer remember what it might have been like with anyone else. And just so we're clear, I have absolutely no regrets."

She was in the act of rolling toward her when she heard a cell phone vibrate. "Yours or mine?"

"Yours."

Mumbling under her breath, Emma picked up the offending phone and answered it. "This had better be good."

That it wasn't came as no surprise, as she listened as Dom relayed a message from Catherine Winters. Telling her they were expected in Washington for an urgent meeting. "I'll swing by and pick you up. There'll be a jet waiting for us, flight plan filed and ready to leave as soon as we get to LaGuardia."

She hissed softly. "I'm not home."

"Where are you?"

Emma glanced at Paxton beside her on the bed, and as their gazes met, she wondered if the need and desire she saw was Paxton's or a reflection of her own. "Pick me up at Paxton's. And I'll need a change of clothes. You'll find my emergency bag in my office."

She was greeted by a long moment of silence before Dom finally spoke. "I'll be there in half an hour. Will that give you enough time?"

"It'll have to do," she murmured and disconnected the call before turning back to Paxton. "I'm sorry. It seems Catherine Winters has called an emergency meeting. I have to be in Washington in a couple of hours. Dom's picking me up in thirty."

Paxton tilted her head, considering, and her expression stilled. "Why don't you hop into the shower while I pour some coffee for you? And maybe some toast?" She started to slip out of the bed.

Emma knew it was the right thing to do. Anything else would leave her pressed for time. But she nonetheless stopped Paxton's forward motion with just a touch to her arm.

"I've a better idea." She drew her back and kissed her, deep and quick. "Why don't you share the shower with me and I take a thermos of coffee to go?"

She was rewarded with a glimmer of a breathtaking smile and knew she'd made the right choice.

❖

"Damn it. We need to figure out a way to get him to come out of his rabbit hole."

Paxton empathized with the frustration evident in Sam's voice and wished she could do more. She knew the team was looking to her for answers. Or at a bare minimum, for direction.

It was akin to a declaration of trust. The initial suspicion and wariness that had existed between them had dissipated, leaving in its place a mutual respect for the craft that connected them—along with a desire to eliminate a common enemy. In their eyes, she'd proven herself and they trusted her talent. Her intellect and her instincts. That was what mattered.

She had the added advantage of bringing firsthand knowledge of the enemy. She had, after all, been partly responsible for teaching him how to leave no tracks. No footprints. How to be invisible.

She considered that, and in the dim light of the multiple monitors, gave a firm shake of her head. There was no sense in dwelling on what had been. She'd deal with it later. For now it was enough to know that even if Luther's skills exceeded long-ago expectations, hers were still better.

She knew they were making progress, but it was much too slow and there was an undercurrent of fear shadowing everything they did.

Fear that Luther would strike again before they were ready for him. Fear that this time he would cause more than chaos and panic. He would cost people their lives.

That particular knowledge—and fear—helped them maintain a sure and steady focus. But they'd been at it nonstop since early morning and as the clock ticked inexorably by, exhaustion was taking its toll on everyone. As was frustration. Worse, as her adrenaline rush faded, it was being replaced by a pounding headache.

Paxton wanted nothing more than to close her eyes, if only for a few minutes, and briefly she turned her thoughts to Emma. Wondering how she was doing in Washington. Allowing her mind to wander, she drew up an image of Emma. Made it so detailed, so realistic, she almost believed she could smell the subtle scent she wore. Could all but touch the smooth planes of her face. Could all but feel the curve of her—

No. Don't go there.

But it was already too late. Along with the memory of touching Emma, came the remembered sexy sound of her erratic breathing, the smoke and velvet moans of pleasure caught in her throat, and the taste of her sweet heat.

Releasing a deep shuddering breath, Paxton leaned back in her chair and forced herself to turn back to the job at hand. She ran an experienced eye across several of the computer screens in front of her. Rapidly scanned available imagery, signal intelligence, human intelligence, and open source data. She found it ironic that in spite of state-of-the-art technology, powerful computer systems, and sophisticated software, it still came down to the skill of the team. The people who put the bits and pieces of scattered information together in order to read the enemy's mind and anticipate his actions.

Touching several keys in rapid succession, Paxton called up the file she'd been putting together. Over the next few minutes, she steeped herself in it, in the images and the data streams. Brought herself up to date on all things related to Darren Luther. Aware Sam and Kinsey were looking over her shoulder, she stared at a current photograph of Luther and tried to superimpose it over the image in her mind.

What she saw was a man with an intense stare and a sullen expression lurking behind unremarkable features, offering a hint of darkness. What she remembered was a largely ego-driven man who'd wanted to wield power and wanted to win, but preferred for others to take all the risks.

He'd been a man whose most important considerations were his own skin and his own interests. And everything she'd learned so far indicated he hadn't changed much in that regard. Luther had been—and apparently still was—a man who liked to run things from a distance. It made him difficult, but not impossible to find.

What still remained unclear was his motivation. They were no closer to determining what was driving him.

In the years that had passed since she'd last seen him, standing near the gravesite at Ben's funeral, he appeared to have drifted through a variety of less-than-challenging roles in small to midsized tech firms. That would have rankled—that no one saw the genius he believed he possessed.

Perhaps that was the driver behind his current acts. Perhaps his ego had taken as much rejection as he was prepared to accept and he was now demonstrating his capabilities for the world to see.

He had to know US operatives would track him down and bring him in, no matter where in the world he hid. It was simply a matter of time. But in spite of succeeding with his initial tests and his escalation with Flight 192, there had been no demands to date. He wanted something. That much was certain. And sooner or later, he would let them know what that was.

Paxton knew they couldn't afford to wait. They needed to take him out of his comfort zone. Force his hand and force him into the open. The question was how.

Occam's razor: the simplest answer was most often correct. And there was only one simple solution she could think of. Luther was a man who liked to run things from a distance. Use others to do his bidding. If they could find and tie up his finances before he could regroup from the damage the reverse worm had caused, it could force him to the surface.

A few deft key strokes granted her access to the US Treasury Department.

"What the hell?" Kinsey muttered. "Are you doing what I think you're doing?"

Paxton shrugged and shook off some nerves. It wasn't as if she hadn't bent rules before. Just never in the presence of federal agents.

"Luther likes to keep his distance. That means he needs support. People to run interference for him. To do that, he's got to have money stashed somewhere. To buy technology and pay for help along the way. Treasury has the software that can sort through millions of financial transactions. This will save time."

With a sigh, she continued going deeper and began extracting secrets and data and personal information.

"Multiple caches would be smarter," Sam murmured as she launched a secondary search.

Paxton glanced over and started to smile. But her expression froze as she watched a message suddenly flash on Sam's monitor.

Good-bye Pax.

Below the words, an image of a bomb with a lit fuse appeared, followed by a timer, its bright red numbers inexorably counting down. *4:59...4:58...4:57...* A quick glance around the room confirmed what she already knew. The same message had simultaneously appeared on every monitor.

"Oh, shit." Feeling adrenaline pumping through her as she met Sam's gaze, she saw a fleeting question, followed by a flash of understanding. "We need to get everyone out of here. Now."

❖

After what felt like an endless day in hell, instead of Washington, Emma was pumped full of caffeine but barely had the energy to speak on the flight back to New York.

Sinking into her seat, exhaustion battered her and her eyelids felt heavy. She closed her eyes, hoping for an uneventful flight. And as the jet rumbled down the runway and began to gain altitude, she used the ambient sounds of the engines to lull her. Allowed her mind to drift, replaying the events from the day, while trying to make sense of it all. Aware there were more questions flooding her mind now than had been there earlier.

It wasn't that she'd been blindsided or caught unawares. Indeed, much of what she had anticipated had come to pass. Everyone was looking for answers regarding what had happened with Flight 192. More importantly, everyone wanted to know what was being done to prevent a reoccurrence.

And that, Emma knew, was on her and her team.

The people in attendance at the meeting had been surprisingly limited, but she could still count several people she knew personally and some she knew only by reputation. The latter included the slim, soft-spoken behavioral scientist from the FBI. They'd not previously met, but Emma knew Kendra Walker's work, respected her opinion, and wondered yet again what it might take to convince her to move her skills to NSA.

The last to enter the conference room was Catherine Winters, who immediately demanded answers no one could as yet provide.

Once everyone was settled around the rectangular conference table, the profiler took the lead. "Our subject is Darren Luther, a thirty-six-year-old white male. His dossier shows he was born in Chicago, completed his undergraduate degree in computer science at Northeastern, and his master's at MIT. He withdrew prior to completing his doctorate after being convicted of vehicular manslaughter. He was driving under the influence in an accident that killed a classmate."

Beside her, the FBI's Jacob Hardy ran his hand over his dark, closely cropped beard. "Based on the findings of our initial research, there is nothing to indicate Darren Luther is affiliated with any known terrorist group, either foreign or domestic. No indication he's been radicalized. And there is nothing in his psychological profile to indicate he is politically motivated."

"What his psychological profile does indicate is a narcissistic personality disorder, and there is nothing in his behavior that is contradictory," Walker continued. "He has an inflated sense of his own intellect and importance, along with a deep need for recognition and admiration. But while he tests in the top ten percent of the general population in terms of intelligence, his career has failed to match his potential. He's tried unsuccessfully for a number of high-profile jobs, but has been dogged by his past—a manslaughter conviction and the suspected hacking incident while he was still a student at MIT. He's unable to get necessary security clearances."

The commander in chief leaned forward, frowning. "The report I read indicates an attempt to hack into the CIA."

Patrick Bender, a dark-haired man from CIA, looked up. "It was his first known attempt and it failed. Our records indicate Luther and another student attempted to replicate a successful hack previously accomplished by another student. Both were placed on probation by MIT."

"Given his personality, that failure will not have sat well," Walker said. "And his subsequent work history shows a pattern of low-level jobs that will have left him generally unhappy and disappointed because he's not gotten the recognition he believes he deserves."

"What about the other student?"

"His name was Ben Davis," Emma said. "He was killed in the accident that led to Luther's manslaughter conviction."

"But unless I'm mistaken, the MIT student who successfully hacked the CIA and tutored Luther and Davis is now working with the NSA," Bender said. "Is that not right, Thorpe?"

Emma stiffened, too surprised by the implication in his question to even absorb it completely. For a moment, the room was silent as they each took stock of one another. "If you mean Paxton James, then yes. She's not only working on my team, she was actually responsible for thwarting the attempt to bring down Flight 192. If not for her, a lot of lives would have been lost."

"Maybe so, but can you trust her?"

"What?"

"I'm just wondering if there is any way to be certain she's not helping Luther from within. I understand you had to pull her out of jail so she could work for you. And while I understand she was set up, perhaps that too was part of a greater plan. To establish trust. To get her on the inside."

Emma worked hard to contain her temper, wondering why Bender was fixating on Paxton. Possibly because the long-ago hack happened not only at his agency but on his watch. Regardless, she knew she had to proceed with care. "We've vetted her quite thoroughly and are satisfied she's exactly who and what she claims to be. And if you want to see the case file, I'll be happy to share it off-line."

Bender backed off, but it didn't get much better. And after going endless rounds, Emma was tired. Frustrated. Her patience worn thin. Willing to tell the next son of a bitch who questioned if Paxton could be trusted to fuck off.

Dom had helped, deflecting some of the heat. But Emma was tired of the questions. Tired of having to explain that the two hackers involved in this case—one black hat, one formerly black and now ostensibly white—had known each other at MIT years ago, but were not now working together.

Was there another connection, one she wasn't seeing, or was it simply coincidence?

Damn it, she just didn't know.

Throughout the day, Emma was aware the president had been closely watching her, monitoring her reactions and responses. It was frustrating, because it would have so easily put an end to most if not all the questions and insinuations if Catherine Winters had simply stepped forward and explained Paxton was on the NSA team at her request.

But that couldn't happen. And to make matters worse, Emma could ill afford to have people question her judgment if it became known she had broken all the rules by entering into a personal relationship with Paxton. An intimate relationship.

How had things gotten so complicated?

"Do you want to talk about it?"

Opening her eyes, Emma turned to look at Dom. "I don't know what you mean."

"Bullshit. I've known you too long and I can hear the wheels turning. I know today would have been tough at any time, but I also happen to know where you spent last night—who you were with when I picked you up this morning."

Emma's eyes narrowed. "Is there a question you want to ask?"

"Only one. You looked happy this morning. Happier than I've seen you in a long time. Are you now having regrets?"

Denial—of Paxton and what she was coming to mean to her—was on the tip of her tongue. An instant later she ran a hand through her hair and released a soft sigh. "No. As strange as this may sound, I'm feeling many things at the moment. But regret isn't one of them."

Dom studied her closely. "You sound surprised."

"I guess I am," Emma said softly, feeling emotions still new enough to be frightening. "Time will tell, but for the first time, work is not the most important thing in my life."

"Hallelujah."

"I'm serious. In a very short time, Paxton's become very important to me. I don't know what that means. We both know I don't do relationships worth a damn. I'm obsessed with my job, forget to call, and screw things up. But this time—"

"This time?"

"I want to know what happens when the job stops and life begins. I want to see where this thing with Paxton can go."

"Whatever it is, it looks good on you," Dom told her. "You know I like the kid. I think she's good for you, and whatever you need, I've got your back."

Emma swallowed and closed her eyes. "Thanks, Dom."

She was still feeling mixed emotions as they drove into Manhattan, stopping when they were less than a block from their destination. The brownstone was still and quiet and she found herself hoping Paxton would still be there. Hoped that last night had been the start of something and they could go home together. Soon.

Emma felt it before she saw it.

Earthquake? The ground beneath her car shivered and bucked. A moment later, she and Dom were surrounded by a dark cloud as dirt and dust, glass and concrete flew into the air. As the blast spread, a large jagged piece of metal went through the windshield like a spear, hitting with such force the glass shattered.

Emma ducked, suddenly feeling as if there wasn't enough air to breathe. Coughing and doing her best to ignore the ringing in her ears, she stared ahead in disbelief. Orange-red fire erupted, close enough that she felt its heat on her face, and gray smoke billowed high into the night sky.

Her chest tightened and her throat ached as guilt threatened to overwhelm her.

Oh, God...oh, God...oh, God.

CHAPTER FIFTEEN

If the timer flashing brightly on every computer screen was accurate, they had less than five minutes to evacuate the building. Not a lot of time—but hopefully enough time. The one thing Paxton knew for sure was she didn't have time to question or second-guess her own actions.

Jumping to her feet, she instructed Kinsey to pull the fire alarm, then called out to Shelby and told her to help clear everyone from the main floor. She paused long enough to pull the security disc out. She then sprinted toward the stairs and headed for the second floor.

She was taking the stairs two at a time when she heard footsteps keeping pace, following close behind her. Turning her head for a brief second, her features tightened and she sent a scowl in Sam's direction. "What are you doing? This place is going to blow. Get out of the building."

Sam stayed with her as they raced in lockstep to the top of the stairs. "Two can search quicker than one. Plus I'm your shadow, remember? I'll be damned if I have to be the one to tell Emma I left you alone in the building before Luther set the hounds of hell loose or whatever he's planning on doing."

Sending Paxton a cheeky grin, she turned right as they reached the second-floor hallway, leaving Paxton to go left.

What the hell. Putting aside any thoughts of the clock ticking its way to zero, she briefly wondered why she wasn't hearing the fire alarm. Knowing there was nothing she could do about it, she emptied her mind and began to check the warren of offices that housed computer tracking surveillance posts and listening stations, hurrying about a dozen confused analysts down the stairs and away from the building to safety.

When she met up with Sam once again in the hallway, they repeated the process on the third floor, then simultaneously looked toward the narrow stairway that led to the rooftop patio. It was impossible to tell if they'd gotten everyone out. Impossible to tell if there was anyone up on the roof without checking.

"I'll go. You really need to get out of here, Sam," Paxton said. But she was no longer surprised when Sam disregarded her instructions. Releasing a halfhearted snarl, she followed her up and onto the roof.

It was a cool, damp night, with a low-hanging mist, and it didn't take a lot of time to confirm the rooftop was empty. "We need to get out of here now. If he sticks to his deadline, we might just make it," she told Sam. But she knew they had cut it too close.

"The fire escape's closer," Sam responded.

Strain was evident in her eyes, but her voice remained calm and Paxton nodded her approval. "Clock's ticking. Go. I'm right behind you."

Are we going to make it? Or are we seconds away from dying?

The logical part of her brain kept asking the questions as she broke into a run while trying to visualize the fire escape. As she followed Sam toward the edge of the roof, all that came to mind was a less than sturdy structure of open steel gratings clinging to the side of the building. Still, it was better than any alternative and she was grateful that the mist obscured the deadly drop from the rooftop.

Knowing they were all but out of time, her heart pounded in her throat as she helped ease Sam over the edge of the roof before following her onto the fire escape. The platform and stairs were rusted and damp from the mist, but appeared to be fairly solid, rattling as Paxton and Sam clambered down toward the ground.

For a moment, Paxton was convinced they would make it. But then Sam abruptly stopped, and when Paxton sidestepped and skidded to avoid running into her, she saw what Sam was staring at. She softly groaned, wishing she had the energy to rage.

Ordinarily, the ladder from the second-floor level of the fire escape to the ground was hinged so it could slide down along a track.

The moveable design was meant to allow building occupants to safely reach the ground in the event of an emergency, but prevent people from accessing the fire escape from the ground to gain entrance.

Except in this case, the sliding ladder was padlocked. It would not be aiding their attempt to reach the ground.

An instant later, she felt the building quiver as if a giant fist had slammed into it. They were out of time. "Jump."

Sam screamed and reached out, her hand clamping tightly on Paxton's wrist like a vise. Biting painfully.

Bet this is going to hurt more, Paxton thought as adrenaline fueled her muscles. There was a fleeting moment when she found herself hoping everyone else had gotten out safely. And then, with her pulse beating out a frantic rhythm, she and Sam vaulted blindly into the darkness, hoping they weren't too late.

They were still midair when hell broke loose and the blast erupted. It sent glass, concrete, wood, and steel soaring into the sky while a blinding, orange-red fire stretched upward, lighting the night sky. An instant later they hit the ground, separating as they rolled several times in opposite directions.

The impact left Paxton stunned. For five seconds, maybe ten, it was difficult to think as pain screamed through her. Disjointed images flashed through her mind, her lungs strained, and it felt as though there wasn't enough air to breathe. Before she could move, a secondary blast caught her. Shrapnel clipped her shoulder, her head, her back, and she flinched, but the debris kept falling, dropping like stones, pummeling her.

Getting to her feet, she began searching for Sam, fear burning her throat more than the smoke inhalation. But all she initially saw were flames licking greedily out of the windows the explosion had blown apart. Through the thick screen of smoke she could see where walls had crumbled, where huge chunks of ceiling had fallen in. There were other explosions, one after another until the night echoed like a war zone, and the remains of the building collapsed.

Then she saw her. Coughing, choking, she dropped to her knees and crawled toward her. Sam wasn't moving and Paxton covered her as best she could with her body while debris continued to rain down on them. She felt a trickle of warm blood run down her face and drip onto

Sam and she tried to brush it away, but discovered her arm no longer responded and it was getting more difficult to breathe.

Her vision dimmed. And then her world became quiet, while behind her an inferno roared and burned bright into the night.

❖

Edgy with increasing panic, Emma fought her way through the gathered crowd of locals. People staring in disbelief at the destruction that had visited their small neighborhood. And then she stopped.

Oh, God. Please, no.

Panic clawed at her throat. One minute it had been there. In the next instant it was gone. Total destruction. She wanted to close her eyes, to go into the dark, but forced herself to keep them open. She felt her hands tremble and fisted them.

Where the station had stood, all that remained was a pile of bricks and stone and broken glass. Nothing but rubble. The house was gone. In its place was a smoldering hole while smoke and flames were visible from the buildings on either side.

And everyone in the house—people she'd worked with, laughed with, and cared about—it looked as if they were gone as well.

Grief clawed at her. Choked her. Covered her like a cloak. Emma could feel her body tremble and her breathing quicken. She slowed her forward momentum as jagged pieces of cement and other rubble got heavier, some of it still burning. And then she was forced to stop.

Dimly, as if through a long, narrow tunnel, she heard the first sirens. Staring in stunned disbelief, oblivious of the fire trucks and emergency personnel that had started to arrive, she sank to her knees under the weight of her grief. She blinked, felt a helpless rage, and angrily brushed back tears.

"Emma?" She felt Dom's hand on her shoulder and looked up into his concerned face.

"It's gone," she said softly. "All of it—all of *them*—gone. I need to do something, but I don't know what it is."

"We don't know they're all gone. Not for sure."

Emma's chest tightened as she got to her feet and shook her head in despair. "Are you crazy? Are we looking at the same thing? Dom, for God's sake. Tell me how anyone could have survived that." Her voice broke as she scanned the area, but all she could see was total destruction. "It would take a miracle and I'm afraid we're all out of miracles."

The flash of anger was over as quickly as it began and Emma allowed Dom to take her in his arms. She fought against the scream that was building up inside her. And then she sagged as if she'd broken inside leaving nothing except grief.

How long she stood there was uncertain. Awareness returned as she felt more than heard Dom say something. "What did you say?"

Dom started to laugh. "I said maybe we're not out of miracles. Look."

She turned in the direction he indicated and nearly lost her balance, saved at the last minute by Dom's strong arms. "Kinsey?"

She blinked several times, but the image of Kinsey didn't waver, while behind her other team members appeared. Shelby was leaning on Theo for support as they clambered over rubble toward her. Others followed. "Oh, God. I'm so glad to see you. Are any of you injured?"

Kinsey shook her head. "We're okay, but you look like you might need a couple of stitches." She gently probed a cut on Emma's head.

Emma hissed and pulled back. "Later, maybe. For now, talk to me. Is anyone missing? Did we lose anyone in there?" Feeling as if she was riding an emotional roller coaster, her gaze snapped to Kinsey's and she saw her expression change. And then she knew. "Where's Paxton? And Sam?"

The look on Kinsey's face was not encouraging as she shook her head, her eyes swimming. "I'm sorry. The two of them ran upstairs to make sure everyone got out. The last thing Pax said—she asked me to set off the fire alarm so people would hurry, but it didn't work. It meant they had more to search and…they must have run out of time."

Shelby draped her arm around Kinsey's shoulder. "We've not been able to get close, to search under the rubble," she added. "All I can tell you is we saw people streaming out of the building right up to the time it exploded. But we never saw Sam or Paxton. I'm sorry."

Emma glanced at Dom, Shelby, Kinsey, and Theo. She read the sympathy in their eyes and it crushed her again. She couldn't help imagining Paxton being torn apart by the explosion and felt a pain deep in her soul.

Slowly the street filled and mayhem ensued as the fire spread and more people evacuated nearby buildings, while squad cars, unmarked cars, fire trucks, and ambulances battled for space beneath a sky that glowed with fire and smoke. Emma continued to watch, feeling numb and uncertain. Not knowing what to do.

"I promise, we'll find him," Kinsey said.

"Who?"

"The bastard that did this. Darren Luther." There was unmistakable anger in her voice. "He'll pay for this. We'll see that he pays."

Emma saw the others nod their agreement, but no one moved to leave. Instead, they stood as a group caught by the brightly colored lights of emergency vehicles and searchlights, watching the first responders battle the blaze that continued to spread to other buildings.

She knew they needed to leave. She needed to report what had happened to the president. It would do no one any good to have it discovered that the Institute where the explosion had initiated was a front for the NSA. And Darren Luther was still at large. Still posed a threat.

But she couldn't make herself leave. It would mean acknowledging the truth, that Paxton and Sam were gone, when she needed to believe in the possibility, no matter how small, that they'd somehow survived. *Please, be alive.*

She tipped her head back, stared at the sky, and tried not to think while silence reigned with the numbness of loss. But finally, knowing too much time had passed, she turned to Dom. "We need to get everyone out of here."

Just as Dom nodded, a murmur went through the group. Emma turned to look. She inhaled, felt her heart pound with expectation. And then felt her soul fill with an unbelievable joy because she knew she'd never seen anything more beautiful in her life. They were there, in the smoke and shadows, leaning against each other, but unmistakably moving toward them.

Emma's eyes teared and then she was laughing, pure delight filling her as the group drew apart, surrounded them. First Kinsey, then Shelby reached out to touch them. As if unsure they were real.

Both Paxton and Sam looked bruised. Wrung out. Their faces blackened with soot and dirt. And then there was the blood. So much blood. Paxton's hair was matted with it, and one arm of her shirt was soaked red, while Sam's face was washed of color but for the blood that was trickling down her cheek, and there was blood covering one pant leg.

"How bad, Pax? How bad are you hurt?"

Paxton shrugged and grimaced. "Not bad. Nothing that can't be fixed."

Judging from the blood, her injuries were worse than that, but Emma could think of nothing to say. There were no words for a moment like the one she found herself in. Gratitude, relief, fear. They all fought for dominance in her head and she couldn't decide which one to yield to first.

She closed the space between them and touched Paxton's cheek, her lips. A gentle move. And then she drew Paxton to her. Closed her eyes and held on, savoring the reality of her presence.

Even as her lips quivered, Paxton managed a shaky, slightly mischievous smile. "You were worried about me, Agent Thorpe?"

"From your tone, I'm guessing I don't have to be any longer."

Paxton shivered and sank into Emma's embrace. She found herself needing her solid strength. Needing to feel her heartbeat close to her own and the soft feel of her breath on her neck. Hanging on as she felt her own energy abandon her, she slumped against Emma as the adrenaline wore off and the pain rushed in.

"Come on. We need to get the two of you to a hospital," Emma whispered against her. "You're covered in blood and I've no idea how much of it is yours and how much belongs to Sam."

"A bit of both, I'd say," Paxton responded wryly before becoming serious. "But no hospital. We can't afford to have me turn up associated in any way with what happened here. It'll raise more questions than anyone is prepared to answer."

Emma started to protest, but Dom intervened. "Paxton's right. As of right now, no one knows the NSA is involved in what happened here, but sooner or later it's bound to come out. And Paxton's presence would be impossible to explain. I know a few doctors who actually make house calls. We can give one of them a call as soon as we get Paxton and Sam settled somewhere safe."

It was clear Emma wanted to argue, but it was equally clear she knew Dom was right as she quickly conceded. "Where? We can't take them to Paxton's loft. Chances are Luther already knows where it is. If anything, we should send the bomb squad in."

"I'd appreciate if you could do that sooner rather than later. I'd rather not lose any neighbors," Paxton said. "We'll also need at least three clean vehicles. Nothing connected to any federal agency, and I don't want to rent. Nothing that can be traced."

Emma frowned. "Why three? And what are you planning on doing in your condition? Steal them?"

"I'll leave that for another time." Paxton grinned tiredly. "Actually, I've had some time to think and I have a couple of ideas. But I need you to trust me. Trust that I know what I'm doing. Give me a few minutes, let me make a call, and I'll see what I can set up."

Emma didn't look entirely convinced but she nodded.

Paxton's cell phone looked slightly worse for wear, but it still worked and her call was answered on the first ring.

"About time you called. Are you all right?"

"Yes, for the moment," Paxton said. "But I need your help."

"Always. Tell me what you need."

On a wave of relief, Paxton closed her eyes. "I need three completely clean vehicles. They'll need to have both power and handling—just in case. But keep it subtle. And preprogrammed GPS systems. All following different routes, but all ending up at the same location."

She felt multiple eyes watching her with interest, but it was Emma's gaze she met as she looked up. She sent her a brief wink before continuing her conversation. "I'll need a couple of first-aid kits—"

"You're hurt?"

"Not bad, Tommy. I swear. More banged up than anything. I'll also need cash. Put some in the glove box of each of the vehicles. Make mine a blue one so I'll know."

"Consider it done. Anything else?"

"Yeah. One more thing." Paxton felt her energy waning and waited for the waves of pain to subside. "I need the beach house prepped, and I need you to pull out all the stops for me. Do you understand what I'm saying, Tommy?"

"You got it. I'll have my boys follow discreetly and keep you protected for as long as you need. Where do I meet you?"

After some discussion, they settled on a location in East Harlem, where Tommy's boys could keep an eye on things and provide any protection that proved necessary.

The call ended, but Paxton continued to stare at the phone. Lost for a moment in thoughts and memories.

"Are you all right?"

Paxton nodded. Looking up into Emma's concerned eyes, she gave a faint smile. "We'll need to split up the group for a bit. I'm thinking Kinsey with Shelby and Theo. Dom with Sam. You with me. Everyone takes a different route and uses a combination of subway and cab. There's a bodega at 103rd and Lex. We'll meet up there."

"All right." Emma's gaze never left hers. "Can I ask who you called?"

"Of course. His name's Tommy Cho. He's—"

"A hacker. I know him by reputation," Emma said. "He's supposed to be brilliant. Not quite as good as you, of course, but then, who is?"

Paxton laughed. "Well, yes. But he's also—"

"One of the good guys," Sam interjected. "He helped Pax get rid of everything her ex left behind in the loft. He's okay, Emma. And he's almost as beautiful as Pax."

Dom choked back a laugh. "Well, I guess that settles it then. What happens after we meet Tommy and get those cars you arranged?"

"We head out on separate routes and meet up at a property I know of."

"Pax?" Emma clearly was uncomfortable with the direction things were going. Her words were calm, but her mouth was tight and her knuckles were white as her hand tightened on Paxton's arm. "We can't just disappear. I have a job and a boss you know quite well. The task force needs to continue looking for Darren Luther. He still poses a major danger. We can't just stop everything and go into hiding because we've been threatened."

"I'm not suggesting we go off grid to lick our wounds and hide. I'm suggesting we go somewhere that will be equipped with anything and everything we'll need to search for and find Luther. I'll even go so far as to guarantee it will be everything you ever wanted in technology, along with some things you may not even be aware exist."

Emma's hand loosened its grip on her arm and a faint smile touched her lips. "This place—you own it, don't you?"

"Yes." She waited, making no move until she saw Emma nod.

"I guess if we don't want to attract a lot of attention, we're going to have to figure out how to cover up all the blood you and Sam have on your clothes. I've a suitcase in the trunk of Dom's car—"

"And I've got a couple of extra sweatshirts," Dom added. "They might be a bit big, but they should at least cover up most of the gore you've both got on you."

Paxton rolled her eyes. "You think?"

❖

His heart pounded.

Tapping his fingers in a sharp staccato against the desk, Luther willed the satellite feed to stream faster. An instant later his wish was granted and he smiled as he saw the fire. Watched it spread and reach high into the night sky.

Beautiful. Nights like this didn't come along very often. He'd have to find a way to thank the NSA for providing the satellite imagery of their own station house going up in flames. It had been so damned easy to establish a link, with a little inside help. And the results were spectacular.

He tried to imagine her expression when she saw his farewell message appear on her computer screen. She would have known by then who was taking her down. The code would have told her. And she would have tasted the bitterness of defeat in those last few seconds before the explosion killed her.

Still, for a moment he wondered if perhaps he'd overestimated her. She shouldn't have been so easy to take down. As his elation faded, he realized he'd been looking forward to the challenge of proving himself against a worthy adversary. And if anyone could have come close to presenting him with a challenge, it should have been her.

He felt the sting of disappointment and terminated the feed. His work in New York was done. There would be no more obstacles standing in his way. No more distractions.

When the phone rang, he answered it on the first ring. For the next several seconds, he listened without speaking. He wanted to scream into the receiver, but instead asked only one question in a low, calm voice. "Are you certain?"

He maintained control long enough to disconnect the call. And then in pure reaction, he screamed out his rage as he smashed the phone against a far wall. Not yet done, he methodically began to pick up and throw anything within reach with a satisfying violence. A lamp. Some books. A glass paperweight. The sharp sounds of their destruction echoed in sync with his heartbeat and fed his anger.

She was still alive. The damned woman had more lives than a cat.

He continued to rage until there was nothing left to throw. Breathing harshly, standing in the midst of the destruction that surrounded him, he paused. And then, in the act of looking for another projectile, it suddenly occurred to him.

He began to laugh. Perhaps all was not lost. He felt exhilarated as he realized it was good that she still lived. It meant the game was still on. And Paxton James might yet prove to be a worthy adversary.

CHAPTER SIXTEEN

Interstate traffic was steady and relatively light, and though she couldn't say so with any certainty, Emma didn't believe they were being followed. She set the cruise control to just above the speed limit, allowing other vehicles to pass at will while she kept an eye on them, and tried to figure out where they were going based on the directions the GPS unit was giving her.

So far, it made no sense. In fact, she was fairly certain they were going in ever-widening circles. But then, after the day she'd had, why should things start to make sense now?

Paxton would know, of that she was certain. But she didn't seem inclined to offer any input. She'd been quiet, almost withdrawn, since meeting up with the enterprising Tommy Cho, who had brought someone with him to tend to Paxton and Sam's injuries.

Tall and lean, with reddish-brown hair pulled back into a ponytail, and dressed in jeans, high-tops, and a Chicago Bulls jersey, the fortysomething woman's face had reflected an almost ethereal calm as she'd smiled at Paxton. That Paxton was clearly taken by surprise was evident, but after an initial shock, she seemed happy to see her. She called her Sister Kate, insisted she take care of Sam first, and then spoke with her at length in fluent Spanish while she tended to the cut on Paxton's arm.

"The kids want to know when you'll be by to play another game of basketball with them," Kate said. "They miss you coming around and want to thank you for your last donation."

Paxton's smile turned into a wince as another stitch was added to

*an already lengthy row. "I trust that means you put Carrie's wardrobe
to good use?"*

*"Of course." Kate nodded and laughed. "We negotiated a very
good price for everything Tommy brought us and used the proceeds to
put a down payment on the derelict house next door to the center. Our
numbers have been growing. We could use more beds. And no"—she
stopped Paxton from speaking with a quick motion of one hand—"you
don't need to do more. You already do more than enough."*

"You play basketball?" Emma asked Paxton, tongue in cheek.

"And you clearly understand Spanish," Paxton responded in kind.

*Kate watched their interaction with an ever-widening grin. "It
seems to me the two of you have much to learn about each other. I'm
surprised, Pax."*

The affection between Kate and Paxton had been evident. Not
unlike the bond that she had with Tommy, who clearly came prepared
for all contingencies, bringing the vehicles Paxton had requested,
money, clothes, and an eclectic group of young men—some black,
some Asian, some Hispanic—who maintained a protective watch over
the proceedings while Kate attended to Sam and Paxton.

A gang of sorts, Paxton had informed her, answering her unasked
question. A gang of hackers.

Just one more facet that made up the enigma who was occupying
most of her thoughts, Emma acknowledged wryly. A woman now curled
up in the passenger seat beside her, reviewing something on her laptop.

It seemed to be code of some kind, but from the driver's seat, it
was impossible to tell. Perhaps when they stopped—Emma glanced
over as Paxton stretched and released a soft groan. "What's wrong?"

"What do you mean?"

"I thought I heard a sound. Like you were in pain."

"Just a little stiff, that's all." Paxton shifted and failed to bury a
wince as she rubbed the back of her neck. "Comes from sitting in one
position for too long."

Emma frowned at the response. She hated to hear the pain in
Paxton's voice. Hated knowing there was nothing she could do. But she
could respect Paxton's privacy when the details weren't being shared,
and over the space of several breaths, she managed to clear the emotion
from her face. "So how do you know Sister Kate?"

"Kate? I met her about seven or eight years ago. She'd just come back from a tour in the Middle East as a medic."

"Wait a minute. A nun working as a medic in a war zone?"

"Well, she's not really a nun." Her laugh was throaty and sexy. "The kids initially saw her as a do-gooder and gave her the nickname Sister Kate. And it stuck. When we met, she was in the midst of organizing a basketball tournament for a bunch of street kids. Mostly former gang members."

"How did you happen to be there?"

Paxton shrugged. "Tommy and I were looking for the kid sister of a mutual friend. She'd gotten mixed up with one of the gangs and we'd gotten word she was hanging out in the area."

"Did you find her?"

"Yeah." A small wry grin appeared. "And before we knew it, Kate had roped us into the tournament. After that, it was helping to paint the old building she and the kids were using as a community center. Then getting equipment and setting up computer classes. Turned out her list was endless."

Emma smiled as things became clearer. "So how much of the center and its activities have you funded?"

"Some." Paxton shifted. "Everyone helps, including the kids. A group of local cops pitched in. So did some organizations I knew. People I'd…um…helped with their network security issues. Everyone contributed and it just kind of grew."

Emma heard it. The discomfort in her voice. She wouldn't want to be in the limelight or be seen as a do-gooder like Kate, any more than she had liked the earlier comparison to Robin Hood. Not Paxton. She was a tough girl. But a hacker with a huge heart. It was time to cut her a break. "That's a nice story. By the way, you should know that Sam's right."

"Oh? How's that?"

Emma grinned. "Tommy really is almost as beautiful as you. Not quite, but close. Must be the long blond hair. He reminds me of the elf in *Lord of the Rings*."

"Oh, Lord, I'll have to tell him you said so." Paxton laughed and for the first time since they'd gotten into the dark blue SUV and left the others behind, some of the tension left her. But not the pain that was evident in the lines around her mouth, Emma noted and came to a decision.

It had been a long day. A very long day. Neither of them had gotten much in the way of sleep the night before, they'd been on the road for nearly two hours, and they could both use an extended break. Plus, with no disrespect to Sister Kate's skills, Emma wanted to check Paxton's injuries herself.

"There's an exit coming up that has a sign for a motel. It hasn't been programmed into our GPS and I can't attest to how nice it might be, but at the very least, it should provide a hot shower and a bed, and we could both use some food. What do you think?"

If she'd expected an argument, she didn't get one. Instead, Paxton reached into the glove box and withdrew a handful of cash.

"Jesus, how much cash did Tommy put in there for you?"

Looking at the cash in her hand, she raised a brow. "I'm not sure. Probably around ten thousand. Why? Is there a problem?"

Emma didn't know how to begin asking the question. "It's just so much. Is it—?"

Her hand flexed against her jeans. "It isn't stolen, if that's what you're trying to ask. Tommy withdrew it from one of my bank accounts."

"Why?"

"Because I asked him to. Cash doesn't leave a trail. The same goes for these cars, why we're all taking different routes to the same location, and why I had Tommy give some cash to Dom and Kinsey. I don't want to leave anything to chance."

Emma gave her a glimmer of a smile. "Well, from where I'm sitting, you appear to have thought of everything."

"No, not everything." Paxton sighed. "If I'd thought of everything, Luther would never have gotten close enough to plant those bombs in the station, the house wouldn't have blown up, and people wouldn't have almost been killed."

The self-recrimination in her voice was clear and Emma watched a calm mask slip back into place as Paxton buried her emotions. She responded instinctively, reaching out a hand to her and waited for Paxton to take it. "Please try to remember no one *was* killed. Focus on that. And remember that the only reason no one was killed is because you and Sam risked your lives and made sure everyone got out."

"Maybe so."

"Without question. Have I told you how very grateful I am?"

"That we got everyone out safely? Gratitude isn't necessary. It was the only thing to do."

"That may be." Emma smiled. "But I'm also very grateful that *you* got out. That *you're* alive and nearly in one piece and that you're sitting here beside me." Her smile slowly faded and she paused. Swallowed. Felt the silence return and settle around them for a moment before she could continue. "When I saw the station, or what was left of it, I was so damn scared. I thought—well, it doesn't matter what I thought. Not anymore. What's important, what truly matters to me right now is that you're okay. Or you will be as soon as I can make it so. Do you understand what I'm saying?"

Paxton looked at her. "I think so."

"I'm not so sure. What I'm trying to tell you is that having you here with me is important. We're not distractions for one another. I know right now it feels like a lifetime ago, but you and I started something last night, Pax. Something beyond work and Catherine Winters and Darren Luther. Something special. One look from you and I feel alive. I don't want to lose that. More importantly, I'd like to see where it can go, even though, to be perfectly honest, it scares the hell out of me. You scare the hell out of me."

"I don't know what to say."

"You don't need to say anything." Emma swallowed. Riding on too much emotion, she feared she'd said too much. Or maybe not enough. "Or you could put me out of my misery here. Maybe tell me you'd like to do that too. That you'd like to see where things between us could go."

"I don't know what *this* is," Paxton answered slowly. "Relationships—they're not my forte. In the past, other than Carrie, I didn't even try to extend things beyond a night or two, and we both know how things ended up with Carrie. But if it helps, you make me want something I've never had before. And just so we're clear, you're not the only one who's scared. I am too."

"Well, all right, then." It was as good as she had any right to hope for or expect. Probably better, and Emma didn't say anything else until she pulled in front of a nondescript motel, parking the SUV near the office before taking a long look.

"Okay, it's not quite the Ritz, but at a glance, I think it might be at least a step up from the Bates Motel."

Paxton's eyes sparkled with barely suppressed laughter. "I've stayed in worse."

"Then remind me not to let you choose our accommodations. In the meantime, let me get us checked in and then see about ordering some food from the coffee shop that's still open. Maybe you can have a shower and try to loosen up a bit while you're waiting."

Paxton nodded and clearly failed in her attempt to stifle a groan as she rolled her shoulders. "Whatever you think."

❖

As she unlocked the door to their room, Paxton noted her hands were unsteady. Pain hummed in the back of her head and she held her breath, waiting for it to abate. It left her only vaguely aware of Emma, standing by her elbow looking solicitous and worried.

"Can I do anything for you? Get you anything?"

She stared at Emma blankly and found herself having difficulty formulating thoughts. "Sorry. I'm not really operating at top speed. Why don't we stick with your original plan? You check the coffee shop for some food while I have a long, hot shower." She paused, tried to find something else to say that would wipe the worried look from Emma's face, and failed. "If they have some kind of soup that would be great. And maybe some aspirin?" She could see Emma standing on the edge of her vision. Could see the fear lingering in her eyes.

"Should I see if I can get a doctor?"

"That's not necessary. Emma, I promise, I'm really okay. Something hit my head after I jumped from the fire escape. It's left behind a nasty headache. That and the smell of blood and smoke will do it to me. Take whatever money you need and I'll see you in a little while."

Emma hesitated. She was close enough that Paxton could see the gold flecks in her eyes. And close enough that she could see her consider any number of words before disregarding them, clearly deciding that this was not the time—for which she was grateful.

"All right. Go have that shower, then lie down. I'll be back before you know it."

After Emma left, Paxton paused at a mirror and stilled as she studied herself, eyeing her reflection critically. She reached out and placed a hand on the wall, steadying herself and taking a deep breath. She blinked several times, but the image didn't alter.

She still looked pale, restless, bruised. Her eyes were gritty and burning, her skin twitchy from a combination of adrenaline overload and simple lack of sleep, and there were traces of blood still on her face.

"You're a mess," she told her reflected self. No wonder Emma looked so worried.

She was shivering as she climbed into the shower, where she stood for a long time hoping the heat would soothe her battered body. Using a lot of soap, she worked to erase the sensory memory scent of blood that still filled her head and let the hot water beat down on her. But the heat sluiced off her skin just like the water, none of it soaking in to thaw the bone-deep cold that held her in its grasp.

She remained there until she couldn't smell the blood anymore, then reluctantly shut the water off and dried her body, wincing as she discovered new bruises. But there was no question, the shower had helped and she was feeling refreshed. Wrapping a towel around her waist, she returned to the room and slipped her earbuds into place before falling facedown on the bed.

An instant later, music blared in her ears. Rock seamlessly shifted to classical—this time Beethoven—and she sighed. Here she could keep the pain at bay.

Emma returned sometime later. Paxton felt her presence and pulled out the earbuds. "I'm just getting my second wind," she mumbled. "I'm sure it'll come any moment now."

"I can see that." Emma chuckled. "Sadly, the coffee shop didn't have much to offer, but I convinced them to heat up some soup. Would you like it now or would you prefer to rest?"

She heard the strain in Emma's voice and opened her eyes. Noticed that she was staring unhappily at the freshly stitched cut on her arm. "It's funny, but I can't remember doing that. I didn't even feel it."

"That's the good and bad of adrenaline," Emma said as she sat on the bed beside her. "At least it's not too deep and it shouldn't leave much of a scar, if at all. Sister Kate. She did a nice job of stitching it. Do you know when you last had a tetanus shot?"

"I'm good," Paxton said, enjoying Emma's gentle, soothing touch as she brushed back the still-damp hair from her face. Just a whisper of fingers that somehow managed to be intimate and caused heat to spear through her like lightning. "I always make sure my shots are up to date before I travel, and if you remember, my last trip ended just before I was arrested."

"That's good to know. One less thing to worry about."

She cupped a hand over the one Emma held to her cheek. "Maybe we can have the soup later?"

Emma smiled. "You really need to eat now and then get some sleep."

"Maybe so." She wound her arms around Emma's neck, drawing her down toward her until she could rest her head on her shoulder. It felt good. Very good. "But I think I found my second wind. It's a gift, you know."

"A gift?"

"Mm-hm. You seem to have an innate ability to make me forget I hurt."

"I'd believe you more if you weren't so pale and I didn't see the pain and fatigue in your eyes," Emma said as she gently found her lips.

Maybe so, Paxton thought, releasing a small, throaty sound of pleasure. Maybe so. But as their mouths met, even the whisper of pain fled and she felt like she was floating in a half dreamlike state.

❖

"Oh, shit. You're bleeding again. I'm sorry I was selfish. I shouldn't have started anything or touched you, but…damn it, I should have known better. I knew you were hurt." She feathered her shaking fingers over Paxton's face. "Let me get something for it."

"Emma, don't worry about it. I'm fine."

"You're humoring me. Please don't." She turned and faced Paxton squarely, her expression serious. "You know damn well you're lucky you didn't break something, or worse, when the station blew up. And now—"

"Emma." Paxton reached out with one hand and gently stopped her. "It's all good. I'm good. See? The bleeding's already stopping on its own. I promise. If it gets infected, I'll go see a doctor. Now come back here and kiss me. I find myself missing your mouth."

"Paxton, no."

"No?" Paxton's eyes narrowed.

In the half-light, with the taste of her still sizzling on her tongue, Emma found herself unable to do anything but comply. She found Paxton's mouth and responded with a kiss as soft as shadows. And instantly, the rise of desire became a deep and liquid yearning that spread and became an aching need.

"Damn you. I shouldn't want you this soon. But I do." She swallowed. "And I shouldn't need you again so soon. But I do."

"Thank God."

The soup was cold by the time Emma got up and brought it back to the bed. But neither of them cared. She topped it off by feeding both of them pieces of the Hershey bar she had purchased, the intimacy of the simple act and the moment somehow making it seem special. It made her forget the dingy motel room. Almost made her forget the events that had gotten them here.

Almost.

Through it all, she was also watching and waiting for Paxton to talk to her. There was clearly something on her mind. Something troubling her that went beyond a building blowing up under her—as if that wasn't enough.

So far she'd not said anything, and Emma had briefly considered how to raise the subject. She wanted Paxton to feel she could trust her. Would have preferred for Paxton to willingly share what was on her mind. But time wasn't on their side.

Before she could speak, almost as if reading her thoughts once again, Paxton sighed. "Have you given any thought, maybe wondered how Luther was able to get bombs planted inside the station without tripping alarms or running into someone?"

Emma went still and didn't allow herself to show any reaction. It wasn't that she hadn't already thought along those lines. But the reality of hearing the question spoken out loud was worse than she'd expected. "Do you mean beyond the obvious?"

"That he had help from someone on the inside?" Clearly restless, Paxton got up from the bed. For an instant, she looked dizzy and Emma watched her struggle to maintain her equilibrium, ready to assist if needed. But the moment passed as Paxton grabbed and put on a T-shirt, then began to pace. "I'm sorry. I don't like the thought, but I can't see it happening any other way."

Emma followed her with her eyes for a moment, knowing Paxton was right. Of course she was right. The only way the bombs could have been set was for someone who worked with her—someone she trusted—to have made a conscious decision to help the enemy. The thought left a deep slice of emotional pain inside her.

"At a guess, it all started in Washington."

She caught something in her voice. "Paxton?"

Paxton walked away, walked toward the window that faced a near-empty parking lot. But Emma doubted she was seeing anything. "The accident outside our hotel. I know you assumed you were the target. But you were wrong. I guess we both were. He's not after you."

She turned around to face her and Emma saw Paxton's eyes go dark and flat, and then her lip curled at the corner. A cynic's smile. "He wants me."

Emma didn't like it, but she had to accept Paxton's read of the situation. That left one question—actually two, but she couldn't decide which disturbed her more. "Why is he coming after you? And who the hell is helping him?"

Paxton shrugged. "As I see it, Luther has been testing his ability to remotely control technology for a while. You previously indicated there had been a number of incidents leading to your task force being formed and my coming on to the scene."

"That's right."

"And the only people who knew you'd brought me on board were Dom, Cat, of course, and your immediate team. Nothing untoward happened until Washington. You stopped for a moment to talk with a colleague just after we landed."

"That's right. But Roger Frederick? Jesus, Pax, I've known Roger and his wife Linda for a long time. I can't imagine—"

"No, you can't. Because most likely, he's done absolutely nothing wrong. The man he was with, however, is another story. He recognized me. He brought up the link between me and Nick Perry. And he asked if I was now working with you."

Emma blinked. "Jeff Strong. I knew that. Damn it, what's wrong with me?"

"He's a colleague."

"So was Nick Perry."

"And he was with a man who's not only a colleague but someone you consider a friend."

Emma nodded slowly. Reluctantly. "I'll talk to Dom. Have him watched. I'm still sorry. I put you in jeopardy. You were almost killed."

Paxton moved close to the bed and reached out her hand. As Emma took it, she felt it tighten around hers. Felt its strength and warmth. "You've done nothing wrong. This is Luther's to own."

"But that still doesn't explain why he's tried twice now to kill you. And this last attempt"—she stumbled on the words—"the death toll could have been so high if you and Sam hadn't acted as quickly as you did. He could have killed everyone in the building. Why? Why does he want to kill you so badly?"

She watched as control smoothed all the emotion from Paxton's face, until calm was the only thing that showed through. "Because I'm the one person he fears."

"Why?"

"Because he knows I can stop him."

❖

Where was she?

Luther's heart hammered in his chest as he paced. All he could think was she had somehow managed to disappear. And he had no idea how the hell that had happened. He'd had people who were supposed to be watching. People he'd bought and paid for. And still she'd managed to vanish into thin air.

He read through the reports again and tried to disregard the nagging voice inside his head. The one that kept telling him he'd made a mistake when he'd destroyed the New York station house.

As long as it was there, he'd always known what she was up to and where to find her. Now she could be anywhere. Worse, not only had she disappeared, so had Emma Thorpe and most of her team. They were all in the wind.

Where did that leave him?

He willed himself to calm down, unclench his hands, relax his shoulders, slow his heartbeat. He had to proceed as planned. There was too much at stake. He was too close to realizing his goal. But he would need to be more careful. She was out there.

The reverse worm she'd hit him with had slowed him down. It had also proven one thing. She could stop him. He knew that now. Perhaps he'd always known it. But he couldn't allow that to happen. It was time to pull out all the stops.

Little did they know the worst was yet to come.

CHAPTER SEVENTEEN

An hour before dawn, Paxton awoke to the vibration of the satellite phone Tommy had given her as it danced across the top of the small bedside table. She glanced at it and in spite of a faint annoyance at receiving a call so early, smiled. The phone was the latest incarnation of something the two of them had been playing with for quite some time. Tommy had added the recent enhancements, which he'd said included a long-life battery to go with the built-in scrambler.

After a brief glance at Emma, still sleeping with her breathing soft and even, she willed away other thoughts that kept intruding and eased out of bed. In the dim light, she found a T-shirt and her jeans and slipped into the bathroom. The shower told her what she already knew. The headache was almost gone and she was moving more easily. On that positive note, she dressed quickly, walked back into the room, and hit the speed dial on the phone.

"Is everything all right?"

"Everything's good," Tommy responded. "We've verified no one's been followed by anyone other than my crew. The news reports have had little to say about the explosion, hinting at some kind of gas leak, so someone's doing a good job of covering it up. And even though I'm not crazy about what you've got planned, everything you asked to have at the house has been taken care of and should be ready when you get there."

Good was all she needed for now. Holding the phone to her ear, Paxton walked to the window where she could peer outside. An old habit coming back to haunt her. Or maybe it was part of the woman she'd become after her time in prison. She didn't know for certain. In either case, the SUV was still parked where they had left it, covered in mist, and appeared untouched. And nothing in the vicinity was moving as far as she could see.

She stepped outside, quietly closing the door behind her. "I want to come straight in. Today."

"Is there a problem?"

"No. I think I'll just feel more comfortable when we've got everyone inside the gate where we can keep an eye on them. Keep everyone protected. And I've got the security disc from the station. Hopefully we can see who it is we shouldn't have trusted."

Tommy grunted unhappily. His voice grew muffled—he'd apparently turned away from the phone—and he said something she couldn't clearly hear. A minute later, his voice came back to her ear. "Okay. Give me thirty minutes. I'll drop off a new vehicle for you and pick up the SUV you drove yesterday. You'll have a full tank. Cash in the glove box. Two cars following you. One a mile or so in front of you."

"Sounds good. In fact, do me a favor. Do the same for everyone. Fresh vehicles all around."

"The others will take more time. Two or three hours."

"No problem. I'll call Dom and Kinsey and let them know to stay wherever they are until they're equipped. Thanks, Tommy."

"Anytime. Keep that disc out of sight. And keep your eyes open and stay safe, Pax. It's going to rain and the roads will be slick."

She made two quick calls after that and discovered there was a joy in working with professionals. Both Dom and Kinsey took her request to stay where they were until new vehicles were delivered to them without question or challenge. It simply was. Dom passed along the good news that Sam was recovering well from her injuries.

When she was finished making the calls, she slipped back into the room. But she remained by the window. Looking out but seeing nothing in the early morning stillness, she formulated plans, considered alternatives. A moment later, she picked up Emma's scent and her whole body immediately heated as she turned.

Emma didn't initially say anything as she slipped closer. But Paxton could feel her heat and sighed as Emma's arms reached up and wound around her neck. Gentle lips touched her throat and the air changed. Became charged with electricity. Shivers danced along her spine and her head spun, while hunger and desire surged through her.

❖

When Emma awoke, dawn had broken and she was alone in the bed, tangled in the thin comforter. There was no sign of Paxton. The bed beside her was cold to the touch, the room was silent. An instant later, nerves struck. Hard and fast.

Where was she?

For a heartbeat or two, all she could think was that Paxton was gone, leaving nothing behind but the towel she'd used to wrap around herself the night before. Feeling foolish, Emma picked it up and brought it close to her face. It had managed to retain the faint scent of soap and something more. Something distinctly Paxton.

Damn. Not what she needed right now. What she needed was clarity and objectivity. Except she really didn't want Paxton out of her sight for any length of time.

Paxton had something that weakened her. Not her looks, although there was no question she was stunning. It could be her kiss, she thought, melting a little at the memory. Yes, that could be part of it. But mostly she suspected it was Paxton's capacity to touch her in places she'd never wanted anyone to touch. Like her heart.

When had that happened?

And where had Paxton gone? She'd acknowledged that Luther was after her now that he knew she could stop him. Had she decided the personal risks were too great? Would she just walk away?

Emma sat for a long moment, her mind free flowing. Conjuring images. The light in Paxton's expressive blue eyes, the softness of her mouth, the strength in her body. Would she—could she just have left?

It was then she heard Paxton, talking softly just outside the door. On the phone, she realized, and recognized she'd been foolish.

Trust much?

Feeling somewhat reassured and partially angered at her own over-the-top reaction, she realized she had no idea who Paxton was talking to. But as she listened, the only thing that was clear was that Paxton was making plans. Without discussing things with her. Without consulting her. That sent up another red flag.

They would need to talk about her penchant for doing that. She would have to explain that while she understood Paxton typically worked alone, she was not on her own this time. There were others whose opinions mattered and needed to be considered. This was still Emma's task force. Her job.

When had she lost sight of that? The question echoed in her brain as she watched Paxton let herself back into the motel room.

In a moment of decisiveness, Emma slipped out of bed and approached her. But the instant her fingers touched Paxton, she almost let go. How had she forgotten what simply touching Paxton could do to her?

Her thoughts scattered and fell by the wayside. Paxton carried the scent of leather and rain and fresh air. Now all she wanted to do was draw her back toward the bed and spend the day there. Memorizing her amazing body. Enjoying her taste—seductive as a dark, sultry night. And eliciting the sounds she made deep in her throat. Sounds that drove Emma to the edge just by listening to them.

"Good morning." Paxton smiled and Emma caught the faint look of pleasured surprise on her face.

She tried to smile back. Tried to hide the emotions that had suddenly roared to life within her as thoughts jumbled in her mind. Included was a flash of a dream she'd had shortly after meeting Paxton. A dream that had left her wondering if, like smoke, Paxton would always remain too illusive to hold on to. A dream that was likely responsible for the mixed emotions she was now experiencing.

A premonition? Was her head telling her she should be slowing things down or even halting things with Paxton? Maybe spending all her time with Paxton was skewing her thoughts and making her forget priorities.

"You've been making plans without including me in the discussion." Even as she said it, Emma knew the words had come out too strong. Too harsh. But before she could say anything or make any kind of course correction, she saw Paxton's smile diminish then fade altogether as she sighed. And a heartbeat later Paxton shrugged her off and stepped out of her hold, a tangible frustration simmering in her eyes.

"I've arranged for Tommy to drop off a fresh vehicle for us within the hour. You should grab a shower while I pick up some coffee to go. I'd like to hit the road as soon as possible."

Emma studied her for a minute. Uncertain, she started toward her. But Paxton immediately backed up. "Pax—"

"No. I'll be back soon." She licked her lips, backed away farther, then slipped out the door without pausing to reach for her jacket, leaving behind a void filled by silence, the smell of rain, and the soft scent of aspens.

Paxton hadn't come back by the time Emma finished taking a shower, so she filled in the time by packing up their few possessions. Then she began to pace. She was contemplating going out to find her when she heard the sound of a car door. Glancing out the window, she saw Paxton and Tommy exchanging both conversation and keys before Tommy got into the blue SUV they'd been using and drove away.

By the time Paxton returned to the hotel room, her hair was dripping onto her shoulders and her T-shit was soaked through. Without saying a word, she handed Emma a coffee, then reached for her bag. "Thanks for packing. The coffee's not much, but at least it's hot. We can always stop for something better once we're on the road, if you like."

"All right." She accepted the coffee and tried not to think about how utterly polite, how proper they'd suddenly both become. Leaving last night as a quickly fading, distant memory. Emma looked away, but could still feel the weight of Paxton's gaze on her. "Thanks."

"No problem. Now, if it's all right with you, I'd like to get on the road."

"All right." She tried not to wince at the chill in Paxton's tone. "But don't you want to change into something dry?"

Paxton glanced down at herself and seemed surprised to discover she was wet. Muttering softly to herself, she quickly stripped off the T-shirt while Emma dug into her pack and pulled out a dark blue Henley. Heedless of the bruises liberally covering her torso, she muttered a quick thanks as she slipped into it.

After grabbing her jacket from the chair, Paxton picked up the bag with their meager possessions and walked out the door, keeping the vehicle keys and staking claim on the driver's seat.

Experience had taught her the value of strategic silence, so Emma said nothing.

❖

They drove in silence, with only the steady beat of the windshield wipers and the tires cutting through pools of standing water to provide background noise. The wet weather had come accompanied by a low-lying fog and although they were traveling through an area Paxton was intimately familiar with and she was suddenly feeling pressured by time, she stayed within the speed limit and stopped only for the coffee she'd promised Emma.

Once the drive began, Emma settled quietly into the passenger seat beside her. Paxton had been concerned that she would want to continue the conversation they'd started in the motel room, about the need to discuss things and consult prior to making decisions. But in spite of maintaining a fine edge of nerves, the topic did not come up and Emma seemed content not to talk.

The silence lasted until they'd been on the road about four hours. She had just finished refueling and picking up fresh coffee when Emma finally spoke. "I'm not sure if I'm imagining things—"

"What's wrong?"

"Well, I'll be the first to admit fieldwork is definitely not my forte, but I think the two cars behind us have been following us for quite some time. Sometimes it's the silver Honda, sometimes the black Malibu. But always the same two. Everyone else has passed and gone on their way or turned off."

Quite aware of the two cars Emma spoke of, Paxton picked up her cell phone and speed-dialed Tommy. "Hey. If those are your boys behind me—one in silver, one in black—could you get them to flash their lights?"

Two heartbeats later, both cars complied.

"You're telling me the two cars behind us belong to Tommy's group of hackers?"

Paxton gave a small laugh. "There's also one about a mile in front of us. Just keeping an eye on things and being available to help if the need arises. If you were to contact Dom and Kinsey, you'd find much the same. They're both surrounded by Tommy's crew."

"Oh."

"I'm sorry if you were concerned," Paxton said, her humor vanishing as quickly as it had appeared. "It was something Tommy and I arranged before leaving Manhattan. With all the chaos, I didn't really stop to consider talking to anyone about it. I just wanted to get everyone away from the explosion site, away from the city, and somewhere safe before Luther made another move."

That pretty much summed it up, she thought, as she let the silence return. Without knowing what they were facing, without any answers as to how the bombing had even happened, Paxton had done her best to protect people—Emma and her team. That was just who she was. Who she'd always been. She couldn't even imagine operating in any other way.

But it was clear her automatic reaction had pushed a hot button in Emma and beyond anger, she could feel her pulling back. Putting distance between them. What did that mean? Did it mean any chance for something real developing between her and Emma was no longer possible?

Surprisingly, she realized she wanted it. She wanted to love a woman in the truest sense of the word. To be in love with a woman. Not out of desperation or loneliness. And not just to have someone in her life. For the first time ever, she wanted to leave herself open to the endless possibility of it.

She'd always thought wanting was different from needing. Now she wasn't so sure. The only thing she knew for certain was that Emma was the first woman she'd allowed to get close to who she really was, and the woman was messing with her head.

She drove for another forty minutes. By then the rain had stopped, and as the breeze kicked up, she could catch the faint scent of the ocean on the wind. Only a little farther, and then she pulled onto a narrow side road, continuing for ten minutes longer before stopping. "We're here," she said pointing to a driveway all but hidden by landscaping.

She turned in and stopped at the gate, then punched in a security code.

❖

Emma glanced around, tried to take it all in, and then gave up trying. Beyond the gate, her trained eyes picked up a number of cameras placed along the shrub-covered fence. Whatever this place was, it had a hell of a security system.

She knew the place belonged to Paxton and she wanted to ask how she had managed to become the owner of a prime ocean-view estate, but as they made their way up the winding drive, she wasn't certain how to bring it up without offending her.

The property—the grounds and the building—was huge. And as she exited the vehicle, she got a better look. From where she stood, she could see the house itself appeared to be nestled into the rocky cliffs rising above the sand and sprawled across three levels, discernable by graduated flagstone terraces.

The top level was even with the road, with glassed walls looking out toward the ocean, while the lower two levels appeared to follow the natural cropping of the cliff.

The total effect was stunning.

Stepping closer to the low stone wall that defined the edge of the driveway, Emma saw that the lowest level came close to what appeared to be a small private beach, accessed by a few stone steps.

The whole property appeared designed around ensuring privacy. An isolated, private cove, a huge house, clinging to the side of a jagged cliff, and a bay, shielded from view by the craggy rocks that made up the northern and southern points.

She took one more look down the cliffside and then turned to watch Paxton greet Tommy Cho and two other men—one distinctly Hispanic, the other an intriguing blend of Asian and possibly Mexican. Moving closer, she waited until Paxton turned toward her. "This place—it's beautiful."

"Yes, it is. And this"—Paxton indicated their surroundings—"will be home, at least for the next twenty-four hours. You'll be safe here and if there's anything you want or need, just ask."

Emma immediately zeroed in on the one thing that rankled. "Twenty-four hours? What happens after twenty-four hours?"

Paxton shrugged. "I guess that's up to you."

Surprised by the comment, Emma searched Paxton's eyes. "I'm sorry. I'm not following. What does that mean?"

"You became angry when I made decisions without consulting you or getting your input," Paxton said softly. "So the next decision is all yours. By this time tomorrow, the rest of your team will have arrived. From there, you can choose whether you want to stay here, make your base here, or take your team back to some NSA-approved space in which to continue your work."

"Take my team?" Emma frowned. "Does that no longer include you?"

"On the contrary. Luther's made it clear he intends to kill me, which means I've a vested interest in stopping him. And after you pulled me out of prison in Bali, I promised to work with you. I meant it then, I mean it now. I will continue to support your task force, but at least for now, I want to do it from here."

"Why here?"

"Because here I have access to technology not available to me anywhere else. And here, I control the security of my environment, along with everything and everyone in it. Something that, quite obviously, I couldn't do in Manhattan."

Emma took a deep breath while she tried to read the closed expression on Paxton's face. "And if I choose to stay here? Do I get to access all the unbelievable technology you're hinting at?"

"Maybe." Something indecipherable flashed in her eyes. "There's no hurry to decide, Emma. Take your time. Look around. If you have any questions, Julio and Zack are always around. Tommy and others will come and go."

"What about you?"

"I've got a couple of things I need to do, but after that, I'll be around as well."

Before Emma could respond, she saw Paxton hand Tommy a disc. "It's a miracle I didn't lose this while jumping off the fire escape. Make two copies and then lock the original in the safe," she said, then turned and disappeared into the house.

Tommy stared at her for a long time. "What the hell happened between you two? The last time I saw you—" He paused as if uncertain what to say.

Emma shrugged. "We had a disagreement."

"Shit," he said on a breath, somehow acknowledging what she didn't say. "I think maybe I should explain something."

"If you think it will help."

Tommy took in a quick breath, suddenly impatient, concerned. "All right. It took me months to find Pax when she disappeared after trekking in Cambodia. And then it took a bit of time to put a plan together."

"What kind of plan are you talking about?"

"We were going to get her out. We figured out a way to make it look like she died—"

"Are you crazy?"

Tommy shrugged. "Yeah, maybe. All I know is we got a drug that would slow down her heart rate to the point it would look like she was dead. We had someone lined up who would get it to her, and tell her how and when to take it. Then we were going to collect her body on behalf of her family."

"Paxton doesn't have family."

"She has us," Tommy said vehemently. "Once we got her away from that place, we would give her something to resuscitate her, and then bring her home."

"Jesus, Tommy. You've been watching too many spy movies. That kind of thing doesn't happen in the real world."

Tommy stared at his feet and kicked at a nonexistent stone on the driveway. "The real world was planning to execute an innocent woman. We may just be über hackers, but we weren't about to stand by and let that happen without trying something—anything—to save her."

That Emma could understand. "I appreciate the sentiment. I really do. And I'm very glad you didn't have to test your plan, or all of you would likely have been imprisoned with her by the time I got to Bali. One question, though. Why are you telling me this?"

"Because I want you to understand how much Pax means to some of us. How far we'll go to see she comes to no harm."

"You think I mean to harm her?"

"I don't know. You tell me. All I know is I see the way she is with you. The way she looks at you. You can tell a lot by how a woman looks at someone she cares about, and in all the years I've known Pax she has never once looked at a woman the way she looks at you. You mean something to her."

The snap of his voice had her eyes narrowing and sent a flare of heated temper through Emma. "Why do I get the feeling you're about to ask me my intentions?"

"Maybe I am."

"If you're worried about Paxton, don't," Emma sighed softly. "I care about her. I just don't know how we fit."

"If you play it straight with her, you'll fit like a lock and key," Tommy said. An instant later, his beautiful face changed. Hardened.

"There's just one thing. If you hurt her, my boys and I will take you out. I don't care that you're NSA. No one will find your body."

Emma balled her hands into fists and leaned back, stunned by the intensity of Tommy's threat. Stunned by the fact that he issued the warning at all.

CHAPTER EIGHTEEN

Eyes closed, Paxton rotated her head, cracking out the tension that seemed to have found a permanent home there. A quick shower and a change of clothes had been a good start. It also helped that she was in her own space, in a place where Luther would be unable to draw near without the security system alerting her.

Tonight she would paint and listen to music. That would bring some order back into her life. For now, she needed to work.

Decision made, she headed for the computer room in the heart of her home. A dust-free, static controlled environment with soft white walls and stable temperatures designed to keep all systems running smoothly.

Walls covered with dozens of monitors displaying radar views, satellite views, multiple websites and databases. And a bank of computers networked together that, while no match for the Chinese Tianhe-2 supercomputer or the American Titan, still gave her all the computing power she needed with some to spare.

Of course, when more than that was needed, through some creative hacking, she could temporarily link to other computers around the world, tapping in to borrow the power necessary to handle things. But that was only in the event the primary core got overloaded.

Not surprisingly, she found Tommy there, viewing what appeared to be the security tape from the brownstone. "Anything so far?"

Tommy shook his head. "A lot of activity. A lot of coming and going. But so far, no one's done anything suspicious."

"You mean like planting a few bombs?"

Tommy laughed. "Yeah, something like that. Do you suppose you'll recognize the person when we finally find something?"

Paxton thought about that for a moment. "Probably not. There were a lot of analysts I never interacted with. People manning listening posts and gathering intel."

"That means you'll have to get Emma or one of her people to identify whoever tried to kill all of you."

"Probably."

Tommy looked at her more closely and she knew he was seeing pale skin and dark, bruised eyes. "You look like you've had a rough couple of days. At a minimum, I can tell you've got a headache, and I'm guessing that cut on your arm is hurting more than you're letting on. Do you want to talk about it?"

What she wanted was to close her eyes, to go into the dark, but instead she kept them open and on Tommy's. She knew he meant well. She also knew herself, and at the best of times, she wasn't given to opening up.

She shook her head. "The headache is manageable and the cut on my arm is healing, which means it's starting to itch. You can help me in a couple of days by taking the stitches out. For the time being, I want to run a test with the neuro headset. We need to see how far we can push it, so we'll have to program different scenarios."

Tommy became immediately serious, but his eyes gleamed and she knew he was intrigued. "What kind of scenarios?"

"I now know I can stop Luther manually when he has control of one jet. That gives us a baseline, and with the headset, I should be quicker." She lifted one hand and pressed her fingers to her lips. "But whatever he's got planned won't stop at just one jet. So we need to know what it will take to stop him if he controls two and then three or more aircraft. I don't know how much he's capable of doing. Probably three. I hope not more than that, but who knows. We just need to be ready for whatever he throws at us."

"Are you sure you're up to it?"

"I have to be, don't I? I only slowed him down with the reverse worm. We have to be ready when he's back up and running, if he isn't already. And that means we have to stay ahead of him. So move over, Tommy-boy, and let's have at it."

Tommy smiled, just a twitch of his straight mouth, as Paxton sat beside him and they began to program the different scenarios, both sets of hands flying over keyboards. Just like the old days, she thought, knowing this was his favorite thing to do. Programming all the technological toys that she dreamed up and they created together.

As for her, she loved it all. Dreaming up new technology, programming it, watching it fly. And without a doubt, using it. This was her comfort zone. Her world. Technology she had always understood. People? Not so much.

And in the meantime, she kept an eye on another computer that was running the security video, looking for a would-be killer.

❖

Emma gave Paxton the better part of the afternoon. And then she went looking for her. But as it turned out, that was not an easy thing to do, especially because the house was huge and had a seemingly endless number of places a person could hide in.

It might have taken longer, but the young hacker named Zack took pity on her and showed her the way.

Walking into a spacious room, she found Tommy at a keyboard in front of two large central monitors. A few feet away, Paxton was stretched out in a large leather recliner. She looked as if she was comfortably resting—except for the fact she was wearing a wireless headset that finished in something that looked like wrap-around glasses.

Tommy acknowledged her with a silent nod and Emma took his silence as tacit assent to her being and remaining in the room. Moving closer, she began to watch over his shoulder, and slowly the readouts on one monitor started to make sense. It was some kind of telemetry unit, and the output was allowing Tommy to continuously monitor Paxton's well-being, including her breathing, heart rate, blood pressure, blood-oxygen level, and more, if she was interpreting the data correctly.

What Paxton was doing was another question altogether. One for which Emma had no answer. But the longer she watched, the more changes began to appear in the readouts and Emma felt her level of concern begin to increase.

Finally, she could no longer remain silent. "Her blood pressure is getting too high," she whispered.

Tommy nodded calmly and engaged a mic. "Pax, your stress level's a bit high and is starting to concern our guest from the NSA. I need you to get your blood pressure down or we're going to have to stop, at least for now."

Paxton never responded or gave any indication she had heard Tommy's instruction. But over the next minute her breathing deepened and her blood pressure slowly came down.

"Good girl," Tommy murmured.

"Impressive."

"It's one of the lessons she learned from her childhood," Tommy said. "She's got a remarkable ability to control her body's reactions to stress, pain. Probably helped her while she was in that prison."

"No doubt." Emma remained thoughtful for a minute. "But it still almost makes me wish her stepfather was still around."

Tommy turned and stared hard at her, then slowly started to laugh. "I'll be damned."

"What?"

"I can't believe she told you about her stepfather."

Emma shrugged. "Only a bit of it."

"Still," Tommy said, reappraising Emma. "The fact she told you anything says a lot—damn."

Emma didn't have to ask what was wrong. The readouts on the computer had suddenly jumped and she could see blood begin trickling from Paxton's nose. "Shit. Whatever you've got running, it needs to stop. Now. Her blood pressure's going through the roof."

"Already on it," Tommy said. His voice remained calm while his hands moved quickly. "There are some towels in that cabinet."

Leaving Tommy's side, Emma found a towel, then moved closer to Paxton, registering the discomfort on her face.

"Don't touch her until I get this shut down. It'll just be additional stimulation she won't be able to handle."

Barely containing her frustration, Emma watched Paxton as she slowly came out of wherever she'd been and whatever she'd been doing. She watched her shudder, then saw her struggle to reach up and remove the headset. Emma immediately moved to help her, then gently wiped the blood from her face.

"Whoa."

Emma stared at Paxton with narrowed eyes. "Whoa? You sit here doing God knows what to that brain of yours, to the point you start bleeding, and all you can say is *whoa*?"

❖

Paxton looked at Emma's concerned face and couldn't determine the problem. Mostly she was annoyed with herself. As first tests went, it had gone fairly well but had ended much sooner than she had hoped. It also reinforced what she already knew. They had a lot of work to do if they were going to be ready to stop Luther. Taking the towel from Emma's hand, she pressed it firmly against her nose.

"Do you need anything? Water?"

"No, I'm good."

Emma nodded, as if she'd gotten the answer she'd expected to get. "Then do you mind explaining what this is"—she indicated the headset with one hand—"and just what the hell you were doing?"

Paxton turned to Tommy for help, but saw him shake his head and grin. "It's a neuro headset. It's designed to provide direct brain computer interface, interpreting the brain's signals and responding directly to the computer. It's much quicker than using eyes, hands, and a keyboard."

"I see. Since I've not seen anything quite like it, I assume the design is yours. Is it patented?"

"The patent's pending on this one, but we have other devices that are already patented." She gave a slight shrug. "They don't always end up where we think they will when we start out—like this one. It's got a lot of uses beyond what we're doing with it right now. It actually started out as an idea to help paraplegics after Zack's brother lost the use of his legs in a motorcycle accident."

"Impressive," Emma murmured. "And what scenario were you testing just now?"

It was at that point that Tommy jumped in. "Actually, we programmed a number of scenarios, all revolving around someone—Luther—taking remote control of aircraft. We knew Pax had been able to wrestle control back when he had control of just one jet, so we used that as a baseline."

"But zero day won't be about him controlling one aircraft," Paxton continued. "He'll want something bigger. So we're trying to see what could be done if we assume he can control more than one."

"How many more?"

Paxton shrugged. "I crashed and burned trying for three. We seem to have a way to go."

Emma released an exasperated sounding sigh. "And it didn't occur to either of you two geniuses that maybe resting for a bit would be helpful? For God's sake, Paxton, you're barely a couple of days away from nearly being blown up."

"Emma?" Paxton reached out and grabbed one of Emma's hands, holding it tightly. "I'm all right. Honestly. The truth is I let myself lose focus for an instant." She wasn't about to admit it was briefly catching Emma's scent that had distracted her. "I know better. And Tommy was monitoring me and would have shut things down before any real damage occurred."

"Still—"

"Still, you're right," Paxton conceded. "We should have waited until tomorrow. After I'd had something to eat and rested a bit."

A slight smile touched Emma's lips. "There," she said. "Did that hurt much?"

Knowing she was being teased, Paxton did the right thing and shook her head. "Speaking of something to eat, have you had dinner yet?"

When Emma indicated she hadn't, Paxton eased herself from the chair, made sure she was reasonably steady on her feet, and then offered her arm. "Why don't we go and see what's to be had in the kitchen?"

With Tommy following close behind, they walked along a hallway offering spectacular views of the ocean. Emma looked out, clearly appreciating the panorama as evening descended on the cove. After a moment, she turned back to Paxton, questions visible in her eyes.

"This place—it really is amazing. If you don't mind my asking, how on earth did you come to own it?"

"I got a heads up from a contact that it was coming on the market," Paxton said as they continued toward the kitchen. "It previously belonged to a mid-level gun runner who wanted to move up the food chain and diversify into drugs."

"And—"

"And some people are superstitious about buying a place where someone's been murdered. So I got it for a song."

"Someone was murdered here?"

"Well, actually more than one someone."

Emma frowned. "How many?"

When Paxton prevaricated, Tommy laughed and coughed and muttered, "Seven."

"Seven? Jesus, Paxton. What did they do? Try to replicate the St. Valentine's Day massacre? At least I understand how you got it for a song."

"It just needed a bit of fixing and cleaning. And smudging."

Emma's eyes crinkled with laughter. "Smudging. Right."

"If you decide to stay, you'll have to wander around and get acquainted with where everything is." Paxton swallowed through a sudden surge of uncertainty. "Nothing's off-limits. Just make note of the codes for the security system and be careful if you decide to go down to the beach alone. The stone steps can become quite slippery from the spray, depending on which way the wind's blowing."

"And you'll have to get Pax to show you the secret tunnels," Tommy added. "It's how they used to bring the guns and drugs in from the boats. Very cool."

❖

Dinner turned out to be a quiet affair for two after Tommy, Julio, and Zack begged off and headed out to search for pizza. Left to their own devices, Emma told Paxton to sit at the island and be lazy, while she chose to make a stir-fry from an assortment of fixings she found in the freezer.

Paxton continued to respond to most comments Emma made, even managed the occasional start of a smile, but mostly she seemed tired, quiet. On the edge of subdued. It left Emma feeling concerned, especially by the mixed emotions she was picking up from her. So she began to talk. Got her laughing at stories of her early days going through training to be an NSA agent while they waited for the rice to finish cooking.

She continued to talk while they ate dinner, realizing she'd uncovered one of the biggest differences between them. She normally processed things by talking, using sounding boards. Paxton was clearly the opposite, withdrawing and seeking her own counsel.

Not that it posed a major problem. Emma knew she could easily grow accustomed to Paxton's preference for silence, even as she wondered how much the silence was learned behavior from less happy times.

Mostly she was pleased to see that Paxton ate with some semblance of a real appetite and they both did justice to the meal.

Once dinner was over, by unspoken agreement they cleaned up the kitchen together. And then with nothing left but time, Emma asked, "I know you'll want to paint tonight, but it's a lovely evening after all that rain. Before the next rains hit, do you suppose we could go for a walk on the beach? I'd love to see the ocean up close. It's been a long time."

"Of course." Paxton stretched as she got up and gave her a sheepish smile as she hunted for the shoes she'd somehow kicked off over the course of dinner. She then extended her hand, waited until Emma's hand slipped into hers and entwined their fingers, seeming to welcome the connection as they walked to the lowest level of the house and out onto the beach.

Emma mimicked Paxton and immediately kicked off her shoes and sank her feet into the cool sand. The beach appeared to stretch out for almost a mile before it was cut off by the boulders that made up the boundaries of the cove. But she was determined to walk all of it. "Oh, God, this is wonderful."

Paxton remained content to let her lead before finally stopping about a foot from the high water mark. Standing still and quiet and with a slight smile on her face, she stared out at the breaking waves, watching the water ebb out of the bay, toward the sea, and then turn and push its way back in.

The wind was blowing across the water, straight from the Atlantic, carrying the promise of more rain before morning, but Paxton didn't seem to mind. Her words a moment later confirmed it. "I love it here. This beach is why I fell in love with the property and had to buy it. I love the quiet. The privacy. The sense of endless space. And the smell of the ocean. It's my refuge."

"I can tell you love it," Emma said. "And who can blame you? In fact, I can literally see you relaxing as you stand there."

"That's because I am."

Emma nodded, knowing she was about to disturb the moment, but feeling she had no choice. Taking a breath, she spoke as casually as she could. "Then will you tell me what's bothering you?"

She watched Paxton kick at the sand as she weighed her answer. "I feel as if I'm being pulled in different directions and I don't know what to do about it."

"What do you mean?"

"Luther, for one. We all know he's out there, even as we speak. Making plans we can only imagine for reasons we may never understand. I need to focus on that. On expanding the capacity of the neuro headset as a potential answer to stopping him."

"What does that mean?"

"At a minimum, it means we need to build better sensors and expand the capabilities of the brain-controlled interface. That will allow it to detect and identify the brain signals more quickly and then translate them, converting them to language the neuro headset will understand, then adjusting the programming to match so the computer responds faster."

"Paxton, darlin'?" Emma grinned and waited until she had Paxton's full attention. "You're talking geek. Assuming I understand what you just said, what's the problem? Do you need materials? Technology? If that's the case, I can try to get whatever you need. I have connections I can access. Just tell me what you need."

"See, that's the other thing that's pulling me." Paxton turned toward her, and in the fading light of day, her mouth was serious and unsmiling as their eyes met. "What if it's you I need?"

"Is that all?" Emma whispered. She slid her hands around Paxton, cradled her back, and then raised her head to brush Paxton's lips with her own. "Why didn't you just say so?"

CHAPTER NINETEEN

A day was only twenty-four hours. Not so long. And yet it felt like a lifetime had passed since she had last held Emma in her arms. Made love to her. Did that explain why she was feeling inexplicably nervous?

Possibly because she knew there'd be consequences. Then again, there were always consequences. She would deal with them tomorrow. A smile tilted at the corners of her mouth and the faint tension in her shoulders eased.

Holding Emma's hand, she led the way and opened the door to her room. It was located on the second floor near the stairs leading to the beach, convenient should circumstances ever dictate the need for a swift exit. Inside, it was dark and silent, but for the soft breeze that whispered in through the open sliding glass doors, carrying the scent and sound of the ocean.

The setting was right, but not the darkness. Emma had a face made for candlelight, Paxton mused. Separating from her for just a moment, she lit a group of slender white candles and watched the shadows and lights flicker and dance over Emma, saw her eyes glint in the shifting light. For a lingering moment, she studied her.

"You're a romantic," Emma said.

"I want to see you," she responded, moving toward her again and taking her by the hand to draw her closer to the candlelight. With surprise, she felt a quiver run through Emma's hand. "Your pulse is racing and you're trembling."

"I know." Emma took a deep breath and exhaled quickly.

"Emma, if you're not sure…if you don't want to do this—"

"I am. I do." The words, hardly audible, thundered in her head. But before she could respond, Emma silenced her as, with her eyes wide open, she fisted her hands in Paxton's hair and dragged their mouths together.

Oh, God.

She couldn't breathe without breathing her, and Emma's scent stirred every hunger Paxton had ever known. She felt desire grip her as if it had claws. Wants, needs bubbled to the surface and lay exposed. She felt a quickening in her blood, a driving need to take Emma swiftly that she had to fight back. She didn't want tonight to be about fast and furious. She wanted to take her time.

Drawing back, she brushed the hair away from the nape of Emma's neck and touched her lips to the sensitive skin, trailing them around the side of her neck. Her scent was more vibrant there, she discovered. Just there above the collarbone. She skimmed her tongue over the spot and listened to Emma's quick, unsteady inhalation of breath.

"Pax—"

Not wanting Emma to think, not wanting her to do anything but feel, Paxton moved to her mouth and used the tip of her tongue. Outlined and tested the fullness of her mouth. So softly, so slowly. All sensation, all arousal. Then she captured her bottom lip between her teeth and felt Emma's breath start to shudder.

Encouraged, she nibbled, then drew the flesh inside her mouth to suck until she felt the answering, unrelenting fire deep inside her. Had her heart ever beat so fast? She loved the way Emma's body seemed to mold itself to the lines of her own, the way the sound of her name came in a whisper through Emma's lips.

Paxton wanted to touch, to taste all of her, but slowly, thoroughly. She used her teeth, scraping them along the long line of Emma's lower lip. Feeling the warmth, the softness of it, and then absorbing it. Emma made some sound, something that seemed to claw up from her throat and was every bit as primitive as the need that raged through Paxton.

Her hands were eager, hurried, but oh, so gentle as they stripped the clothes away from Emma's body, finding her already hot and wet. Slowly, carefully, she loved her, her body attuned to her every need, anticipating them and satisfying them with a passion designed to leave her reaching, longing, aching, and then blissfully sated.

The next groan came from both of them.

It built slowly, this pleasure, layer over layer of heat tangling with layer over layer of need. And then suddenly aggressive, all fire, all flash, Emma moved with her, against her, for her, until any semblance of control was ripped apart, shredded, and forgotten.

❖

Emma's eyes opened as the first light of morning broke across her face. From where she lay, she could see pale purples and blues paint the sky with their opalescent hues, while the soft sound of the relentless waves and the scent of the ocean filled the room.

She was alone. Again.

What did that mean?

She was trying not to analyze this latest occurrence when the bedroom door opened and Paxton walked in. Her hair was wet and she was clearly fresh from a shower, although there were still smudges of paint on one hand and on her chin, leaving no doubt about what she'd been doing.

As was often the case, she was barefoot, wearing a white T-shirt and faded jeans that fit entirely too well. Even better, she was carrying a tray holding a covered basket, large mugs, and a carafe that smelled enticingly like chocolate.

"Hey," Paxton said and smiled. It was one of those slow, easy smiles that could touch without a trace of physical contact. And though she was still too pale and her eyes too shadowed, she looked wonderful.

"You're still here," Emma whispered.

"Of course I'm still here. Sorry. I just wanted to surprise you." She was still smiling, but there was nothing cheerful left in her eyes.

Paxton stared out the window for a long moment before putting the tray down and passing the basket to Emma. "Have a croissant," she said. "Zack made them while I made the hot chocolate."

They were big and hot and flaky, and Emma's mouth watered as she took a bite and watched Paxton fill two mugs with steaming chocolate, its rich scent filling the room.

"When I was a kid, I loved to sneak out to watch the sunrise. The old man who ran the bakery down the street, he loved to watch the sunrise too and sometimes he would join me and bring the most amazing hot chocolate. He's the one who taught me to make it."

Emma listened without question, filing this unexpected glimpse into the personal history that had shaped Paxton. When the mugs were filled, she accepted one gratefully, letting the sheets slip and pool around her waist. The chocolate was thick, creamy, and rich, and had her sighing. "God, this is wonderful," she said as she took a sip. "Thanks so much for doing this."

"I suppose that's better than thinking I was gone," Paxton said.

Bending her head and looking away, Emma nodded. "I know. I'm sorry. Could you please forget I said or even thought that and just forgive me?"

"It's okay, Emma. You and I—we came together unexpectedly and now we're just trying to find our way, while at the same time trying to deal with what's going on out there. With Luther and whatever he's planning. None of it comes easy and it doesn't leave us much time to figure out the personal stuff while trying to stay alive, so we're bound to get it wrong a few times."

Emma felt a flush of relief and looked back up. "Does that mean we keep on trying?"

Paxton looked a little more than surprised. "I hope so."

She said it with a smile that hit Emma like a punch. Putting the mug on a side table, Emma reached up with one hand, drawing Paxton to within inches. Pushing the still-damp hair out of her eyes, she studied her for a minute. "You look...you haven't slept, have you?"

Paxton arched a brow then shrugged. "I really needed to paint after you fell asleep." A slow, reluctant smile appeared. "And so I did until I got tired. Then I got the idea to come back and join you in bed and was heading back when I saw Zack making the croissants and thought I'd bring you some. And then I thought they'd be really good with hot chocolate. So it became eat first, then sleep."

"A good plan."

Without any further comment, she tugged Paxton's hand. A quick pull and she tumbled into the bed beside her. Only a few heartbeats later, she was curled into Emma's side, her breathing slow and even as she drifted into sleep.

❖

Paxton stood still and stared at the image frozen on the computer screen in front of her with detachment. There was no point in getting emotional. Just because she was watching a man place bombs intended to kill her and everyone else who happened to be in the New York station was no reason at all.

She hadn't met him. She would have remembered. But she now knew everything she needed to know about him. His name was Cal Finch. He was forty-six years old and had spent some time as an analyst in military intelligence, before being honorably discharged. He'd joined the NSA shortly after leaving the service and had spent time in a listening post in East Asia.

There were no ties to radical terrorist groups, either foreign or domestic. In fact, nothing stood out as unusual in his background check. Not until six months ago—about two months after he transferred into Emma Thorpe's team. That was when weekly cash deposits began to appear. Varying sums of money, all between five and nine thousand dollars.

From there, it took only a few keystrokes for all the deposits to be traced to a relative. A second cousin named Darren Luther.

The deposits were wire transferred into accounts Finch held in different banks in and around New York. But eventually all the money was funneled to an offshore account in the Cayman Islands. And when everything was tallied, it added up to two hundred fifty thousand dollars.

Is that the cost of a life?

Paxton looked once again at the dates on the screen and wondered about the timeline. Was it simply a coincidence that Finch began receiving payments from Luther only two months after joining the team? Or had his transfer onto the team been planned?

"A nice bit of change for doing some work on the side for a cousin," Tommy said, looking at the bank statements he'd printed. "Are you going to show this to Emma?"

"As soon as she's free." Paxton stepped away from the computer. "Her team got in just a little while ago and she's meeting with them right now. I'm guessing she's making sure they're all okay and giving them the option of staying here or going someplace else. Someplace no doubt selected and controlled by the NSA."

"Any doubt which way her decision will go?"

"I don't think so. Not to say I can't be surprised every now and then, but there's nothing the NSA can offer that we can't surpass. Not security and certainly not technology. So it wouldn't make sense."

"Not to mention whatever it is the two of you have going on?"

Paxton's lips tugged into a half smile. "There's that, too."

"So where do we go from here?"

"My guess"—she gave a shrug and pointed back to the man on the monitor—"is that Emma and Dom will need to go and deal with Finch quickly, leaving the others here with us. In the meantime, we'll keep things going on two tracks. Continuing to search for Luther and expanding the neuro headset's capabilities so we can deal with as many possibilities as he's likely to throw at us."

"Sounds like a good plan."

"What's a good plan?" Emma asked as she walked into the room.

She had managed to keep her tone neutral, Paxton noted wryly, but a slight edge was still detectable if you listened for it. If nothing else, it confirmed that she and Emma still had a way to go before they managed to build a solid foundation between them.

"We've identified our bomber," Paxton said, indicating the man on the monitor, forever frozen in time as he placed bombs inside the station.

Emma immediately went pale as she turned to look. "Calvin Finch? Oh, Jesus. Why would he do that?" She continued to stare at the image as if she was picturing the house in flames, her people dying.

"Other than the money he was paid?" Paxton kept a close eye on Emma. She looked paler and more upset than she would probably want to admit. "Is he a friend?"

"No. The truth is I don't know him very well. He applied for a transfer to the team as a replacement for one of our analysts who got badly hurt in an accident. I remember Finch had the experience we needed and his boss spoke highly of his skills. He just wasn't certain he wanted to live in New York, which is why the idea of a temporary transfer appealed to him."

Paxton stiffened. "What kind of accident did your analyst have?"

"A hit-and-run, actually. The car that hit her turned out to be stolen and the driver was never found. Shit." Emma closed her eyes as if she wanted to block out everything around her, then opened them again. "I know Kim really well. She's gone through months of pain and physical therapy just to learn to walk again. Was her accident deliberate? Is it possible Calvin Finch and Darren Luther put a plan into action months ago?"

Paxton reached out and placed a hand on Emma's shoulder, squeezing it gently. Emma appreciated the gesture and indeed felt comforted, but her head was still reeling.

"If you're asking whether your analyst was deliberately injured so that Finch could replace her on your team, I'd say it looks more than likely. Luther has planned whatever he's doing for some time. And by putting someone close to the ground, he could stay ahead of the manhunt."

Emma shook her head. "But that doesn't make sense. Eight months ago I was directing the American Cyber-Research Institute working cyber threats. But the task force hadn't even been formed. Why would he want someone on my team?"

"Because you were seen as the person most likely to be picked to head up any group dealing with a new and serious cyber threat. Your reputation is solid. And Luther would have known it."

"But why go to such an extreme? Why blow up the station?"

Paxton's eyes became as dark and unyielding as Emma had yet seen them. "Because you brought me into the mix, and he simply couldn't afford to have me there." Paxton gave her shoulder another squeeze before walking away and moving toward the window. "Your team is good, Emma. But Luther didn't see them as a threat. And if by chance you started getting too close, he still had cousin Calvin there to keep an eye on things for him."

"Damn," Emma said. "It's what you said before. He knows you can stop him."

"Because I can."

"So what do we do? You and Tommy were talking about a plan when I walked in. What are you thinking?"

Paxton turned back toward her and let out a long, slow breath. "I guess that depends on whether you intend to stay here—you and the team."

"Was there any doubt that would be my decision?"

"It was my hope."

Frowning slightly, Emma murmured, "Damn it, Pax. I need you to be more sure of me than that. Now tell me about this plan you and Tommy have concocted."

Emma listened while Paxton and Tommy shared their thoughts. That she would go with Dom to Fort Meade and deal with Calvin Finch. Arresting him and interrogating him might yield some information on Luther's whereabouts.

"There's something quite terrifying about the feeling of handcuffs being locked around your wrists," Paxton said quietly. "If he knows something, maybe feeling the noose tightening might just be enough to get him to talk."

Emma moved closer, slipped her arm around Paxton's waist, and squeezed. She knew there was nothing she could say or do that would erase what Paxton had experienced—being set up by her then girlfriend, her arrest, and the months she'd spent imprisoned in Bali. All she could do was offer comfort.

"If he knows where Luther is," she said thoughtfully, "then hopefully he'll give him up. Calvin didn't kill anyone when he blew up the station, thanks to you and Sam. If he thinks it's still possible to cut a deal, he may give Luther up."

"That's the idea," Tommy said. "And in the meantime, we'll keep working on increasing the capabilities of the neuro headset. Maybe some of your team can help, in between trying to track Luther."

Her eyes narrowed as she looked at Paxton, and Emma tried to hold back some of the intensity she was feeling. "I know only too well you'll do what you will do regardless of what I say or the risk involved—"

"Emma—"

"No, please don't argue with me. Just listen to me for a moment." In no apparent hurry to get to the point she was trying to make, she traced a fingertip along Paxton's lower lip. And felt inordinately pleased when she heard her sharp intake of breath and felt her muscles tense and shiver. "All I'm going to ask is that you try to limit the risks you take. I need you to somehow ensure your mind will remain intact by the time I get back. It will serve no purpose if you do yourself any harm, and I find I've grown rather fond of your mind—among other things."

❖

This was who he was.

Staring at his own reflection in the monitor, Luther felt old memories stir. He reminded himself that he liked pushing himself and the limits of his capabilities. He liked challenges. The problem wasn't him. The problem was Paxton. He blinked and shook his head as he reordered his thoughts.

He knew there were only so many things in the world he could control. And he was starting to believe Paxton James wasn't one of them.

He'd come close years ago. But his inability to fully see or understand what drove her had resulted in her slipping beyond his grasp. And by the time he realized what had happened, Ben was dead and she was gone.

Things were different this time. His talents far exceeded what anyone might suspect and he had the resources to carry through with his plans. The problem remained Paxton. As much as he would enjoy pitting himself against her, she remained a wild card.

She could blow his entire plan to hell if he didn't manage to get her under control. He'd come too far and failure wasn't an option. He needed to be in control, and if he couldn't control her…well, he'd simply have to destroy her.

Closing his eyes, he took several deep breaths, feeling his blood pulse with life. Fury and determination began a slow burn in his gut. He could feel it simmering. Boiling. Growing. Ready to be unleashed.

He could do this.

Just try to stop me.

Chapter Twenty

With Emma gone, Paxton fell into a pattern. In the early mornings, she ran on the beach, sometimes with Sam, sometimes alone. In either case, she found she needed the mental release that a long run would provide. She then spent her day working on programming, testing, and reprogramming the headset while helping Emma's team as they widened the scope of their search for Luther. And when darkness descended on her corner of the world, she painted.

She began having nightmares. Every time she closed her eyes, she was assailed by images and sounds, none of which were conducive to sleeping.

She started hearing the screams of people that she now considered colleagues and friends as they burned while trying to escape the flames spreading through the brownstone. They were inconsequential to Luther, she realized. They would simply have been collateral damage resulting from his attempt on her life.

She started hearing the rats again. The ones that came out in the darkness, each and every night she'd been locked up in prison.

She started hearing the priest's final words, garbled and unintelligible, as she stood by a rainy graveside and said good-bye to her mother. To Ben.

She started hearing the sound of the belt as it slashed through the air before striking her as her stepfather beat her to within an inch of her life.

By the time Emma was gone four days, Paxton had stopped even trying to sleep altogether and it was wearing on her. It was like something had broken inside her and she didn't know how to put it back together.

So she did what she could. She ran. She worked. She painted. And she tried to figure out how to put an end to Luther's zero-day threat. But she couldn't figure out what had started, let alone how to stop, the sounds echoing in her head.

Tommy had approached her about it, his eyes uncharacteristically serious. "Whatever it is, you're not alone, Pax. So don't think you have to solve everything by yourself. We've been friends a long time. Tell me how to help."

She knew her answer was important to him. She simply didn't know what to say. "You are helping, Tommy. We're making good progress and I couldn't do it without you."

"Maybe so. But it doesn't explain why you're not sleeping. If you don't want to talk about it, that's totally okay. But don't tell me I'm wrong. The shadows under your eyes don't lie. You're losing weight and you look, I don't know, unhappy."

He was right and she knew it. She hadn't been eating. Most of the time, she simply wasn't hungry. And when it occurred to her she should eat, she was usually past caring.

But Tommy cared. That was the problem. Unable to find an appropriate response that would explain what was happening, she just shook her head and muttered a small self-conscious apology.

Emma's team was another matter. Theo looked concerned, while Sam, Kinsey, and Shelby were less delicate and threatened to put in a call to Emma. It was a meaningless threat, of course, and they all knew it. Because if Emma had been in a position to get on the phone with them, she already would have done so.

And having Emma with her wouldn't necessarily help. At least Paxton didn't know for certain. Yes, she missed Emma's presence. Missed her sharp insights, missed her dry humor. More than that, she missed her warm laugh. Missed her touch and missed her heat. Damn, she was in trouble and it wasn't going to get any easier.

This was no time to consider and contemplate what-ifs. She couldn't afford to lose sight of priorities and right now her attention needed to be on solving Darren Luther, whose malevolent presence orbiting her world she could all but feel. He was in complete control right now—

He was in control.

Paxton's thoughts spiraled. Could that be the key? She could feel her heartbeat accelerate at an unhealthy rate as she considered all the possibilities. So far, Luther had controlled everything. Timing. Location. Everything. What would it take to change that?

Feeling more energized than she had in days, she headed to the computer lab.

❖

Emma breathed a sigh of relief as Dom turned off the highway and onto the side road that led to Paxton's beach house. It almost felt as if she was coming home, and the idea was so crazy she had to laugh at herself.

Still, there was no question she had missed being here. The ocean. The beach. The gentle sound of the surf. Just as she had missed her team—and had missed Paxton.

She'd called earlier in the day to say she and Dom were heading back, but Paxton had been unavailable. Shelby had been cryptic, simply saying it was about damn time she came back. But when Emma had pushed for clarification, Shelby had not been forthcoming.

Faintly frustrated, Emma had disconnected and turned her thoughts back to the past week. Calvin Finch had been picked up and charged with treason, a crime against his country. The moment he'd seen her with Dom, he had known it was over. He had given up without a fight and had been placed in solitary confinement, locked in a steel cell, ironically not far from Nick Perry. A cell where the slot in the door for passing food would be his only contact with the real world.

Interrogation had gotten them nowhere. The only admission Finch had made was that he hadn't wanted to be responsible for killing all the people in the station. That was why, contrary to the instructions he'd received from Luther, he'd programmed the five-minute warning that had appeared on staff computers.

Emma knew Finch was still hoping to cut a deal. But while he knew the brass ring had slipped through his fingers, he was still fearful enough of Luther's revenge, and fear was keeping him from saying anything.

Perhaps some time in isolation would encourage him to talk more openly. And maybe tell them where Luther was hiding.

In the meantime, they had some new avenues to pursue as they searched for Darren Luther. Teams of analysts had already begun the intensive task of combing through Calvin Finch's life. They would seek out every bit of communication he'd had and expand their search in ever-widening circles. At the same time, they were still attempting to trace the money transfers Luther had made.

The irony was that considering Finch and Luther were both technological experts, they had somehow overlooked the fact that cyberspace truly was forever and highly resourceful people would always be able to find anyone. It was simply a matter of time. The only question was how much time they actually had before Luther set his plans in motion.

Someone was clearly monitoring security at Paxton's house, because the main gate opened up for them without their having to enter the pass code. A nice welcome, although there was no one near the front foyer when they let themselves in.

"It looks like someone's been busy," Dom said as they walked toward the kitchen.

Emma nodded. It was hard to miss the number of new canvases leaning haphazardly against bare white walls. "Damn. They look amazing, but do you think she got any sleep?"

"I don't know about sleep, but it looks like the blonde that's been haunting her is starting to take form."

Shit. Something in Dom's tone had Emma pausing and bending down to take a closer look. The last thing she wanted was to discover the ever-present face in Paxton's paintings was really meant to be Carrie Nolan. But as she stared at the latest rendition of the blonde, she felt a sense of relief that it most definitely wasn't Carrie. In fact, although still not totally defined, the face was beginning to look a little bit like—

"It's starting to look like you," Dom said.

Wide-eyed, Emma turned and stared at Dom. "It's not possible. The blonde has been a recurring theme in her paintings from long before we met in Bali."

"Whatever you say." Dom laughed. "But you and I both know that stranger things have been known to happen. Who knows?"

Still shaking her head, Emma preceded Dom into the kitchen to discover the team seated over the remains of dinner while the scent of freshly brewed coffee filled the air. And one look at the grinning faces that turned in her direction told her all she needed to know.

"Yes, indeed. I'd say she caught your good side," Shelby teased before adding, "Welcome back, boss."

All Emma could do was groan softly and smile back.

❖

"Damn it all." Paxton whipped the headset off, stopping herself from throwing it at the last instant.

"Thanks for not throwing it," Tommy said as he took the headset from her hand. "It'll take a lot longer to put all the pieces back together than it will take to fix the programming glitch."

Not feeling placated in the least, Paxton glared at him as she accepted the towel he handed her and used it to clean up the blood trickling from her nose. "That programming glitch just gave me one hell of a headache."

"I know. And I'm sorry. But if there's good news to be found in all of this, it's that it's taking longer each time before it knocks you on your ass."

Because she wanted to press her hands to her throbbing head, she tucked them negligently into her pockets. It would only make Tommy feel worse, which was the last thing she wanted. Instead, she tried for a small smile and nearly succeeded. She knew there was a measure of truth in his statement. But even as they made strides, Paxton couldn't help but be concerned that it was taking too long.

"Why don't you take a break? We both know you need one. And I know you hate pills, but maybe you should take something for the headache before it gets worse. And get something to eat while I work on this."

She shook her head and quickly realized the movement only served to increase the dull throbbing in her head. "Food's not high on my list right now. I think I'll get some fresh air instead. A walk on the beach should do it," she said. "I'll be back in a bit."

"No need to hurry. And make sure you grab a sweatshirt and a jacket. It's going to be cold down by the water."

Paxton smiled wryly and rolled her eyes. "Yes, Mother."

Tommy's surmise about the weather proved entirely accurate. The evening was clear, the sky already filled with stars, the air cold. As always, she was staggered by the raw beauty of nature around her and fell more deeply in love with the place than she had ever thought possible.

She hadn't thought to grab gloves, so she shoved her hands deep into her jacket pockets and she walked along the water, breathing deeply. She laughed at herself, knowing the sweatshirt she'd put on was one of Emma's. But she found being surrounded by her scent comforting. Almost as if Emma was here.

Drugs, she decided, were highly overrated. This was what she needed. And as the silence and crisp, salty air began to work their magic on her headache, she worked on a different problem. Getting Luther off stride and wresting control away from him.

Easier said than done.

After twenty minutes of walking, she finally stopped, dropping down to her knees. The sand was cold, but the silence, broken only by the surf, felt like a benediction. An idea had begun to percolate in her mind, and with her brain on overload she needed more time to think it through. To pick apart the pieces and then put them back together. To consider all the risks and ramifications.

She found herself wishing more than ever for Emma to hurry back. Emma was a perfect sounding board. Her years of experience as a threat analyst and her logical mind would help her sift through potential holes in her idea.

Of course, she knew she had other reasons for wishing Emma would come back from Maryland. Much more personal reasons.

❖

Once Tommy confirmed where Paxton had gone, Emma didn't bother waiting inside for her to reappear. She was exhausted and on edge. But ignoring her own fatigue, she grabbed her jacket then slipped outside and down the stone steps, searching the darkened beach for any sign of Paxton.

Dark jeans and a black jacket didn't help matters any, but as she made her way along the beach, it was only a matter of time before she finally spotted Paxton. And then—

Damn it all. She was pale, her eyes shadowed, her mouth grim. Even as she watched, she pressed her fingers to her eyes as if they burned. Hurrying forward, Emma stepped quietly into her space.

Paxton must have somehow sensed her as she drew near. Better yet, as she looked up, the sad brackets on either side of her mouth vanished and the light came back in her eyes.

"Hey," she murmured and slowly stood up. "I was just thinking of you and here you are. Awesome to think I can conjure you."

They faced each other in the darkness, heedless of the cold breeze coming in off the water. And for the moment, it was simple as Emma spread her arms out in invitation. "Come here, you." Her frosty breath hung in the air between their faces as Paxton stepped forward without hesitation. Who knew a week could be so long?

Too long for Paxton, apparently. Angling her face, she found Emma's mouth. And in an instant the kiss went from welcome to hot, greedy, and full of edgy need. "Welcome home, Emma. Damn, but I missed you."

With her heart pounding in her chest, and the blood roaring loud and fierce in her head, Emma didn't hear herself say the same words in response. But she felt them.

She couldn't think. Couldn't breathe. Suffused with heat, she felt consumed with wanting to kiss Paxton. Touch her. Have her. She struggled to focus as she tipped Paxton's head back with a fingertip on her chin. She studied her and frowned. "You've got a headache."

"It's not as bad as it was earlier—and definitely getting better."

"Tell me you're finished whatever you're working on," she said urgently. "At least for tonight."

Paxton laughed. "If it means I can have you, I can be finished for quite some time. How long can I have?"

They made it to Paxton's room without running into anyone else. Coincidence or collusion? Emma wasn't certain. Neither did she care.

But in the glow from a corner lamp, she could clearly see what she hadn't noticed on the beach. She could see just how tired Paxton was. And how thin she'd gotten in just one week.

As Paxton reached for her, she held her back and shook her head solemnly. "We're not going to make love tonight."

Paxton looked at her for an instant with an expression that was unreadable. "We're not?"

"No." In that moment, her disappointment became so tangible Emma almost relented. Almost. "That's for tomorrow. Tonight, I just want to hold you while you sleep."

"Emma—"

"Trust me," she responded softly. She raised her hands to Paxton's face. Stroked the planes of her cheekbones, ran her thumbs across her lips, and then kissed her. "Tonight, we're both too tired to do much more than want. Tomorrow, I promise to make it up to you. Now come to bed and let me hold you."

Paxton met her gaze and then capitulated. "All right."

Emma smiled. "Good. Now will you answer one question for me?"

"Don't I always?"

The laugh that bubbled out felt good. "Not really. Now tell me. Why haven't you been sleeping?"

At first, she didn't think Paxton would answer her. But a heartbeat later, she heard her say, "I've been having flashbacks...nightmares."

"The bombing? Your time in prison? Your stepfather?"

Releasing a shuddering breath, Paxton covered her face. "All of it."

"I wish I could change things for you, but I can't. All I can do is promise that tonight, if you have nightmares, you won't be alone to face them." Reaching for her and drawing her close, Emma moved them onto the bed and then continued quietly. "Nothing will touch you tonight, Pax. Nothing will hurt you."

CHAPTER TWENTY-ONE

Paxton awoke still held firmly in Emma's arms. The light through the windows was thin and gray from the storm rolling in with morning, but she didn't mind. She felt good. Refreshed. Better than she had in days and ready to tackle whatever came her way.

The night had not been completely free of nightmares. She could remember waking on a couple of occasions with a scream trapped in her throat. But true to her word, Emma had been there with her. For her. Holding her. Stroking and soothing her with her hands and with her words until Paxton was able to drift back to sleep.

Shifting slightly, she watched Emma sleep for a moment or two, studying the classic beauty of her face before reaching out and using her fingertips to make slow circles on silky skin. She could feel the heat rising as Emma released a soft pleasured moan, igniting Paxton's visceral response to having her so close, to touching her.

It was impossible to deny the nature or depth of her response. There was no other place she'd rather be and no one else she'd rather be with. Need was a low, throbbing beat between her thighs. But for the moment, she was content to continue her slow exploration and the gentle touches. Emma was here beside her and there was no reason to hurry. No reason at all.

Moving closer still, Paxton let herself forget everything but the way Emma's scent filled her, clouded her vision. And then there was the way she tasted as she brought her mouth closer and gently kissed her skin. Her teeth closed delicately over a nipple before her tongue slid over the captured point.

Slowly, with alternating licks and nips and butterfly kisses, she made her way across Emma's belly and lower still. Emma's hips arched for her even as she cupped them, lifted them. She opened her. Found her hard and hot and wet and feasted on her. Devoured her until she felt the first orgasm rip through her. Then slid up her body and fused their mouths, swallowing her gasps and moans and the sound of her name on Emma's lips.

Her head was still spinning when she managed to push herself up on her elbows and met Emma's laughing eyes.

"Good morning. What are you doing?"

Paxton raised both brows. "If you have to ask, then I've lost my touch at the ripe old age of twenty-seven."

"Oh, you've not lost anything. Trust me on that," Emma said with a laugh. "And you look like you're feeling better."

"I am." Paxton smiled. "You look like you're feeling better too. If you give me a few minutes to get dressed, I'll go and get us both some coffee."

Or not, she thought when Emma wordlessly flipped her onto her back and stretched out on top of her, making her intentions all too clear. "Let me have you, Pax."

Unprepared for the onslaught of competing sensations and emotions, Paxton felt her heart rate accelerate and reminded herself to breathe. Without thinking she closed her eyes, feeling Emma's kiss brush against her cheekbones, her eyelids, then down to her mouth again before moving on, down the side of her neck.

It wasn't something she allowed to happen often, not in any aspect of her life. But as Emma's soft, feathering kisses made her want more, she relinquished control and let herself drift. Let herself enjoy.

❖

Fresh from a second shower, it was early afternoon before Paxton and Emma headed down to the kitchen. And as fate would have it, the entire team—along with several young men Emma had yet to meet—was gathered there. In mid-debate about the best tactics for dealing with Luther, all conversation stopped and they were met with open stares and covered-up grins.

Paxton met their looks with an intense blue gaze just as the storm that had been threatening all morning finally hit. A flash of lightning split the sky, distant thunder rolled, and a steady rain began to fall. Watching reactions across the room, it took all Emma could muster not to lose her composure and start laughing.

Without a word, Tommy jumped up to pour them coffee, Dom quickly added two more chairs at the table, and Sam slid a tray filled with various kinds of pizza toward them.

At the same time, Emma was beginning to appreciate how difficult this had to be for Paxton. She didn't normally let her guard down. As a rule, she held her emotions tightly in check and kept people at a distance. For a woman who admitted to not dealing well when surrounded by people, to now have them constantly around, all watching her, knowing where she'd been and what she'd been doing—

"You look better," Tommy said, breaking the awkward silence. "And you'll be happy to know I think I got the programming glitch fixed. It should give you an extra fifteen minutes or so before you get knocked on your ass."

Paxton rolled her eyes. "You think?"

Slowly the conversations resumed. Ideas were tossed out, argued, and disregarded. Emma knew Paxton was mulling something over in her mind. But until she actually put it out there, she had no idea how far she had thought through her idea. Whether it would even fly.

Selecting a slice that looked vaguely vegetarian, she put it on the plate in front of Paxton while holding little faith that she would eat it. Emma then grabbed some pizza for herself, poured them both more coffee, and sat back to listen as the group brainstormed.

"It's not that Luther's exceptionally clever or better equipped than we are," Paxton finally interjected. "He's not. His advantage is that he has control."

"What do you mean?" Sam asked as the others fell silent.

"He's been calling the shots all along. He gets to decide what target he's going to hit, when and how he's going to hit it. All we've been able to do is react in the moment to whatever he's done."

Intrigued by where she could be going with this, Emma regarded her with interest. "How do you propose we change things?"

"We need to shake him up. Force him to act before he's ready."

Emma pushed. "How?"

"What if he thinks he has competition? What if he thinks I don't just want to stop him, I want to beat him at his game."

"Jesus, Pax." Emma was looking at her with a stunned expression. "You're talking about directly challenging him. Calling him out. You can't do that."

"Why not?"

"Wait," Dom interrupted. "Emma, wait just a minute. Just hear her out. I think she's got something here."

"Yes. A damn death wish. We all know Luther wants nothing more than to eliminate her. The first time he tried for her was when we were in Washington. There she got lucky. But if Finch had done what he was told to do, what he was supposed to do, Luther would have succeeded in killing not only Pax, but everyone else at the station that day. And now she wants to call him out?"

"Emma." Paxton covered Emma's hand with her own. "Please. Just think about it for a minute."

"Think about what?"

"Luther. We all agree he knows I can stop him."

Emma frowned, confused. "So what?"

"The only thing he knows for sure is who I used to be. What I used to be. If we want to make him think I want to beat him at his own game, all we need is to introduce a flicker of a doubt. Make him think that's what I'm doing. He won't like it and it could force him to act before he's ready. That means he won't be in control like he usually is and we'll be ready and waiting when he acts."

Emma sat back and met her eyes. "Suppose I agree that there's something in what you're saying. What are you proposing to do? Are you planning to start taking control of jets?"

"If Paxton starts taking control of airliners, all we'll succeed in doing is scaring the daylights out of the American flying public," Kinsey said. "Somehow, I don't think Catherine Winters will be too happy with us."

"Actually," Dom said. "Paxton wouldn't actually need to do anything. What if we simply give her the credit for what Luther's already done? Her reputation would do the rest."

Emma frowned. "How do you propose we do that?"

"Simple." Dom laughed. "We arrest her."

❖

Emma was looking at Dom with a stunned expression. "Are you crazy? We got Pax out of prison hoping she could help us. Not so we can exchange the prison she was in for a stateside one."

"I'm not suggesting we lock her up. I'm suggesting we make Luther believe we've arrested Paxton and given her credit for what he's been doing."

"He's got a point, Emma," Paxton said. "The Darren Luther I used to know isn't going to want anyone—but especially not me—taking credit for what he's been doing. Especially before he shows his hand and lets us know why he's doing all these things in the first place."

"You'd rock his world," Sam said.

"Right," Dom added. "He's going to want to correct the error. Not because he gives a damn that Paxton's been arrested for something she didn't do but because his ego won't let someone else take credit for his brilliance. We force his hand. Make him move up his schedule."

Paxton nodded. "In the meantime, we set up everything we need to catch him when he comes up for air. Between your people and Tommy's crew, we have the talent. We can distract him and keep him busy without letting him destroy anything or kill anyone. At the same time, we locate him so you can arrest him."

"We can do all of that?"

"Yes. And if need be, we can tap into the NSA and borrow some additional power to make sure we outperform Luther no matter what."

Emma groaned. "I don't think you should be telling me that."

"Maybe not."

She saw it on Emma's face the moment the facts crystallized and it all became clear.

"You and Dom are remarkably in sync already, aren't you?"

"Yes. But there is one thing."

"What's that?" Emma asked.

"Please make sure you've got my back covered." She managed a shaky laugh, her chest suddenly aching. "I don't want to end up in jail again for real. Especially not in federal lockup in a cell between Nick Perry and Calvin Finch."

Leaving the group in the kitchen to discuss logistics, Paxton went to the computer lab to check the programming enhancements Tommy had implemented. But it really wasn't what she wanted to be doing, and she was much too restless and on edge to concentrate.

Putting the headset down, she stopped to grab her jacket and headed down to the beach.

❖

Emma found her there nearly thirty minutes later. Cold and wet, standing near the water's edge in the fog-bound cove. The heavy rain that had been falling earlier had turned into a light drizzle, but the temperature was dropping, and Paxton had wrapped her arms around her body, shivering.

"Come back inside," she said, reaching for Paxton's hand. "You're soaked to the skin and shaking like a leaf."

Leading her inside and to her bedroom, Emma ignored the uneasy silence between them as she helped her undress. "Turn on the shower as hot as you can stand it and don't come out until you've thawed. I'm going to get you something to eat and come right back. All right?"

Taking Paxton's silence as assent and leaving her on her own, Emma ran into Dom as she went to the kitchen.

"Is she okay?"

Emma nodded as she searched through the cupboards for something to entice Paxton's nonexistent appetite. Nerves and adrenaline might have wiped out her desire for food, but hadn't eliminated the need for calories. "I think she'd already overextended her stress levels and although this is partly her idea, the thought of being arrested again so soon after the last time scared her more than she anticipated it would."

"I'm truly sorry about that, but I can't see any other way. Not if we want to make it look real." Dom opened a can of soup and handed it to her, then busied himself cutting bread and cheese and placing it on a tray along with two glasses while she put the soup on to heat.

Emma raised an eyebrow when she spotted the wineglasses, but then Dom opened a bottle of Russian River Valley pinot gris and added it to the tray. "I thought it might make whatever conversation you're going to have go down a little easier. You need to assure Pax that we'll make everything as quick and painless as possible."

"After Bali, I'm not sure any of it will be painless. She's still dealing with recurring nightmares from her experiences there."

"Damn. I hadn't realized that. Look, all I can tell you is it should take a day at most. We just need enough time for her to be booked and processed—"

"You're actually going to book her?"

"We have no choice." Dom shrugged. "If we're going to make it look real, it needs to be real. And it has to be real if we're going to get Luther to believe it. Make sure Pax really understands that."

By the time she returned to the room, Paxton was not only out of the shower, but she had a fire burning brightly in the fireplace, was wearing a long-sleeved navy T-shirt that brought out the blue in her eyes, and was sitting cross-legged on the bed.

She quickly got up and helped Emma put the tray on a table in front of the windows looking out at the ocean. She poured wine for each of them, then drank most of hers quickly while watching Emma finish setting two places for them.

"Go easy with that," Emma cautioned. "Especially on an empty stomach."

Paxton shrugged. "Can't seem to help myself. The fact you brought wine has me nervous about whatever conversation it is you want to have."

Emma disregarded the potential opening and they ate their meal in almost total silence, broken only by the hiss and crackle of the fire, and the sound of the rain beating against the windows. When Paxton finished eating, she got up and walked to the window, staring out at the fog and rain. She twisted the wineglass in her hands, and Emma could almost see her mind working as she processed what would happen over the next few days.

Her participation was critical. But Emma wanted to ensure Paxton knew exactly what she was getting into. That she was clear on the personal cost that would come with what they planned in order to bring Darren Luther out of hiding.

Finally, Emma touched Paxton's arm. "Can we sit and talk?"

Paxton nodded and sat on the bed. "Is there a problem?"

"I don't know. I guess I want to make sure you know what you're getting yourself into. That you've thought through all the consequences of what you're undertaking."

Paxton narrowed her eyes. "I thought I had, but clearly you've got something in mind and you're starting to make me nervous. You're not planning to leave me in jail, are you?"

"Good God, Pax. Just the thought that you're going to have to go through booking and processing is making me sick."

"Then what is it, Emma? You're as tense as a cat on a hot tin roof. What's going on?"

"I just—" Emma sighed. "You do realize that it's your reputation, specifically your reputation as a hacker, that's going to sell this, don't you?"

"I know that."

"What you may not realize is that once you're arrested"—Emma stopped and visibly struggled to start again—"the people who freely do business with you, people you respect who are interested in your incredible designs, they're going to take a step back. And even when the truth comes out, when it becomes public knowledge that you were actually working to help your government, your country, there will always be people who won't believe it and won't want to be associated with you."

"Emma—"

"No. I need you to listen to me because I'm trying to give you the unvarnished truth. Because there's the other side as well, don't you see? The people you work with on the darker side of your business. Once they know the truth, once they understand that you were working with and cooperating with the NSA, they're not going to trust you anymore. So no matter what, you'll be the one for whom nothing will ever be the same. The one person who'll make this all possible, the one who is risking everything of value is the one who will pay."

"Don't you think I've thought it all through?"

"I honestly don't know. Have you? Because once we set off on this path, there's no going back. You'll be the one in the line of fire."

"Are you trying to talk me out of helping you?"

"No. I just want you to make a choice you can live with, because once you make it, no one can live with it for you."

"The only real question to be answered is whether I could live with myself if I said no," Paxton said flatly. She held Emma's eyes for a long moment before she got up and poured herself another glass of wine. But she might as well have been drinking water, for all she tasted the oak-aged wine. "I think maybe we need to get a couple of things out in the open."

"Like what?"

"The first is that I don't really need to work. I've made enough and continue to bring in enough income that I will never have to worry. And while I won't deny that some has come from my black-hat days, most comes from the tools and technology I've designed. Things like the neuro headset."

Emma smiled faintly. "You're telling me you're well off and I needn't worry about you."

"I'm telling you I will be more than okay. But no matter what, I will also continue to work, to create, to program and design things because it interests me."

"All right. What's the other thing you believe I need to know?"

"The other is that the people I work with know who I am. I've been vetted quite thoroughly by some of the special interest groups I've done work for. Like Mossad and MI6."

"You've done work for Mossad?"

"I no longer dabble in what you so delicately called the darker side of my business and am quite clean. So that's not going to be a worry. As for anyone else, they will believe what they choose to believe."

"And you're all right with that?"

"Absolutely. Because the truth is there are only four people whose opinion of me matters. The rest…" She shrugged.

"Someday I'd love to know who's on that list."

"Why wait? I can tell you now." Paxton held up her hand and checked each name off. "There's Cat and Paul Winters. They saw something in me at a time when I didn't, and even though I never agreed to be their kid, they will forever be family to me."

"I think they know that." Strong emotions were visible on Emma's face.

"They'd better." Paxton laughed softly. "Then there's Tommy. He's been with me, stood by me, a very long time and he will always be the brother of my heart if not my blood."

"I would have guessed that one too."

"And then, of course, there is you."

Emma stilled. "Me?"

Paxton finished her wine and placed the empty glass on the table before she approached where Emma was still seated.

"You," she whispered and stroked Emma's face before bending down and placing a line of slow, soft kisses along her jaw and the side of her neck. "And now, if it's all right with you, I find that I'm all talked out. Come to bed with me, Emma. Let me show you what you mean to me. How much I want you."

CHAPTER TWENTY-TWO

It took five days to put plans into place and get everyone ready. Each member of Emma's team was paired with someone from Tommy's crew and each newly formed team was trained and primed to act the moment Luther revealed himself.

Over the course of five days, Paxton drilled them, shaped them. Her eyes constantly scanning everything in view. Hunting for anything not working. Anything out of place.

In the mornings, regardless of the weather, they ran and did qigong on the beach, then ate as a group. After that, they reviewed computer records of Luther's previous attacks. They learned his methods, his tells, and studied the defense Paxton had successfully used to defeat his last attempt on Flight 192. They brainstormed. They ran simulated attacks until their responses were automatic and they were ready for anything.

Emma watched with pride as her newly expanded team became something bigger and better than they had been. Highly skilled and more agile cyber warriors. Capable of detecting cyber threats. Capable of taking action and defeating any attacker. This had been Catherine Winters's vision. The goal when the American Cyber-Research Institute had been formed.

She found it fascinating to watch how her original team integrated with Tommy's hackers, accepting them, and learning from them. A sign if there ever was one of where the next generation of NSA cyber specialists would come from.

She knew there would be those who would object. Traditionalists.

Unable to see the young hackers as anything other than thugs and criminals. But Emma believed those who could see beyond their own preconceived notions would appreciate the value of this initial merger and see the truth.

Beyond having an enhanced team on hand, this time there would be one other clear difference when Luther's next attack finally came. Paxton and Tommy would be able to use the neuro headset and not only help shore up any cracks in their line of defense, but also identify the source of the attack. They would pinpoint Luther's exact location. The information would be relayed to Dom and Emma, who would coordinate with law enforcement to bring Luther down.

With the clock ticking down, they were as ready as they were going to be. It was now time to shake Darren Luther's world. There was no reason to delay. Paxton would be credited with Luther's acts of terrorism and arrested. It would make a grand show, and above all, it would get Luther's attention. Force him to act. All according to plan. Except Emma was dreading it.

Now that the time was here, what was Paxton thinking about all of this? How did she feel about being placed in this position?

"It's all right. It's all going to be okay. You'll see." Somehow, Paxton had come up behind her and was now standing next to her, speaking in an easy conversational tone.

Turning to look at her, Emma saw a curious light in Paxton's eyes. She already knew her emotions were in turmoil at the thought of being arrested again. The past and everything that had happened to her following her arrest in Bali was still much too close. But now, along with fear, there was an equal amount of determination showing. She was part of something and it wasn't in her nature to let anyone down.

"I know," Emma finally responded. "I just wish—"

"Me too." Paxton closed her fingers around Emma's hand and squeezed, then bent forward to touch their foreheads together, seemingly oblivious to the smiles on the faces of the team. She gave a small smile of her own, then turned back to the team and continued the exercise at hand. The conversation ended, debate lost by default.

❖

It was still dark when Paxton left the house, the air cold and unnaturally still. There was no birdcall, but she could hear the soft sound of the waves washing in on the sand and smooth stones.

Nonetheless, it looked like everyone was up to see her off, accompanying her to the driveway and the waiting car.

Most simply reached out to touch her shoulder, her hand. Zack gave her a travel mug filled with hot chocolate, Tommy and Sam wordless hugs. Incredible comforts. Especially for the child she'd been. The one who'd had no one in her corner when she was growing up.

Emma was standing by the door as she approached the car. Just as she reached the car, she felt a light breeze touch her face. It was as though someone unseen had just caressed her. Her involuntary shiver was delicious and she smiled, then saw Emma's mouth reflecting a similar expression and wondered if she had felt it too.

"I'll be back before you have a chance to miss me," Paxton said softly.

"Not possible," Emma responded. "I miss you already."

After that, there was nothing left to say.

As the car pulled away, Paxton tilted her head back and closed her eyes. She wasn't planning on sleeping. Dom would know that. But she hoped he understood she was in no place or mood to hold any kind of conversation.

She remained silent as they boarded their flight and for the duration of the trip to Washington. It was only when they landed that Dom finally broke the silence.

"I'm sorry, Pax. You know I have to do this." He pulled a pair of handcuffs from his belt and pushed the bracelets through the ratchets. "I have to ask you to put your hands behind your back, wrists together."

Paxton's heart rate jumped and her throat burned, but she complied in silence. Both Emma and Dom had briefed her on what she could expect. So she'd known they would be met once they landed. And that there would be expectations, protocols dictating how a federal prisoner would be handled.

But expecting and experiencing were two different things and there was a sense of finality to the sound of the handcuffs locking into place that immediately transported her to Bali. She could smell the scent of the sea and an abundance of tropical flowers—hibiscus, bougainvillea, jasmine, and water lilies—like a memory and a ghostly presence all at once.

"Pax? Are you all right?"

She shook her head to clear it and felt as though she was coming out of a daze. But what was she supposed to say? That she was all right or fine or even hanging on by a thread? The lie would be obvious because she clearly wasn't. So she compromised. "I'm as ready as I'm going to be. Let's just do this."

Four men wearing standard government-issue dark suits—clearly FBI or NSA—stood waiting and simply watched her approach. And in that moment, she knew she had just ceased to be Paxton James, cyber wizard, and had become Paxton James, cyber terrorist. Public enemy number one.

She recognized the younger agent that stepped forward. Jeff Strong. He'd been the one who recognized her when she and Emma had flown into Dulles. Was probably behind the first attempt on her life. Emma and Dom had determined to leave him alone, but he'd been watched closely since then. If he indeed was the leak, he would now likely confirm her arrest for Luther.

He immediately grabbed her arm roughly. "I guess you really weren't working with Thorpe, were you," he muttered and checked her handcuffs before tightening them past the point of discomfort.

"Goddamn it, Strong. Back off," Dom said and started to intervene, only to have Paxton shake him off.

They couldn't afford to have this seen as anything other than the arrest of a wanted cyber terrorist. All around them, she knew people were watching. Airport workers and grounds crews. And somewhere some of them would be taking pictures with their phones. Pictures that were being posted to the internet even as she was transferred to a vehicle and taken to a Department of Homeland Security office.

Mission accomplished—*almost*.

For the next few hours, they took turns questioning her. Over and over again, the same questions were asked and not answered. What did she have planned? Who was she working for? Who was helping her? What was her endgame?

Paxton could see her silence angered some of the agents, particularly Strong. She could see the simmering fury in his expression, and the tension in the small interview room increased until it was nothing short of unbearable. But there was nothing Strong could do. Not with Dom towering beside him and unknown others watching through the mirror on the wall.

Finally, just when she thought things would never end, they took a break and left her alone in the interview room. For three long hours. Uncomfortably handcuffed, tired, thirsty, and wishing she could be miles away. Anywhere but here. This was taking much longer than she'd anticipated. But Dom probably needed the time to deal with matters and do what he had to do to get her out of here.

If he managed to wrap things up soon, she might just barely make it home tonight. Much too late, definitely well past midnight, but there was still an outside chance Emma would still be awake.

When she heard the door open, she looked up expectantly. Hopefully. Only the man standing in the doorway was not Dom, and he seemed just as shocked to see her as she was to see him.

"Nick Perry."

"You fucking bitch." He screamed at her and then launched himself toward her, striking her before she had a chance to react. His handcuffed hands caught her cheekbone and his two-handed blow knocked her off her chair, unable to prevent her head from striking the floor as she landed.

Perry immediately fell on top of her, clearly recognizing while his hands were cuffed in front, hers were cuffed at her back, leaving her in no position to defend herself. Taking full advantage of the situation, he bent and squeezed his hands around her throat. "You did this to me, you bitch. I'll kill you for this."

At first, Paxton could only see his face. See the rage and hate that filled it. There was a brief moment when she thought she might have seen someone else come into the room over Perry's shoulder, but her vision was already starting to fade as dots swam in front of her eyes. Choking, unable to wait or hope for rescue, she did the only thing left to her. She drove her forehead into Perry's nose as he leaned forward to secure and tighten his hold on her throat.

She felt the satisfying connection of flesh and bone, heard him curse, and felt his blood spray over her. For an instant, she held out a brief hope. But in the next moment, his hands tightened around her throat and Paxton knew she had no way to stop him. She struggled only in her mind, heard a roaring in her ears, and her world slowly faded from gray to black.

Then, miraculously, her throat was released. She felt Perry's weight come off her and she desperately sucked in some much-needed oxygen past her burning throat. She thought she heard someone call out her name and felt herself lifted from the floor.

It only took a matter of seconds—but then again it might have taken much longer than that—before she was able to open her eyes. Dom had removed her handcuffs and was hovering over her, his face grim and eyes filled with concern. Behind him, she could see three other agents dragging a bleeding and still-enraged Nick Perry out of the room. Dom closed the door behind them, leaving her in sudden and blissful silence.

"Goddamn it, Paxton. I'm so sorry. That should never have happened. Can you drink some water?"

"Please." Paxton nodded. "What was Perry doing here?" she asked, her voice sounding strained and hoarse from the bruising and damage to her throat.

Dom helped her into a sitting position, brought a paper cup filled with cold water, and held it steady while she drank. "Apparently someone picked up some intel and Perry was brought in for more questioning. And while very few people knew you were in this room, I can't say for certain it wasn't deliberate—taking advantage of you both being on-site and letting Perry have at you, even just for a moment."

As he fell silent, he seemed to notice Paxton's injuries for the first time and cupped her chin, tilting her head to one side. "Damn it, you're bleeding. We need to get a doctor to take a look at you. Beyond the bruising, you probably need a stitch or two."

Paxton's adrenaline was subsiding and she was aware of just how much she was hurting. She pushed her hands through her hair and felt the tackiness of blood on the back of her head. But consenting to a doctor? Not as long as she was still breathing.

"It's all right, Dom. I've had worse," Paxton whispered. "And I really don't need a doctor."

"Somehow, knowing you've had worse doesn't make me feel any better. But at a minimum, we need to get some ice on that bruise and a butterfly bandage to close the cut. Emma is likely to kill me when she gets a good look at you."

Paxton discovered it was a mistake to laugh. Damn but her throat hurt. She rubbed some feeling back into her hands where the tightly ratcheted cuffs had left marks at her wrists. Her face hurt like hell, her head was throbbing, and the edges of her vision remained foggy and gray.

She knew from Dom's sympathetic looks that she already had a hell of a bruise on her face. Enough was enough. "Speaking of Emma, did we manage to do what we set out to do? Do you suppose we can go home now?"

If Dom answered her, she didn't hear it as her world shaded from gray to black.

❖

Emma had been disappointed when evening came and went and there had been no contact from Paxton or Dom. Although reports and images were already on the internet, attesting to the arrest of a wanted cyber criminal, it had probably been foolish to hope they could accomplish everything they needed to do and be back the same day.

She hated seeing the images. Paxton, head down and in handcuffs, being led by four agents across the tarmac to a waiting vehicle. Her body was stiff; her face was pale and expressionless. And yet it was exactly the image they needed Darren Luther to see.

But what was taking so long?

It was nearly dawn when her cell phone finally rang. "What is it, Dom?" she asked as she picked up, her voice containing a trace of alarm. "Has something happened? Is Paxton all right?"

"She'll be fine. The doctor just wanted to keep an eye on her overnight."

"What doctor? What are you talking about? And where the hell are you?"

"We're at the White House. It seems we have a president that knows all and as soon as she heard Pax was injured, she immediately had her transported to the residence and had her own doctor waiting to check her out."

Feeling as if she had just fallen down a rabbit hole again, Emma tried to slow things down. "You're in the residence. I get that. But what happened? How did Paxton get hurt? How badly? And why didn't you call me and let me know?"

He described the events of the day. "What I wasn't clear on at first was whether letting him into the room where Paxton was being held was an accident or a deliberate act."

"At first?" Emma closed her eyes. "Does that mean you now know? Was it a deliberate act?"

"Yes. We arrested Jeff Strong about four hours ago. He was caught in the act of contacting Darren Luther. Luther was long gone by the time we triangulated the cell connection and launched a search, but we know he was in New York."

"And Strong?"

"So far, he's admitted to being behind the wheel in the hit-and-run. But he refuses to give up any information regarding Luther's location or plans. I don't know whether he's looking for a deal or if, like Finch, he's afraid of Luther."

Emma felt a wave of anger wash over her. That bastard. She fought to keep her voice calm. Forced herself to concentrate. One breath at a time. But even then, it took all the effort she could muster. "When will you bring Paxton back?"

"The doctor, President Winters, and Dr. Winters are all with her now. As soon as she is cleared, we've got a helicopter standing by to bring us back."

"All right. Make it soon." She sighed with resignation.

"I promise."

"And Dom? I'm counting on you. Don't let anything else happen to her."

CHAPTER TWENTY-THREE

I don't believe this. How could no one tell me?" Catherine Winters paced restlessly back and forth across the antique carpet. She paused momentarily and stared at Paxton. "And you—how could you agree to do this?"

Aware that Cat's reaction had more to do with the visible damage to her face and the report she'd just received from the doctor, Paxton crossed her arms and watched her pace before giving a weary smile. "Cat, you know I love you, don't you? But I really need you to sit down. All this pacing is making my head spin."

Catherine froze in midmotion, her face suddenly pale. "You love me," she repeated softly.

"Well, of course I do."

"My dear Pax, you are the child of my heart and have been since I first met you in that hospital all those years ago. It's why I tried so hard to have you let me adopt you. But do you know this is the first time you've ever said those particular words to me?"

It was Paxton's turn to freeze. Her mind was already muddled by a combination of the earlier blow to her head and too little sleep. But now—could it be? "I'm so sorry, Cat," she said. "I always felt it. I guess I always thought you and Paul could tell and would know without my having to say the words."

"I did know, but it's still—"

"Nice to hear the words." Shaking her head, Paxton wondered how her life had become so complicated. "Still, it's ironic, don't you think?"

"What is?"

"The fact I loved you and Paul was also why I couldn't let you adopt me."

Catherine frowned, turned briefly to look at her husband before looking back at Paxton. "What are you saying? I thought coming to live with us wasn't what you wanted."

"It was everything I wanted." Paxton whispered a truth she'd been guarding for too long. "But I didn't want you to be hurt because of me—like my mother was. So it was better for you to let me walk away."

By the time she realized what she had just said, it was too late. The words were already out, hanging in the space between them. It was clear Catherine was waiting for more, but Paxton was no longer willing to fill in the silence that ensued.

"How on earth would my adopting you have hurt me," Catherine finally asked. "Pax, please. I don't understand and I think I have a right to know."

Paxton closed her eyes, almost instantly finding herself going back nearly fifteen years. She saw Gerald Hughes. Heard his words all over again. And was surprised to discover it could still hurt. "Allowing you to take me in, to adopt me…it would have damaged your reputation, your credibility, and hurt your chances at achieving your political aspirations."

"What on earth would make you think that?"

"It's what he said."

"Who?" Catherine moved to Paxton's side and knelt in front of her while Paul came and stood behind her. "Who told you that? Pax?"

Paxton opened her eyes, focusing again on Cat. "Senator Hughes."

Catherine's eyes narrowed. "Gerald?"

"That bastard," Paul said. "I should have known. He didn't want anyone distracting Cat or taking her eye off the prize—including me."

"You're kidding?" Paxton swallowed hard, uncrossed her arms, and took a deep breath. "He really was a controlling bastard, wasn't he?"

Catherine released a low laugh. "He still is. But where you're concerned, all he can do is posture. He can't touch me. And once what you've been doing on behalf of your country becomes public knowledge, we could get you elected as the next president, and there would be nothing Gerald could do."

Paxton gave a look of mock horror. "You wouldn't do that to me, would you? I thought you loved me?"

"I do, child. Paul and I both do. But try, if you can, to remember the one thing we taught you."

"How to counter a roundhouse kick?" Paxton grinned.

Paul laughed. "Good point. And after that?"

"To never look back with regret, only to learn."

"Exactly." Catherine and Paul spoke in unison, before Catherine continued. "Keep that in mind as you deal with Luther and what's to come. Now, if you can focus for a minute or two longer, there are some things I need to understand. But there will be no holding anything back, all right?"

"As if you'd let me. And I promise you won't have to wait as long before I tell you I love you again."

Looking pleased, Catherine moved to sit beside her and held her hand while Paxton explained the plan they'd devised to take Darren Luther out of his comfort zone. She explained it all calmly, rationally, and was fully prepared to bear the brunt of Cat's anger.

Cat listened, nodded, then turned to look at Dom who had been remarkably invisible until now. "And how much of this plan was your brainchild and that of Emma Thorpe?"

Dom shifted and straightened to his full height. "I am prepared to accept full responsibility, Madam President."

"Oh, stop it, Dom," Paxton interjected. "It was both Dom's idea and mine, Cat. We came up with it together. Emma had nothing to do with it."

Cat gazed at her a moment before turning to Dom once again. "Does she always jump so quickly to Emma's defense?"

Clearly caught between a rock and a hard place, Dom stared straight ahead for an interminably long moment. And then he started to laugh. "Yes, ma'am. I believe she does."

"Interesting." It took Catherine several seconds to digest the words. "And you, Paxton? Is there anything you want to tell me?"

Paxton felt a blush heat her face and she dropped her gaze. "I don't think so."

Catherine's eyes remained fixed on her a moment longer before she relented. "Another time, perhaps? But don't make me wait too long, Pax."

On a wave of relief, Paxton felt some of the tension leave her body. "I won't."

"Good. Right now, if I understand correctly, you both intend to go and prepare for Darren Luther's imminent appearance. It doesn't please me, knowing you're concussed. But I have faith in that incredible mind of yours and trust you'll be careful. It doesn't hurt to know Dom and Emma will do everything to keep you safe."

"Yes, ma'am."

"And one more thing. No more surprises. I expect to be kept fully briefed. Am I making myself clear?"

This time, both Paxton and Dom responded in unison. "Yes, ma'am."

❖

Emma's heart skipped a beat and her pulse picked up from the time she heard the approaching helicopter.

Finally.

She went out to meet them, noting the steps were slick with condensation, and the air tasted of salt and wet pine needles. She could see the helicopter was already low over the cove and she waited impatiently while it searched for and landed on a relatively flat spot on the beach.

No surprise, Dom jumped out first. He then stopped to help Paxton, who followed more slowly. Emma lifted her gaze and absorbed as much as she could as they approached her.

Paxton was dressed in unrelenting black. Black jeans, a black turtleneck, a black down vest, and dark Ray-Bans. But Emma didn't need to see her eyes or have to ask if she had slept. The somber clothing accentuated the pallor of her face. Her stiff, unsteady movements told her the rest.

Her eyes continued scanning, looking for signs of fresh damage and finding them. She moved closer, walking to meet them until they were an arm's length apart and she could push back Paxton's hair, slip off the sunglasses. Until she could look more closely at the cut on her cheekbone and the ugly bruise that had formed below her right eye.

"It looks worse than it feels," Paxton said, not that anyone believed her.

"Did the White House doctor want to keep you in Washington longer?"

When Paxton tried to sidestep the question, Dom answered for her. "Yes, but she talked him out of it by promising to rest for the next twenty-four hours."

"Then that's what you'll do." Leaving no room for argument Emma turned silently, reached for Paxton's arm, and walked with her to the stone steps and into the house.

Once inside, she temporarily moved aside while others drew near and welcomed Paxton back, almost as if needing to verify for themselves she was all right. But when her eyes became glassy and unfocused, and her expression distant and vague, Emma cut the reunion short and led her into the bedroom.

Leaving her side while she went to a dresser and got out a fresh T-shirt, Emma saw Paxton make her way to the glass wall overlooking the bay. She swayed briefly as she stared out, but regained her balance without the need for intervention.

Fog was creeping in, already encasing the spruce and pine trees near the shore, and the water was gray, reflecting both sky and the granite boulders. Water, rocks, and sky were quickly becoming indistinguishable. But Paxton clearly found what she was seeking and her expression changed. Grew softer. Almost as if the scent and sound of the water and the breathtaking beauty of the rugged coast were what she needed to recover.

When Emma approached, she leaned back against her with a faltering smile. "Hey there."

"Hey, yourself." Emma wrapped her arms around Paxton's waist and tilted her head to one side to better see her. "You look beat. How are you holding up?"

"Better now. Happy to be home. Happy to be…just happy."

Nodding, Emma tightened her hold. "I'm sorry you had such a rough time. It shouldn't have happened the way it did."

"Maybe not. I mean it really wasn't good. But I'm not feeling sorry for myself if that's what you're worried about."

"Oh?"

"Some good came out of this. Jeff Strong was arrested, which means he won't be leaking any more information to Luther."

"Uh-huh."

"Luther now has every reason to believe I'm trying to steal his thunder."

"Uh-huh."

"And I'm here now, with you."

Emma watched her in silence for the space of several slow breaths, felt her body begin to hum as her blood stirred, then shook her head helplessly and smiled. "That's good too. Anything else?"

"Yeah. I told Cat I loved her. Told both her and Paul."

Stunned. That was the only word Emma could think of to describe how she was feeling at that specific moment in time. Stunned and possibly speechless.

"Surprised you, did I?" Paxton murmured with a touch of mischief.

Emma spun Paxton around while maintaining her hands on her hips. Some things simply demanded eye contact. "Who are you? And what have you done with Paxton James, the über hacker that left for Washington so she could get arrested? That was just yesterday morning, if I remember correctly."

"She's standing right in front of you—*I'm* standing right in front of you. Right where I want to be."

The moment slipped into surreal. "Pax? How badly concussed are you?"

Paxton laughed, and the silvery sound threatened to destroy what was left of Emma's control on her emotions. "Maybe the concussion rattled my brain in a good way. Ever think of that?"

It suddenly seemed to Emma that they were talking about something else. "And what exactly is rattling around in your brain? Care to share?"

Paxton appeared to deliberate for a moment. "Well, I may not get this right. I mean I'm fairly new to this. To talking about my feelings."

An understatement, Emma thought. "Just take your time."

"Right. I always thought Cat and Paul knew—I thought they knew how important they were to me. How I felt about them. And it turns out they did. But it also turns out they really wanted to hear me say it. That saying the words was in some way just as important as what I was feeling. Does that make sense?"

"Very much so."

"Is that how you feel?"

"If you're asking if it's important for me to hear the words, then again, I'd have to say yes. Very much so."

Paxton hesitated for only a single heartbeat. "Then I think you should know—that is, I should tell you I'm in love with you."

Emma stared, unable to respond. Feeling out of time and place as her emotions threatened to overwhelm her.

"Emma? It's all right if you don't feel the same. If you don't reciprocate my feelings. That's not the point. But after my conversation with Cat, I just felt I should tell you—"

She got no further as Emma pulled her closer and kissed her hungrily. "How could I not feel the same," she mumbled against Paxton's mouth as she kissed her again. "I'm absolutely crazy about you and have been for such a long time."

Paxton started to shake. "That's good, then. But tell me. Just now—what were you thinking?"

"I was thinking if this is a dream, I don't want to wake up."

CHAPTER TWENTY-FOUR

It was still dark when someone knocking at the bedroom door woke Paxton from a deep sleep. Groggy from the concussion and possibly an emotional hangover, she slipped out of bed and stooped to pick up and put on a T-shirt before opening the door.

"What is it?"

Sam shifted uncomfortably, while behind her, Zack remained motionless. "I'm sorry. Luther's made contact with the White House. He wants to speak directly with the president and will call her back in one hour."

Paxton processed the information, deliberated for an instant. "Get everyone together in the main lab. I need ten minutes. Can you make sure there's enough coffee to go around?"

Sam nodded, leaving Paxton to wake up Emma and explain what was happening.

"I'm awake," Emma said as she approached the bed. "I also think we have enough time for a quick shower. God knows how long it might be before we get another chance, and I, for one, need to clear my head."

Ten minutes later, hair still wet and the image of Emma, hot and wet and naked, imprinted vividly in her brain, Paxton accepted a cup of coffee, walked to a computer on the table, and quickly established a connection.

"Paxton," Catherine Winter's immediately recognizable voice came through the speakers. "Thank you for calling so quickly."

"Jesus, she's got the president on speed dial," Theo whispered behind her.

"Cat, I've got the team gathered and I'd like us to listen in when Luther calls you. Are you all right with that?"

"Of course. What do you need me to do?"

"Nothing."

"You're tapped into the White House communications system? And no one knows this?"

Paxton laughed. "We can do video if you like, although depending on who you'll have in the room with you, it may make them a bit uncomfortable. Especially since the papers still have me safely locked up somewhere."

She could hear Cat sigh. "That will be cleared up as quickly as possible. You have my word."

"I'm not worried. I just need to listen to what Luther has to say. I need a real sense of how over the top he's gotten so we can plan accordingly."

"All right." The momentary silence that followed wasn't comforting. "Pax? We know he'll take control of airliners filled with passengers. Ordinary people going about their lives. And he'll use them to further his agenda, whatever it may turn out to be. To force our hand."

For a moment, Paxton fought back images of the car in Washington bearing down on her as she pushed Emma out of harm's way. She saw Cal Finch planting bombs designed to kill everyone working in the brownstone. She saw Nick Perry's enraged face as he tightened his hold on her throat, determined to kill her.

And then she stared at the sweet rolls, the warm croissants with butter, the bowls of fruit and carafes filled with coffee someone had placed on the table. All a reminder of normalcy. A normalcy she'd never truly experienced before, but one she hoped to explore and enjoy once Luther was permanently dealt with.

"Cat, what is it you want to know?"

"I know you can take back control of one jet. But Luther knows that too and he's likely to go after more. He'll need to. When he does, how many can you—"

The question didn't come as a surprise and Paxton had already given it a lot of thought. "In simulations, we—the team and I—have been able to take back control of five jets. If pushed, I'm pretty sure we can handle six. Beyond that? I'm sorry, Cat. I just don't know."

"All right." Cat's voice was sure. Determined. She kept her tone unemotional and professional. But Paxton knew that kind of control came with a cost. "I'll be in the Situation Room."

"I understand. We'll be here until this is resolved."

❖

Once the call was terminated, Paxton remained motionless. Staring straight ahead but seeing nothing beyond whatever was foremost in her mind. Emma recognized her stillness and pensiveness for what it was. Paxton's way of containing her own conflicting emotions. And if she needed to remain in that contemplative state until the call with Luther ended, then Emma would see to it that she could.

Around her, people gathered in pairs, the teams to which they'd been assigned, moving as one. Grabbing food and coffee, they moved to their assigned stations, speaking in hushed tones so as not to disturb the others. Amazing, she marveled, how two such disparate groups had melded and come together in common purpose.

Tommy stationed himself to Paxton's left, leaving the seat on her right to Emma. Dom remained on his feet, moving to stand behind Paxton when not pacing.

When the call went through, everyone became perfectly still.

"You'll never find me, you know." Luther's voice was smug, but Emma detected what could be a hint of nerves. Perhaps he'd realized that he was speaking with people who were much better than he'd ever be. Good people. Loyal and dedicated people, united in a common bond against him.

"Why don't we get down to business, Mr. Luther? Tell me what it is you want." Catherine Winters's voice was clear and steady.

"What do I want? I want the recognition I so rightly deserve for *my* mind. My creativity. My genius. I want to be wealthy. Very wealthy. I want Paxton James. Dead. She needs to pay for trying to claim what is rightfully mine. And you, President Winters, are going to see to it I get everything I want."

Paxton had to be aware all eyes in the room had turned to look at her the moment her name had been mentioned. But she remained focused on the computer in front of her and showed no sign of distress.

"You should know the US government does not negotiate or give in to terrorist demands," Catherine said.

Luther laughed. "That will change. I'll see to it. As to what I want, let's start with one hundred million dollars, wire transferred to an account I will provide."

"Mr. Luther—"

"As of this moment, you will have exactly eight hours and not a minute longer to transfer the money I want and bring Paxton James to a location of my choosing."

"And if we don't?"

"You will discover before the time is up that I have taken remote control of a number of aircraft. And for each minute you make me wait beyond the eight hours, one of those airplanes will crash. But not just anywhere, Madam President. Thanks to the information I got from USACE, I now have a number of targets to choose from. And I will choose. The results should be catastrophic, don't you agree?"

"I need to confer with my advisors. How can I reach you?"

"I'll reach you," Luther said and disconnected.

A minute passed. And then Catherine Winters spoke again. "Paxton?"

"I'm here."

"His reference to the Army Corps of Engineers. He's targeting dams."

"Yes."

"I trust you understand we will never allow him to get anywhere near you. But if he goes through with this madness, we may find ourselves with no option other than to shoot down one or more passenger airliners."

"I understand."

"I also know I have no right to ask or put you in this position, but if it comes down to it, if shooting these planes down becomes our only choice, will you be able to at least divert the planes so that the level of destruction they cause when they crash is minimized?"

The room around Emma stayed deathly quiet. She saw Paxton close her eyes. Swallow. And then she heard her say, "Yes."

❖

Paxton felt Emma's hand on her shoulder and appreciated the squeeze of comfort she'd just given her more than she could say. But she remained where she was, with her eyes closed and not saying a word, for a minute. And then two. Her head was hurting and she needed the extra time to regroup.

When she opened her eyes, she straightened her shoulders, looked around at the team that had somehow become her friends, and calmly began to speak.

"Tommy, I need you to run an algorithm and tell me which dams will cause the most devastation if they're destroyed."

"Hoover Dam," Kinsey murmured.

"A good choice, but as a primary target, it would likely prove to be more of a challenge than Luther can handle."

"How so?"

"Think of it. It's anchored into massive granite canyon walls and designed with enough mass for gravity to hold its reservoir in check. It's more than seven hundred feet high. The top is more than twelve hundred feet long. At the base, it's more than six hundred fifty feet thick and at the top it is forty-five feet thick. No conventional bomb or crashing airliner would take it down. Even a nuclear bomb would need to be well inside the dam when detonated."

Sam looked startled. "By now it shouldn't surprise me, but holy shit, how do you know all of that?"

"As soon as I heard the USACE had been hacked, I started studying what information I could find. It's what I do."

"Does it ever get so crowded in your head you can't take in any more?"

Paxton shrugged and smiled, appreciating the humor. "Not yet, but I'll keep the possibility in mind should it ever happen."

Although they were on the clock now, counting to zero, time somehow ceased to matter. More important was anticipating where Luther would strike and being ready for him. And when the team regrouped an hour later, Paxton felt the time had been well spent. Especially when Sam and Theo arrived at the same conclusion she had.

"While federal resources are currently focused on protecting the Hoover Dam from a terrorist attack, it seems comparatively little has been done to safeguard Glen Canyon Dam upstream on the Colorado River or Flaming Gorge Dam upstream on the Green River," Sam said.

Emma leaned back and looked at the map they brought up on the screen. "Why these two?"

"After Hoover, these two represent the second- and third-largest dams, respectively, in the Colorado River Basin," Theo responded.

Paxton nodded. "If either fails, it could set the stage for a series of catastrophic events."

"How so?"

"Think of it as a domino effect causing major damage to the water supply systems in the lower Colorado River Basin. The Glen Canyon Dam sits tucked into porous Navajo sandstone that constantly leaks water around the structure, and large pieces of canyon wall adjacent to the dam routinely break away. Any rupture of the dam's crumbling abutments would release two years' annual flow of the Colorado River toward the Grand Canyon before surging across Lake Mead on its way to the Hoover Dam."

Dom shifted closer and stared at her. "What would happen?"

"In a best-case scenario, the water would flow over the top of Hoover, creating a downstream flood similar to a Hoover Dam collapse."

"And worst case?"

"In a worst-case scenario, the collapse of Glen Canyon could damage Hoover Dam, sending four years' annual flow of the Colorado River heading toward Mexico all at once."

"Jesus."

"It doesn't stop there. The water is filled with silt, and as it makes its way downstream, it could collapse other Colorado River dams. Dams which provide water and power to thirty million people. Without them, the economy of the Southwest would collapse."

"What are you suggesting?" Emma asked.

"I'm not suggesting anything. I'm stating facts. If I were Luther, that's where I'd strike."

Sam and Theo nodded in agreement.

❖

It was done. His plan had been set in motion and there was no turning back now.

Luther thought back to the telephone call he'd just finished. His conversation with the President of the United States, no less. A feeling of euphoria bubbled up inside him and he bit his lower lip, suppressed a laugh. Because at no time would anyone who knew him ever think him likely to have a conversation with the president, let alone to be in a position to make demands.

But that was exactly what he'd done. And for what?

Recognition. What those people didn't understand. He was human. He had an ego. He wanted—no needed—to have his talent appreciated. And all those others, the ones who refused him the jobs that would have allowed him to truly shine, would know the error of their ways. By then, of course, it would be too late. And no matter how this all ended, he would have it. He would be famous. Everyone would know what he was capable of. Everyone would know his name.

His second demand—the one hundred million dollars—was a smoke screen. They didn't understand that either. They'd expected him to ask for a king's ransom, and he hadn't wanted to disappoint.

As for his third demand—Paxton James—if that ever happened, it would simply be icing on the cake. Delicious.

In spite of himself, a giggle escaped his control. He knew the president and her advisors didn't believe he was serious. They likely thought him mad. But that would soon change. They would soon discover just how serious he was. By then, it would be too late to stop him.

CHAPTER TWENTY-FIVE

Emma stared out the window and thought of everything she'd learned in the last twenty minutes. Because while Paxton had painted the bigger picture using broad strokes, there were other implications.

If the Hoover Dam was compromised by an attack at one of the lesser dams, trillions of gallons of water would head down the river in a massive tsunami.

Thankfully, the dam was located in an area that was not overly inhabited, but there were still some sizeable populations. Towns with populations ranging from ten thousand to forty thousand people. There were also the reservations of the Fort Mojave, Colorado River Indian Tribes, Chemehuevi, Cocopah, and Quechan Nations.

All were at risk.

"Have you looked at this?"

Glancing up, Emma looked at the document Dom was holding. Oh, yes. She had definitely looked at it. Read it carefully. Twice. It was a what-if scenario Paxton and Sam had developed that took the initial domino effect further and examined the damage water released from a compromised Hoover could also do to two lakes below it. Lake Mohave and, below that, Lake Havasu.

That's where the greatest impact would be felt, because the water in those two lakes produced hydroelectric power, irrigated farmland, and supplied drinking water to cities including Los Angeles, Las Vegas, Phoenix, and San Diego.

"I've seen it."

"If Luther succeeds, the results will be catastrophic."

"Which is why we need to make sure he doesn't succeed."

"Can we do that?" Dom's expression grew uncharacteristically bleak.

"Dom, if you've got doubts, talk to me. But please don't let the team see them."

"Don't you have questions? Doubts?"

Emma didn't hesitate, didn't need to. "I think this is one of those moments we often talk about and plan for, but hope we never encounter. When I was first training with the NSA, one of my instructors told me that when you're in the fight of your life, you need to trust your instincts. That's what I'm doing. I have data, facts, patterns, and instinct. And my instinct tells me to put my faith and trust in Paxton and the team we've put together. So no, I don't have any doubts."

"Because you want to trust her?"

"If you mean Paxton, then no. It's because I do trust her. She's unbelievably analytical, brilliant, and sees things most of us miss because she sees all the different shades of gray in a situation."

"I suppose, but just tell me one thing. Does this leap of faith have anything to do with the fact that you're involved in a very personal relationship with her?"

"No. And I would say the same thing with equal certainty even if I wasn't mad about her. Dom, if you stop and think about it, Paxton's put everything on the line for this. Her time and resources, her people, her reputation, and even her life. I trust her completely. The team trusts her. And Catherine Winters trusts her. That's why they're on the phone right now. Finalizing plans. That should say something to you."

"I think it says it's a good thing she's on our side."

Emma was still laughing as Dom left the room, passing Paxton, who was standing in the doorway, a cup of coffee in hand and an uneasy expression on her face. She paused, tried to smile, then stepped the rest of the way into the room.

Damn. It wasn't enough that the woman had an issue with trust. What had she heard? Trying to recall everything she and Dom had said, Emma pushed back from the table and approached her. She took in the cut on her cheekbone, the bruises, and the fatigue in her eyes.

Raising one hand, she touched a finger to the corner of Paxton's unsmiling mouth. Trailed a fingertip across her lower lip. "Are you all right?"

"Just a headache."

"Have you taken anything for it?" She watched with concern as Paxton downed the remains of the coffee in her cup. "And how much of that have you been drinking?"

"No. And you don't want to know."

Emma laughed softly. "That's where you're wrong. Because if it concerns you, I want to know." She deliberated for a moment then continued. "Are you bothered by any of the conversation you walked in on?"

"Dom doesn't entirely trust me." Paxton shrugged. "That surprised me more than it bothers me."

"Trust is a funny thing," Emma said. "It's a gift that's offered, it's something you earn, and yet it's so damned fragile."

"I know. I've learned a lot about trust recently. I've learned that without trust, love isn't worth a damn."

"I trust you with my heart and my soul and my life."

Paxton swallowed. "We're good together. The über hacker and the über cyber cop. Who would have thought it possible?"

"That's easy. I did." Emma smiled. "The first time I saw your photograph."

❖

Just as the clock reached zero, Luther called the president. "Are you prepared to transfer my money and meet my other request, Madam President?"

His voice still sounded smug, but there was an undertone of something Emma couldn't decipher. An edge that hadn't been there previously. Nerves?

"There will be no electronic transfer of funds, Mr. Luther. Nor will you be allowed anywhere near Paxton James. Not in this lifetime. And you can forget adding time to your clock. As I explained, the US government does not negotiate with terrorists. Nor do we give in to terrorist demands."

In spite of the tension, the president's words brought smiles to the faces around the room.

There was a momentary silence and then Luther spoke again.

"You may not think so right now, President Winters, but I promise. You will pay. You will pay in the blood of the citizens onboard the passenger jets I will bring down. In the lives destroyed as a consequence of the crashed airliners. And you will continue to pay until the citizens of this country rise up against Washington and come for your head."

"Nothing like over the top. But he sounds more than a bit off," Emma murmured as the call was terminated. "Anyone else pick up on it?"

"I'm inclined to agree," Catherine said. "Is there a chance he's taking something?"

"Drugs?" Paxton considered the possibility and shrugged. "When I knew him, his vice of choice was alcohol. But he needs to stay sharp if he's going to see this through. If he's as tired as I am, it's quite possible he's taken something."

"Paxton?" Visibly tense on the screen, Catherine sat up straighter. "You haven't taken anything, have you?"

When Paxton shook her head, it was as if a collective sigh went through the room. "Hell no. Anything stronger than aspirin messes with my head. Makes it difficult for me to think, and I can't afford for that to happen. But it's possible Luther has taken something and hasn't noticed how it's affecting him."

Emma leaned forward. "I'm not sure. Is that a good thing?"

"I'm not sure either." But it was clear Paxton didn't like whatever she was thinking. "It might help us in some ways. His instincts may be dulled, his reflexes may be slower, and it may leave his problem solving not as sharp. But it can also make him more unpredictable."

"Oh, shit." Sam didn't take her eyes off her computer screen as she spoke. "Pax? We've got trouble. We're starting to get reports of planes being remotely taken over. They're coming from multiple carriers."

"I'm picking up the reports as well," Shelby said calmly. "Three— no, four."

"Ah hell, I'm counting seven," Theo said.

"Paxton?"

Paxton looked up and met Catherine Winters's somber gaze. "It's going to be close."

"The air force has scrambled jets to intercept, Pax. I'll hold off as long as possible, but it's our last line of defense. If it looks like he'll manage to do what he's threatened, we'll have no choice."

Paxton closed her eyes. "I understand, Cat. And I'll be here. Count on it."

Emma placed her hand on Paxton's thigh and felt the tension thrumming through her as she reached for the neuro headset, while Tommy moved in beside her.

"Okay, heads up, people," Paxton said. "We'll work to save them all, but let's focus on any flights within two hours of Las Vegas. He'll want the fuel tanks as full as possible. But I think McCarran itself will be seen as too obvious."

"I've got a possibility out of San Francisco," Sam said.

"There's also one out of LAX," Kinsey added. "And damn, one out of Phoenix."

"I'll take those three," Paxton said.

"Are you sure?"

"No. Don't look for logic. Call it gut instinct. Emma—"

But Emma was already one step ahead. "You do what you need to do. I'll look after the team and the other four."

As Emma moved away from her, all she could think was that this was so not what she wanted. Paxton should have been using the neuro headset to locate Luther, not trying to resume control of three jets on her own.

It didn't help that Paxton was dealing with symptoms from her concussion. And as Emma glanced at the screen monitoring Paxton's vital signs, she saw the concussion would be only one of the problems they would have to deal with.

Damn Darren Luther to hell. Because Emma knew part of what was driving Paxton was the knowledge that somewhere above Nevada, several air force jets were waiting for a signal from their commander in chief. A signal that would unleash death on defenseless passenger airplanes. The deaths of all those innocent people would weigh heavily on Paxton, even knowing guilt would get her nowhere. Especially if she had to use her skill to position the jets where they would cause the least collateral damage.

Before moving away, she tucked her fingers under Paxton's chin and raised it so she was meeting her eyes. "Whatever happens won't be your doing. Remember that."

Paxton nodded.

There was something else in her eyes, and hoping she hadn't

misread it, Emma raised her mouth to Paxton's and kissed her softly. "For luck, not that we'll need it. Not with you on our side."

❖

Paxton was only remotely aware of anything beyond the virtual world she was in. She knew what they were dealing with was time sensitive and on some level, she was aware time was passing. She also knew her skin was hot, her pulse was hammering, and her throat was dry. But not much else.

At some point, she became vaguely conscious of a cheer that went up in the room, which she interpreted to mean Luther had lost control of first one and then a second aircraft. Hoping the jets were able to make safe emergency landings, she resumed her fight with Luther.

The unexpectedly quick loss of two planes clearly distracted Luther and provided the opening Paxton needed to release the Phoenix flight from his control. But with three less aircraft claiming his attention, he turned his sights on her and launched a series of powerful counterattacks.

Fighting what you see is easy, Pax. Fighting what you can't see is the challenge. Paxton could hear Tommy calming her. Helping her focus on what she needed to do. But she found it harder and harder to breathe.

Unlike the first time, with Flight 192, she couldn't speak directly with the pilots. But she discovered she could communicate with them by connecting to their onboard computer system. And she could hear their responses. It was now time to get them ready for what was coming.

Greetings, Flights 8180 and 7176. My name is Pax and for today I am your guardian angel. You can talk to me using your radios. Unfortunately, I can only respond through your computer system. You need to know I am working to return control of your aircraft to you. But I can't do this alone. I will need your help...

The pilot of the LAX flight was the first to respond. "This is Captain Mitch Cochrane of Flight 8180. I don't know who you are, Pax, but I'm mighty glad to have you on board. Especially if it means I get control back before my shadows have to do something none of us will like."

I don't understand what you mean by your shadows.

It took a few seconds before the pilot responded, but Paxton was aware he was still attempting to regain control of his aircraft. "I'm talking about the four air force jets that are shadowing me. I assume they're here to prevent whoever has taken control from using 8180 as a weapon of some kind. That they'll take us out before that happens."

His matter-of-fact understanding and calm acceptance of his situation reassured Paxton. If they were going to prevent Luther from carrying out his plan, she would need both pilots to have their heads in the game.

They will act only in the event I have failed. And Captain? I have no intention of failing.

That was when the flight out of San Francisco joined the conversation. "Roger that, guardian angel. Good to know. This is Captain Dave Anderson, Flight 7176, standing by awaiting your instructions."

Okay, Captains. I'll be going silent for a bit while I deal with a few things, but I will still be here. When I tell you, I'll need you to resume manual control. It's unlikely to happen at the same time for you both, but whatever happens, I will need you to respond immediately. Without question. And I will need you to keep it on manual. Do not go back on autopilot, no matter what else is happening around you. That means manual until you're safely wheels down at the closest available emergency landing site.

"Roger, guardian angel," Captain Cochrane said. "One question. Are you the other shadow tailing me? It would be nice to think you're that close."

Other shadow? For an instant, Paxton lost her concentration and her blood pressure immediately started to rise. She could feel the first trickle of blood from her nose, even as she heard Tommy reminding her to breathe.

Captain Cochrane? Say again. What other shadow?

"It's a private Learjet. Been mirroring my flight plan and tailing me since I departed LAX but doesn't respond to any attempts to communicate. I take it that's not you?"

Paxton's pulse rate spiked further, followed by a headache. Throbbing. Intense. Blinding. It struck like lightning, almost bringing her to her knees, and left her lungs burning and gasping for air.

"Pax—"

She needed to breathe.
She needed to finish this.
"Pax? Are you still there?"
Paxton blinked. Tried to focus.
Sorry. Not me behind you. That has to be Luther...
"What are you saying? Who's Luther? And why is he tailing me?"

❖

While the team worked to reclaim the remaining flights Luther had taken over, Emma had been loosely following the pilot's conversation with Paxton, aware of the smooth Southern drawl coming through the speakers, but much more concerned with monitoring Paxton's vital signs.

With each jet they reclaimed, it became clear Luther was concentrating almost exclusively on his battle with Paxton. The more aggressively she battled him, the easier it became to take back control of the other flights. But the cost? Paxton's face was glowing with an intensity born from adrenaline and exhaustion. Her nose was bleeding, her blood pressure and heart rate much too high.

Luther was doing this to her. He had to be stopped. And then—
Son of a bitch! Emma froze as she heard the pilot say Luther's name. Was he right? Was Luther actually tailing him? It certainly fit his profile. The one they'd been given by the FBI. Paxton had read it and agreed. The profile fit the man she'd known years earlier. That man would want to be close when it came time for the end. He would want to see the total destruction.

"Catherine—*Goddamn it.* President Winters." Emma dragged a tired hand through her hair. "There's a Learjet following 8180. There's a good possibility it's Luther."

It took a long, painfully slow few minutes before a frowning Catherine Winters responded. "We heard. Our birds checked him out, but he's not responding to their orders to veer off." She looked and sounded angry. "Your best advice, Emma. On my signal, they can take him out. Do we know what that might trigger? Will it force the release of the two passenger jets he's still controlling?"

Beside Paxton, Tommy vigorously shook his head. "Not good. If he goes down while still in control of 8180 and 7176, we could lose them both. And there's no telling what it would do to Pax. She's already too tied into him and I'm barely reaching her."

On the screen, Catherine Winters could be seen nodding, indicating her understanding, then turning her head to listen to a four-star general who whispered urgently in her ear.

Emma didn't need to hear to know what was being said. So far Luther had the two remaining jets moving in a wide circle. But she knew—they all knew—that if it looked as if he was stopping whatever game he was playing and got too close to one of the dams, the argument would become moot. The two jets, the passengers and crew on board, and Paxton would all be deemed acceptable losses in the face of the catastrophic devastation Luther's plan could cause.

And for what? It didn't matter. That wasn't happening on her watch. Not if she could help it.

"Sam, Zack. Kinsey, Shelby. I need all of you focused on taking back 7176. It's the other flight he really wants. Let's give Pax a fighting chance." As they moved into action, following her instructions, Emma tried to think of what else could be done.

Dom stared at Paxton. "Is there anything we can do to directly attack Luther and help the kid out?"

Emma looked to Tommy. Next to Paxton, he was probably the most gifted hacker in the room. It didn't take him long.

"Yeah." He stared at the monitor and adjusted something. "I've been running the defense while Pax has been trying to counterhack and break into his server. According to Pax, Luther's got some seriously layered defenses. But she's already breached his primary firewall. That means he's got an open doorway which should make it possible for us to ride the carrier signal back to him. We just need enough time to upload a little gift Pax created."

"Another reverse worm?"

Tommy grinned. "Yeah. And she's a beauty. It's a self-propagating program, so we just need enough time for it to get a foothold. Then, even if he cuts the flow between him and Pax, it will still be too late."

"Meaning?"

"It's a hungry little bastard. It will eat everything in sight."

"So what are we waiting for?"

❖

Paxton wasn't certain whether she saw or felt the bright flash of light. She struggled to refocus on what she'd been doing, but a strange humming in the back of her head kept distracting her. Something was happening. *What* was another question.

It was clear Luther had regained strength and was fighting her with renewed effort. Normally, that would have told her he'd lost control of another jet and would be cause for celebration. Except this felt different. This wasn't Luther trying to maintain his hold on the jets in pursuit of his mission. This was Luther redirecting his energy and coming after her.

She licked her lips as the edgy feeling inside her began to grow exponentially. Aware her vitals were straying into dangerous zones, she tried to bring them back. To settle her mind. She needed to focus. But all she could feel was a chaotic jumble of emotions. She could hear the harsh sound of her own breathing and a loud and erratic drumming she finally recognized as the beating of her heart.

Time slowed. Everything became distorted in a red haze that pulsed like a strobe. Light then dark. But in that instant, she saw the opening she'd been seeking.

Now, Captain Cochrane...

She sensed it the moment the last jet pulled free of Luther's control. She felt a momentary elation along with Luther's rage and frustration. Thought she sensed others nearby. Sam, Zack. Kinsey, Shelby.

Emma.

The thought slipped away in a whirling mist as her mind let go.

❖

Emma's heart froze the instant Paxton hit the floor. She couldn't believe what she was seeing. Couldn't accept it as she raced to Paxton's side, calling out her name. She had to get to her. Had to see her look up and smile, reassuring her everything was fine.

She'd freed Flight 8180 from Luther's hold. They'd defeated Luther, successfully preventing him from seeing his endgame through to completion. The air force would deal with him now. They could take some time to celebrate their victory. And then they could figure out what came next.

Together.

But Paxton wasn't moving, wasn't responding. She simply remained where she'd fallen, utterly still, the blood streaming from her nose slowing down to a trickle. She looked so pale and vulnerable Emma was almost afraid to touch her. Afraid that when she pressed her fingers against Paxton's throat, she would find no pulse. There would be nothing.

Even as she dropped to her knees and reached out with a shaking hand, Sam and Tommy were there ahead of her. Sam pressed her hand to Paxton's throat and smiled. "I've got a pulse. Strong and steady."

"I'll be damned," Tommy said. "I think she's asleep."

Emma frowned. "You're kidding?" And then she realized it didn't matter. She was alive. Nothing else mattered.

Somewhere in the background, through the chaos in her mind, Emma heard someone instructing the air force jets to escort Luther's Learjet to the nearest landing facility where law enforcement would be waiting to take him into custody. Right now, she didn't really care. Her only concern was Paxton.

She could also hear Catherine Winters, demanding to know how Paxton was doing, fear and love warring in her voice.

"She's alive," Emma said, more to herself than to anyone else. She looked lifeless, but no other answer would do. "She's alive."

❖

Luther stared at the blank screen, disbelief surging through him.

How was it possible? How had this happened? He'd planned everything down to the last detail. And his plan had been flawless—or so he'd believed. Emotion gripped him, and for a moment, all he wanted was to rage. To scream.

It wasn't fair.

He closed his eyes, tried to swallow. But all he could taste was failure. When he opened his eyes once again, nothing had changed. The screen was still blank. All the passenger jets he had been controlling were gone. And from the cockpit, he could hear the air force jets trailing him ordering his pilot to land.

What was there left to do?

As a matter of course, he had planned for every contingency. This had been a remote possibility. Now it had become inevitable. He could not face spending the remainder of his life in federal lockup. He knew that likely made him a coward, but it would destroy him as surely as if he put a gun to his head and pulled the trigger.

His mind briefly turned to thoughts of Paxton. She had survived fourteen months in that hellhole of a prison in Bali. And then had returned to beat him at his own game.

Ben had been right all those years ago. She really was the best of them.

He pulled the laptop closer and punched in a sequence of numbers and letters. Felt a prickle of conscience as he thought of his pilot. Whispered good-bye. Then hit enter.

EPILOGUE

Paxton floated in a warm place. She inhaled the scent of the ocean. Felt the heat of a fire. Heard a soft, familiar voice calling her.

Slowly an awakening shifted over her skin and she became more aware. She opened her eyes and realized where she was. In her bedroom. In her bed.

Emma leaned in closer, squeezed her hand. "Hey there. I'm glad you finally decided to make an appearance at the party."

Paxton blinked several times, licked her lips, and frowned as she attempted to reconcile disparate thoughts in her mind. Her head thrummed to a steady beat and she felt dazed. But she was alive, Emma was beside her, and that had to trump everything.

It took a few more seconds before clarity came roaring back. "Oh my God."

"I know. The good news is we won."

"Luther?"

"Gone."

Gone? "What do you mean?"

"His jet—it blew up. Whether deliberately or by accident, we may never know. But he won't be threatening countless lives ever again."

Paxton swallowed. "I guess that's what counts."

"Maybe so." Emma looked away for a long moment. "I thought we were going to lose you. Actually, I thought we had. I know we didn't and that's what's important, but please don't scare me like that again."

"I'm sorry. I didn't plan on it going so badly."

"Then why?" Emma swore. "Can you tell me why you continued fighting him when you had to know how much he was hurting you?

How much damage he had already caused and was continuing to inflict on you?"

Paxton's smile faded. "I'm sorry. Every now and then a challenge comes along and all my good intentions go out the window. But I knew it would be all right because I could feel you there. I knew you'd make sure I came out of it okay."

Emma's eyes welled up. Leaning over, she kissed the top of Paxton's head and murmured, "You had a lot of faith in me, love."

"It's called trust. And I'm here, aren't I? So thank you, Emma. For saving my life. For giving me a life. And for being in my life." Paxton saw a trickle of fear still lurking in Emma's eyes and reached for her hand. "I think what I really need is someone to keep me in line."

Emma frowned, her gaze searching. "What sort of someone?"

"Someone who knows and can accept what I've been and who I am."

"Are you saying you're ready for something more?" She moved closer, trapping Paxton in warmth. "Please be sure, Pax. If we cross this line, there's no going back."

"All or nothing. Is that what you're asking?"

"Yes."

She brought Emma's wrist closer, kissed her palm, then drew her down onto the bed beside her. "I know I don't exactly fit in your life. But I know I love you. Those are facts. They're neither right nor wrong. They simply are. So if my choice is all or nothing, it's going to be all, Emma. I choose you."

"You have me. You have every part of me for as long as you want." An instant later, her warm mouth found Paxton's.

The raw heat that flared between them demanded more, while the sensuality begged for her to go slow. Paxton placed soft kisses at the curve of Emma's neck, the hollow of her throat. "How about forever?"

Pushing Emma's sweater up and over her head, she began a long slow slide of lips and tongue. Emma arched into her, offering more, and watched her take a taut nipple deep into the heat of her mouth before she moved on.

Paxton held her gaze as she moved over her body in an intimate invasion. She listened to her breath shudder and saw her eyes drift closed as she played with her and teased her flesh. But it wasn't enough.

Paxton wanted more, wanted everything, and laid claim with her mouth, while worshipping with her hands.

She devoured even as she whispered her love, her need, her desire. Emma's hands and mouth began to mirror her own, moving in synchronous rhythm.

Increasing the tempo, Paxton felt it. The sharp edge of the moment when Emma's orgasm tore through her and she cried out her name. She held her, continuing to take, continuing to give, until the last of the tremors flexed through them both and they sank breathlessly into the soft mattress.

❖

Wrapped tightly around Paxton's length, Emma was the first to hear someone knocking at the bedroom door. She considered getting up, but realized that would take more energy than she could muster. Instead, she reached for the duvet and covered both their bodies, then called out for whoever it was to enter.

Tommy came into the room, looking more pleased than embarrassed by what he saw. "Sorry about this, but I thought you should know we've company coming. In about ten minutes or so, a helicopter will be landing on the beach."

"Who?" Paxton raised her head.

"Ten secret service agents, the president, and her husband," Tommy answered with a laugh. "That's why I thought I'd give you a heads-up. Oh, and Sam thinks she's found a way to make the neuro headset a bit more user-friendly."

"Bloody hell," Emma muttered. "Does Sam remember she works for me at the NSA?"

Tommy's grin widened. "Yeah, but we figure since you'll likely be leaving the NSA soon, maybe Sam should follow you here. Something to think about while you get ready for the president."

Emma could hear Paxton's laughter before Tommy closed the door. Pretending to glare, she pulled the duvet down until she could see Paxton's face, half buried in a pillow. "What's so funny?"

"Actually, I think Sam joining the team is an excellent idea."

"You do? Should I be jealous?"

"Not at all. I just think she'll be great at keeping an eye on Tommy and the crew for us. At least for a while."

"And where will we be?"

"I was thinking after all this a trek might be in order. Maybe do the Inca Trail to Machu Picchu and then Patagonia. What do you think?"

"That's curious." Emma frowned. "I thought you already did the Inca Trail?"

"I have," Paxton answered. "But you haven't, and it's incredible."

"So I'm told." The thought of going anywhere with Paxton made her heartbeat skip and heated her blood. No work. Just time to explore, to play, and to love. "But I thought your preference was to trek alone?"

"That was because there was never anyone I wanted with me." She paused and gave Emma a soft, sweet kiss, then rolled on her back and took Emma with her. "But that's all changed now, hasn't it?"

"I guess it has at that." Emma leaned in, loving how well they fit together. She closed her eyes, all but purring. "Do you think there's any chance we could sneak away before the president's helicopter lands?"

"Ah, Emma. I do love you." Paxton laughed softly.

"God, I can't breathe when you say that." Emma smiled and drew her closer, knowing in her heart and soul this was where she belonged. Starting and ending each day where she felt loved. Right here, in Paxton's arms.

About the Author

A transplant from Cuba to Toronto, AJ Quinn successfully juggles the demands of a busy consulting practice with those of her first true love—storytelling—finding time to write mostly late at night or in the wee hours of the morning. She's the author of four previously released romantic thrillers: *Hostage Moon*, a Lambda Literary Award finalist, *Show of Force*, *Rules of Revenge*, and *Just Enough Light*. An avid cyclist, scuba diver, and photographer, AJ finds travel is the best medicine for recharging body, spirit, and imagination. She can be reached at aj@ajquinn.com.

Books Available From Bold Strokes Books

Arrested Hearts by Holly Stratimore. A reckless cop who hates her life and a health nut who is afraid to die might be a perfect combination for love. (978-1-62639-809-2)

Capturing Jessica by Jane Hardee. Hyperrealist sculptor Michael tries desperately to conceal the love she holds for best friend, Jess, unaware Jess's feelings for her are changing. (978-1-62639-836-8)

Counting to Zero by AJ Quinn. NSA agent Emma Thorpe and computer hacker Paxton James must learn to trust each other as they work to stop a threat clock that's rapidly counting down to zero. (978-1-62639-783-5)

Courageous Love by KC Richardson. Two women fight a devastating disease, and their own demons, while trying to fall in love. (978-1-62639-797-2)

One More Reason to Leave Orlando by Missouri Vaun. Nash Wiley thought a threesome sounded exotic and exciting, but as it turns out the reality of sleeping with two women at the same time is just really complicated. (978-1-62639-703-3)

Pathogen by Jessica L. Webb. Can Dr. Kate Morrison navigate a deadly virus and the threat of bioterrorism, as well as her new relationship with Sergeant Andy Wyles and her own troubled past? (978-1-62639-833-7)

Rainbow Gap by Lee Lynch. Jaudon Vickers and Berry Garland, polar opposites, dream and love in this tale of lesbian lives set in Central Florida against the tapestry of societal change and the Vietnam War. (978-1-62639-799-6)

Steel and Promise by Alexa Black. Lady Nivrai's cruel desires and modified body make most of the galaxy fear her, but courtesan Cailyn Derys soon discovers the real monsters are the ones without the claws. (978-1-62639-805-4)

Swelter by D. Jackson Leigh. Teal Giovanni's mistake shines an unwanted spotlight on a small Texas ranch where August Reese is secluded until she can testify against a powerful drug kingpin. (978-1-62639-795-8)

Without Justice by Carsen Taite. Cade Kelly and Emily Sinclair must battle each other in the pursuit of justice, but can they fight their undeniable attraction outside the walls of the courtroom? (978-1-62639-560-2)

21 Questions by Mason Dixon. To find love, start by asking the right questions. (978-1-62639-724-8)

A Palette for Love by Charlotte Greene. When newly minted Ph.D. Chloé Devereaux returns to New Orleans, she doesn't expect her new job and her powerful employer—Amelia Winters—to be so appealing. (978-1-62639-758-3)

By the Dark of Her Eyes by Cameron MacElvee. When Brenna Taylor inherits a decrepit property haunted by tormented ghosts, Alejandra Santana must not only restore Brenna's house and property but also save her soul. (978-1-62639-834-4)

Cash Braddock by Ashley Bartlett. Cash Braddock just wants to hang with her cat, fall in love, and deal drugs. What's the problem with that? (978-1-62639-706-4)

Death by Cocktail Straw by Missouri Vaun. She just wanted to meet girls, but an outing at the local lesbian bar goes comically off the rails, landing Nash Wiley and her best pal in the ER. (978-1-62639-702-6)

Lone Ranger by VK Powell. Reporter Emma Ferguson stirs up a thirty-year-old mystery that threatens Park Ranger Carter West's family and jeopardizes any hope for a relationship between the two women. (978-1-62639-767-5)

Never Enough by Robyn Nyx. Can two women put aside their pasts to find love before it's too late? (978-1-62639-629-6)

Love on Call by Radclyffe. Ex-Army medic Glenn Archer and recent LA transplant Mariana Mateo fight their mutual desire in the face of past losses as they work together in the Rivers Community Hospital ER. (978-1-62639-843-6)

Two Souls by Kathleen Knowles. Can love blossom in the wake of tragedy? (978-1-62639-641-8)

Camp Rewind by Meghan O'Brien. A summer camp for grown-ups becomes the site of an unlikely romance between a shy, introverted divorcee and one of the Internet's most infamous cultural critics— who attends undercover. (978-1-62639-793-4)

Cross Purposes by Gina L. Dartt. In pursuit of a lost Acadian treasure, three women must work out not only the clues, but also the complicated tangle of emotion and attraction developing between them. (978-1-62639-713-2)

Imperfect Truth by C.A. Popovich. Can an imperfect truth stand in the way of love? (978-1-62639-787-3)

Life in Death by M. Ullrich. Sometimes the devastating end is your only chance for a new beginning. (978-1-62639-773-6)

Love on Liberty by MJ Williamz. Hearts collide when politics clash. (978-1-62639-639-5)

Serious Potential by Maggie Cummings. Pro golfer Tracy Allen plans to forget her ex during a visit to Bay West, a lesbian condo community in NYC, but when she meets Dr. Jennifer Betsy, she gets more than she bargained for. (978-1-62639-633-3)

Taste by Kris Bryant. Accomplished chef Taryn has walked away from her promising career in the city's top restaurant to devote her life to her six-year-old daughter and is content until Ki Blake comes along. (978-1-62639-718-7)

Valley of Fire by Missouri Vaun. Taken captive in a desert outpost after their small aircraft is hijacked, Ava and her captivating passenger discover things about each other and themselves that will change them both forever. (978-1-62639-496-4)

The Second Wave by Jean Copeland. Can star-crossed lovers have a second chance after decades apart, or does the love of a lifetime only happen once? (978-1-62639-830-6)

Coils by Barbara Ann Wright. A modern young woman follows her aunt into the Greek Underworld and makes a pact with Medusa to win her freedom by killing a hero of legend. (978-1-62639-598-5)

Courting the Countess by Jenny Frame. When relationship-phobic Lady Henrietta Knight starts to care about housekeeper Annie Brannigan and her daughter, can she overcome her fears and promise Annie the forever that she demands? (978-1-62639-785-9)

Dapper by Jenny Frame. Amelia Honey meets the mysterious Byron De Brek and is faced with her darkest fantasies, but will her strict moral upbringing stop her from exploring what she truly wants? (978-1-62639-898-6)

Delayed Gratification: The Honeymoon by Meghan O'Brien. A dream European honeymoon turns into a winter storm nightmare involving a delayed flight, a ditched rental car, and eventually, a surprisingly happy ending. (978-1-62639-766-8)

For Money or Love by Heather Blackmore. Jessica Spaulding must choose between ignoring the truth to keep everything she has, and doing the right thing only to lose it all—including the woman she loves. (978-1-62639-756-9)

Hooked by Jaime Maddox. With the help of sexy Detective Mac Calabrese, Dr. Jessica Benson is working hard to overcome her past, but they may not be enough to stop a murderer. (978-1-62639-689-0)

Lands End by Jackie D. Public relations superstar Amy Kline is dealing with a media nightmare, and the last thing she expects is for restaurateur Lena Michaels to change everything, but she will. (978-1-62639-739-2)

Bitter Root by Laydin Michaels. Small town chef Adi Bergeron is hiding something, and Griffith McNaulty is going to find out what it is even if it gets her killed. (978-1-62639-656-2)

Capturing Forever by Erin Dutton. When family pulls Jacqueline and Casey back together, will the lessons learned in eight years apart be enough to mend the mistakes of the past? (978-1-62639-631-9)

Deception by VK Powell. DEA Agent Colby Vincent and Attorney Adena Weber are embroiled in a drug investigation involving homeless veterans and an attraction that could destroy them both. (978-1-62639-596-1)

Dyre: A Knight of Spirit and Shadows by Rachel E. Bailey. With the abduction of her queen, werewolf-bodyguard Des must follow the kidnappers' trail to Europe, where her queen—and a battle unlike any Des has ever waged—awaits her. (978-1-62639-664-7)

First Position by Melissa Brayden. Love and rivalry take center stage for Anastasia Mikhelson and Natalie Frederico in one of the most prestigious ballet companies in the nation. (978-1-62639-602-9)

Best Laid Plans by Jan Gayle. Nicky and Lauren are meant for each other, but Nicky's haunting past and Lauren's societal fears threaten to derail all possibilities of a relationship. (978-1-62639-658-6)

Exchange by CF Frizzell. When Shay Maguire rode into rural Montana, she never expected to meet the woman of her dreams—or to learn Mel Baker was held hostage by legal agreement to her right-wing father. (978-1-62639-679-1)

Just Enough Light by AJ Quinn. Will a serial killer's return to Colorado destroy Kellen Ryan and Dana Kingston's chance at love, or can the search-and-rescue team save themselves? (978-1-62639-685-2)